# DIRTY WORK
## Part Two

Melodrama Publishing
www.MelodramaPublishing.com

*Dirty Work - Part Two.* Copyright © 2017 by Melodrama Publishing. All rights reserved. No part of this book may be used or reproduced in any manner whatsoever without written permission except in the case of brief quotations embodied in critical articles or reviews. For information, address Melodrama Publishing, info@melodramabooks.com.

www.melodramapublishing.com

Library of Congress Control Number: 2017909509
ISBN-13: 978-1620780879
First Edition: February 2018

Printed in Canada

# BOOKS BY

# *Erica Hilton*

# DIRTY WORK
## Part Two

Erica Hilton

# 1

Kid Kane—AKA The Kid—sat in his wheelchair in silence and looked at himself in the long mirror. He had a lot on his mind. He missed his brother, their conversations, and the bond they had shared. He missed the way things used to be—he missed playing chess in St. Nicholas Park. Kid couldn't help but to feel he had failed his brother. He had the cover of anonymity; he should have squeezed off a couple bullets into Meek's cranium. If only he could go back in time and make things right. But he couldn't. Now he had to deal with living without his brother for the rest of his life.

The Kid was angry and bitter. He thirsted for revenge. All he could think about was killing Maserati Meek and continuing to use Jessica for two betrayals: breaking his heart and sleeping with the enemy. Now, he was the main pieces on the chessboard—the king and queen. Every move mattered. He had to look five moves ahead of his foes. He had to be careful. He had to remain calm and keep up his deception. To everyone besides Papa John, Devon, and Jessica, he was harmless—a smart, lanky nerd in a wheelchair.

Devon was the decoy, looking like he was now in charge of Kip's operation, but The Kid was the brains. If an order needed to be implemented, he would relay it to Devon, who would then transmit it to the crew. Their crew was building in numbers now that they were moving kilos of cocaine and heroin. They were making a serious name for themselves in the streets—leveling up from their stickup-kid reputations. Their crew had taken on Maserati Meek, and it garnered a lot of respect through Harlem for Papa John and Devon.

Kid Kane had a vision, one that his brother had not seen. The Kid wanted to build something massive. He wanted to honor his brother's death with success in everything from drugs and gambling to legit businesses. But first he wanted to kill Maserati Meek and avenge Kip's murder. Once Meek was dead, then Kid could focus on building an empire.

The Kid sat there alone, still thinking. Alone was how he could fully see things clearly. He couldn't shake the feeling that the reunion Jessica was planning was a setup. The thought ate away at him. Why would she go through the trouble of bringing everyone together after all that had happened? Jessica wasn't that kind of person—forgiving or nice. She was selfish and greedy. She was superficial, and from his own eyes, The Kid saw that she was in love with Maserati Meek—or in love with his money and power, anyway.

Had Eshon not been so devastated by Kip's murder and yearning to have a memorial for him, then she never would have allowed Jessica back into the fold after the way Jessica had violated her and Brandy for some foreign nigga. Jessica was a sneaky and heartless bitch. She learned from the best—Kip. She knew how to trap niggas and outsmart women.

Kid called Jessica.

"Yo, I ain't gonna be able to make the memorial."

"What?" she asked, her voice elevated. "You have to come."

"All I gotta do is survive on these streets. All else are nonfactors."

"Homes, what that shit got to do with what I'm puttin' together? You sound crazy right now."

"I am a lot of things, but crazy will never be one. Disrespect me like that again, and I will put you in a deep sleep."

Jessica could hear the seriousness in his already deep voice, which had dropped a few octaves. She felt Kid was a couple grams short of an ounce. There was something loco about a grown man who pretended to be crippled to murder muthafuckas. She thought about all the times they pushed his big ass around, all the times he pulled his seemingly dead legs in and out of that wheelchair, and all the times he appeared to be innocent when he, too, was in fact a killer. She didn't want to aggravate him.

"My bad . . . listen, poppi, I really want you to be there. And to keep it one hundred, I am doing this as much for you as Eshon and Kip. I know how much you loved your brother, and I just want to celebrate that. You know how vain your brother was—shit, he's expecting this," she said and chuckled.

"I'm focused on Meek right now, Jessica. I don't want to be sidetracked."

"And you won't, baby. I give you my word. This memorial is what we all need and I'll be right there by your side. Besides, you ain't got to worry about Meek. Us together will beat him. You're smarter than that puta."

Kid thought, *Did she just call me baby?* Jessica was going hard. And he knew it.

The Kid let her squirm for a moment and then he conceded. "A'ight, I'll be there. But only because you asked me to. When you're throwing your arms around that sand nigga just remember this. Remember that you had and will always have my heart. I'm doing this for you, and for my brother."

"If you show up then maybe we'll slide off together."

"You and me?" Kid sounded as if his interest was piqued. "Stop playing."

Jessica gave a flirty laugh and said in a sultry voice, "I'm dead serious."

"We'll see." He hung up.

Her kindness toward Kid and the others was suspect in his eyes. And something else worried The Kid. Up until now, he had felt that he had the upper hand on Maserati Meek because Meek didn't know about him. What if Jessica had given him up? It was a strong possibility. Jessica was a duplicitous bitch, and Kid would see her dead soon.

He had a plan. He wheeled himself away from the mirror and dialed Devon and Papa John and told them he needed to meet with them. He and his peoples were still going to the mattresses—going to war with their rivals and living in isolation and security.

It was a beautiful summer day with clear skies and warm weather. A much-needed cool breeze came blowing in through the open window. The Kid sighed. Though he was alone, he continued to remain in his chair. He found some comfort in it. It was an attachment to him, and it was the memory he had of Kip before his murder. If only Kip knew he could walk again. What would have been his older brother's reaction? Would it be shock, anger—bewilderment? It was a question had that always plagued Kid's mind. Now he would never know. Kip had always felt responsible for the accident that had crippled Kid, and he had done everything in his power to help get Kid's life back to normal.

An hour later, Devon and Papa John arrived. The men sat and waited to hear what The Kid had to tell them.

"What's good? Why we here?" Devon asked.

The Kid looked at them and said, "This thing with Jessica, this event, I strongly feel that it's a setup."

Devon frowned. Then he barked, "I don't see why we ain't kill that bitch in the first place. Why is she living, nigga? After everything this bitch did, she should be dead. I'm ready to put a bullet in that bitch's head right now."

Papa John agreed.

The Kid looked at the two men coolly. "I still need her alive, Devon," he explained. "She's more useful to us alive than dead at the moment.

Meek is a formidable foe, and the more intel we have on him, the better. She is needed."

Devon still griped, but he halfheartedly understood.

"A'ight, we wait."

Kid wasn't completely honest with them. He was leaving out the fact that he was still obsessed with her and he couldn't end her life at the time. Maybe she was still on their team. Keeping her alive was a huge risk, but he needed to know for certain. How would he know if she had been compromised? Jessica wasn't always easy to read.

Devon and Papa John were furious with Jessica. They had treated her like a sister, and she had violated them. If Kid's suspicions of her were true, then Devon had a special way he wanted to kill her. He would do it slowly and cruelly. She would feel his wrath for hours until she was begging to die.

"Patience, Devon, patience, and we shall have our way," The Kid proclaimed like he was some fifth-century prophet.

The Kid was smart, and so far he had brought them ahead of the game and kept them alive with wits. Devon and Papa John had to respect him. He had many tricks up his sleeve, and they could see in his eyes that he was a lot more dangerous and deadly than his brother.

The two men were dismissed. They left the room. The Kid sat there for a moment, consumed in silence and stillness. It was going to be a long road ahead for them. He was willing to travel it for his brother—for his revenge. He wheeled himself toward the window and looked outside. A deep breath came to him, and he balled his hands into fists. Though departed from his brother physically, The Kid still felt Kip's presence inside of him. He would see Kip in his dreams, and most nights, he could hear his brother's voice, talking to him and guiding him. Some would say it was madness or that he couldn't let go, but The Kid saw it as a sign that they would always be together, as one—even in death.

# 2

Two black Escalades came to a stop on Surf Avenue, and the engines were left idling in front of the iconic Coney Island amusement park in Brooklyn, New York. The first SUV carried armed Egyptian killers, and the second carried a crime boss with his beautiful lady, an armed Egyptian driver, and one bodyguard riding shotgun. The back door to one of the Escalades opened up, and Maserati Meek exited the vehicle first, followed by Jessica. Dressed in white shorts and a white button-up with his long, black hair in a bun, Meek stood elated on the sidewalk packed with people. The sun's rays made his gold and diamond Rolex glimmer. He wanted to enjoy the beautiful day and have some fun racing karts.

Jessica flanked her man wearing a pair of floral skinny jeans, a tank top, and a pair of heels. She was Maserati Meek's eye candy. She was in his ear about the upcoming event, the one where Kid and everyone else would be killed. Her mouth was salivating with the thought of Eshon, Brandy, Kid, and everyone else meeting their demise at the same time. She carried no forgiveness for anyone. They had all wronged her and embarrassed her, and now she wanted to have the last laugh.

Maserati Meek didn't want to discuss business today. He told her that everything was taken care of, and that she should relax. Today was a fun day, a day to chill and enjoy the speed of a racing kart.

"We're in Coney Island, eh. Look around, Jessica. Nothing but sun and fun," he said.

She looked around, and it was the last place she wanted to be. She wanted to leave right away. She wanted to ride off into the sunset with him, but Meek had other plans. He acted like they weren't at war with rival crews—like he wasn't a marked man.

Maserati Meek walked toward the racing karts. His goons flanked him, and it drew some attention. Jessica noticed hungry looks from several women aimed at her man. Meek was handsome and rich, and they wanted to sink their claws into his soft, brown flesh and latch on. But Meek was hers, and she wouldn't hesitate to beat a bitch down if they had the audacity to step. She rolled her eyes at the thirsty bitches and walked hand in hand with Meek toward the karts.

The line was short, the skies clear, and the people around were having a good time. Meek joined the line for the ride. He was all smiles. Soon, it was time to ride the go-karts. He climbed into a black one. He reached out for Jessica and uttered, "Come eh . . . enjoy this with me."

She managed to smile. She climbed into a blue go-kart behind his, and two of his men climbed into similar go-karts. Three strangers climbed into the last three, and the race was soon to be started. Maserati Meek was in front, ready to take off. Like his life, he was in charge, the leader up front.

The attendant made sure everyone's seatbelt was secured, and then he released the gateway. Meek took off down the track, hitting the first curve with his feet completely pushed against the accelerator. Jessica was right behind him, catching up fast. He slammed against the barrier and Jessica hurried by him. Meek soon got back right and slammed on the accelerator and took off; he was now in third place, but he didn't plan on being third for long. He zoomed around the curve at top speed and came barreling behind Jessica. He was determined to win. The two went neck and neck around the track. Surprisingly, Jessica was good at this. Maserati Meek was impressed. Now they both were having some fun.

It was the last time to circle the track, and Jessica was in the lead by a hair. Meek was close—too close. He was gaining speed, and when they were parallel just seconds before crossing the finish line, Maserati Meek sideswiped her. Jessica went crashing into the barrier, and Meek crossed the finish line, coming in first place. She came in third.

Maserati Meek sprung from the kart looking victorious. His huge grin was splattered across his smug face. Jessica was upset.

"You cheated, homes!" she griped.

"You win by any means necessary, eh . . ."

She pouted.

"I'll make it up to you," he said.

"You better."

It was a different side of him, one that was almost confusing to her. How were men like him able to laugh and have a good time when they were crime bosses and cold-hearted killers? Maserati Meek seemed so cool and pleasant today. There was no concern about rival drug organizations or fearing retribution from Kip's crew. How could he put it aside so easily?

"Let's go for a walk near the beach, eh," he suggested.

He took Jessica by her hand, and the two of them walked toward the boardwalk that stretched parallel against the crowded beach with his men close behind him. They moved coolly but with watchfulness. This world was far different from their home across the Atlantic. Their country was in turmoil, torn apart by political strife and civil unrest. A day at the beach and theme park rides were far and few between in their country.

"I love here," Maserati Meek proclaimed. He gazed at the beach flooded with people and the calm, blue ocean.

Jessica remained silent. She couldn't relax like him. She couldn't escape from everything that had been happening. Her mind was forever bothered by what if's—what if Kid and his crew were there, or Panamanian Pete and his killers, the feds? So many enemies. What did Maserati Meek have inside of him that allowed him to come off so cool and collected? The new faces surrounding them—their vibes were disturbing, but Jessica knew they were men from Meek's country there to protect them and were proficient and efficient at getting any job done.

"Are you hungry?" he asked her.

She shook her head. "No, I'm okay."

They traveled farther down the boardwalk, mixing in with the regular civilians as best they could, but there were fleeting and lingering looks thrown their way. No matter how much Meek tried to fit in, he stood out. His man bun, wooly beard, urban attitude, and his jewelry made it nearly impossible for him to blend in. The men with him wearing turbans in the summer heat were the epitome of being racially profiled—*terrorists* was their first thought.

Some fool even shouted out while in passing, "Remember 9/11!"

The comment didn't bother Maserati Meek; he kept his cool and a smile. It was just a fool with his opinion, and even so, he could be a dead fool with one snap of Meek's fingers. Besides, no Egyptians were involved in the 9/11 attacks. Today was a day of peace and enjoyment, no violence—not yet anyway.

After a half-hour on the boardwalk, the couple headed back to the vehicles parked on the avenue. The rear door to the Escalade was opened by one of his men and Jessica slid inside first, then Meek. The door closed. Both SUVs drove off. Jessica was nestled against Meek, and the smell of his cologne was enticing and his touch was stimulating.

"I want you. I want to eat your pussy right now." Meek was spontaneous, and he wasn't shy about expressing his sexual needs and his feelings. He touched her even with the driver and bodyguard in the front seat.

At first, Jessica felt apprehensive with the extra company around, but Maserati Meek was quite aggressive. He undid her jeans and pulled up her shirt.

"Forget that they are even here," he said about the driver and the bodyguard.

It was hard, but she knew she couldn't refuse him. He was in charge. She closed her eyes and positioned herself on her back against the backseat, allowing Meek to remove her jeans and panties, and then spreading her legs. It was electrifying. As the SUV merged onto the Belt Parkway, Meek went down on Jessica and ate her pussy with the vehicle doing sixty miles per hour. She squirmed and moaned. Life was good. She didn't want to give it up for anyone or anything.

Fifteen miles later, she came in his mouth. Her body felt spent. Maserati Meek lifted himself back into the seated position, wiped his mouth, and smiled. It was fun for him. It was mind-blowing for her. The two men seated in the front seat didn't turn around once. Maserati Meek had them trained well.

An hour later, Meek dropped Jessica off in Harlem—the busy 125th Street. Jessica wanted to do some shopping. She kissed her lover goodbye and climbed out of the truck. She felt safe, but Maserati Meek left her with a shadow—one of his goons to watch her back. He wouldn't speak or interact with Jessica; it was forbidden. Where she went, he went, and he would remain subtly unseen in the background, armed and trained to kill.

"Let's go," Maserati Meek said to his driver.

He gave Jessica one last fleeting look as the SUV moved away from the curb. His fun time was over; now it was back to business.

\*\*\*

The dark Escalades rolled up in front of an old Brooklyn residence in East New York. On this sunny, summer day, the urban block was flooded with thugs and drug fiends, while the neighborhood kids played in the blast of cold water from the fire hydrant. A few neighbors enjoyed the sun-drenched day by sitting on their concrete steps or their aged porches, chitchatting and watching cars and people pass by.

One of the Escalades parked on the street, while the other pulled into the narrow driveway and stopped. The back door opened, and Meek climbed out. The backyard had a high wooden privacy fence looping around it. The neighbors on the block knew who the men were and were concerned about their illicit activities, but they minded their business. These were dangerous men, and fear was a strong motivation for silence and cooperation.

Meek entered the residence from the back entrance. The smile he had earlier was long gone, replaced with an expressionless look. The house was where victims were taken and questioned, and sometimes discarded. No drugs or cash were present, though some guns and men were. It was the hub for an operation they planned to carry out. It was hush-hush until it was the right time.

Flanked by his foreign henchmen, Meek walked through the kitchen and descended into the concrete basement. Three men lingered below. Meek's African American goons were not needed for this operation; only Egyptian men were involved in this side of the business. Each man looked more sinister than the next. They were busy with assembling equipment and welding machinery—engrossed in preparation and perfection. Maserati Meek stood in the center of the basement and observed how it all was coming together, piece-by-piece. He would wage a war on the New York streets—one like the city had never seen before. His enemies would tremble with fear, and his name would reign supreme. He smiled at the progress being made and thanked his men in Egyptian Arabic.

"My brothers, Allah is with us today."

# 3

The Kid sat in the room devising his master plan of deception. He once read that during World War II, the Allies used dummy tanks made out of cardboard to deceive German reconnaissance planes into thinking a large armored unit was on the move in one area while the real threat was somewhere else. And it worked. The Kid needed to implement his trickery, but it wouldn't involve a dummy anything. There would be human sacrifices.

He figured that at the event Jessica put together, he and his crew would be gunned down in a hail of bullets when they exited the club—slaughtered viciously on the streets for everyone to see. He would have done it the same way, but there was no underestimating Maserati Meek. He doubted anyone from Meek's crew would come inside the club because it would put everyone on high alert.

How would he attack, and exactly when? The Kid needed to think.

Jessica was also on his mind. He wanted to see her. Though she was a selfish and conniving bitch, he wanted her. But there was no avoiding it; eventually, she would have to die. She was a huge liability, and keeping her alive would make him look weak to Devon and Papa John.

The Kid met with Devon privately to go over his plan. He told Devon everything, and how it should be done. It was a chance, a huge one, but The Kid felt it would work.

"Listen, how can dead men implement revenge?" he said to Devon. "If Maserati Meek thinks we're dead, then let's make it look that way. Let's create it. And then soon after, he won't even see us coming."

Devon was listening, but it was hard for him to wrap his head around what The Kid was suggesting. Kid was the brains, and Devon was the muscle—the killer.

"Yo, why we doin' all this? We should just lay on this nigga Meek and blow his fuckin' back out and that ho, cunt, Jessica too. I'm telling you, this shit don't feel right. Your brother underestimated this Muslim muthafucka and he dead now."

"Don't disrespect my brother," Kid warned.

"How is saying a dead nigga dead disrespect?"

Kid cut his eyes toward Devon. "What's with all these questions? You got a problem wit' the way I run things?"

"It ain't even like that. I got a problem wit' getting a tag on my toe before my time. I know you're smart, but walking into an ambush don't seem smart to me. In fact, it feels the opposite. It feels dumb, Kid. I'm telling you, let's not do this!"

Both Devon and Kid were frustrated. Kid understood Devon's hesitation, but he needed his triggerman to be on the same page.

"Let me paint this picture for you. My brother is six feet below rotting. Maggots are eating away at his flesh and his soul ain't at rest. I know this cuz he comes to me in my dreams. In order for Kip to rest peacefully, I gotta beat this sand nigga not only with muscle but with my mind too. This was cerebral from day one. The moment Meek hired y'all to rob the drop, he positioned his pieces on the chess board, and he doesn't want to lose. When he killed Kip he knocked over our knight. He had no idea that I'm the fuckin' king. I have to finish what Kip started. Meek has to lose twice—mentally and then physically. If you can't understand that, let Papa John step up to the plate. We gonna win, Devon. You just gotta trust me."

Devon nodded. He was ready to go.

The next evening, they all met at Eshon's place to talk. She'd been living there alone since her mother had moved to Brooklyn. There, they had the privacy to meet and talk. Devon wheeled Kid into the apartment.

Eshon was still mourning Kip's murder, but she was getting a little better every day. She had a million regrets. She regretted each time she denied him pussy because she was angry with him. She regretted never getting pregnant because she wanted to be his wife first. She regretted not telling him she loved him more. Her days were filled with regrets.

Brandy was already present, seated on the couch pulling from a blunt, and Papa John arrived soon after. Everyone who mattered was inside Eshon's place.

Eshon looked at Kid and asked, "How are you holding up?"

"I'm okay. I think about him every day," he replied.

"I think about him every minute," she said.

"A'ight, Y'all listen up," Devon hollered. "I called this meeting today because I got a plan."

"A plan? You? For what?" Brandy asked, looking at him skeptically.

Devon cut his eyes at Brandy. "You think I'm just some ignorant killer, huh, Brandy? You don't know much about me. I'm smarter than you think, fuckin' bitch."

"I'll believe it when I see it," she countered.

"Bitch, you think I'm a fuckin' joke!" Devon exclaimed.

"Hey, let's just all be quiet, chill out, and listen to him," The Kid said. "Now is not the time to be going against each other when there's a real threat that wants us dead."

Kid quickly calmed things down between Brandy and Devon. Now wasn't the time for civil war. If they didn't come together as one, then they were going to be defeated and die. Brandy took another pull from the blunt and then passed it to Eshon. After everything she'd been through, she needed to smoke regularly.

The Kid nodded toward Devon to continue. He did.

"Like I was sayin' before I was rudely interrupted, I got a plan, and it's a really good one," said Devon.

The room was listening. Devon stood in the center of the room with his rough appearance. His small Afro was nappy, his hands were ashy, and his clothes had seen better days, his beige Timberlands scuffed and untied. It was clear that he was carrying a pistol in his waistband, and his eyes were colder than the Antarctic. He was in charge, but how? Some people wondered.

Devon was the exact opposite of Kip. Kip had swag; Devon had none. Kip was smart and put-together, twenty-four/seven. Devon was a hothead and reminded people of Oscar the Grouch from Sesame Street, living out of a garbage can and dirty. He had a sixth-grade education but was respected on the streets because of his gunplay. He had no finesse. But this was the man who was supposed to keep the crew alive and outwit Maserati Meek, a criminal kingpin. Brandy, Eshon, and others in their growing crew did have some concern. Papa John was the only one who knew who was really calling the shots.

Devon stood in front of everyone and started to recite the monologue The Kid taught him to remember and say. It took them hours for Devon to get things right and know where The Kid was going with the idea. He started to talk, saying, "What I'm about to propose will involve some human sacrifices."

Whoa, "propose" and "human sacrifices," those were pretty big words for a hotheaded killer with a limited education, they thought.

Devon went on to say, "Maserati Meek will continue to be a threat to us until we're dead to him. So let us make him believe that we're dead. This coming event that Jessica has set up, we will die there."

Brandy and Eshon thought he'd lost his mind. Where was he going with this speech and plan? The Kid remained silent. So far, Devon was doing a pretty decent job outlining the plan to everyone.

There was concern and grumbling, though.

"Hear me out. I been doin' a lot of thinking," Devon said.

He had everyone's undivided attention. The Kid sat coolly, like it was the first time he heard of the plan. He couldn't take control of the meeting. He had to remain seated and meek, and allow Devon to do what they'd rehearsed.

"We need decoys at this party," he said.

"Decoys?" Eshon asked with a raised eyebrow.

"Yes, someone to take our places there—people who look like us from a distance, but they ain't us; ya feel me?"

It was still confusing.

"So you want people to die for us?" Eshon said.

"We're gonna pay 'em."

"So you want to pay muthafuckas to take our place and die for us?" Eshon asked. "And who's gonna take the job to get paid to die?"

It sounded crazy.

"That's where the ruse comes in. They won't expect death but think it will be something else—reality TV maybe."

Eshon and Brandy laughed.

"You think muthafuckas are stupid out here, Devon?" Brandy exclaimed.

"They do what we pay 'em to do," he said.

"Obviously you didn't think this shit all the way through," Eshon said.

The Kid was watching his plan fall apart. The girls were skeptical. They were ready to walk away from it. He had to do something. Devon played his part well, but he wasn't prepared for the backlash.

"I think it's a great plan," The Kid intervened.

"Really?" Eshon said. "And why's that?"

"Look, if Maserati thinks we're dead, then the threat is cleared, and it will be a lot easier for Devon and Papa John to get at him. Ghosts don't kill people," he said, sounding somewhat rational.

"Look, I don't give a fuck who gotta die, as long as it ain't me," Brandy said. "And Jessica, I'm ready for that bitch."

They all wanted to tear Jessica apart, especially Eshon. She wanted to wrap her hands around the traitor's throat and squeeze tightly until there was no more breath inside her body. She wanted to kill her former friend with her bare hands. E&J Brandy bitches were no more. Jessica was a manipulative bitch that didn't deserve life.

Eshon sighed. "So, how we supposed to do this? How we gonna get people—innocent people—to become decoys for us at this party?"

"Like I said, money and a con," Devon said.

"You need to be more specific about the con you want to implement," she replied.

"And I have a way," he said.

They were all waiting to hear the con. The Kid sat and waited, too. He had to sell it to the crew first before they could sell it to anyone else, especially the decoys.

Devon had it memorized. The Kid steered him in the right direction earlier and tried to cover all the bases. Devon looked everyone in the eyes and said, "Everyone wants to get paid, right?"

"Not to die," Eshon said.

"They ain't gonna know they gonna die!" he repeated. "Look, we go out and find five muthafuckas that resemble us—"

"And tell 'em what?" Brandy asked.

"Look, y'all makin' this shit more fuckin' difficult than it already is," Devon griped.

"That's because it is difficult," said Eshon.

"It ain't fuckin' difficult, a'ight? Shit gonna be simple as A, B, C," Devon exclaimed.

Devon was losing control again. The Kid was watching him crumble under questioning. Devon looked at The Kid; he needed help with this one. It was going good so far, but Eshon and Brandy weren't fools. They wanted to know every single detail of his plan. If it wasn't right, then they weren't with it. They were used to Kip having it all mapped out for them. He covered everything. He knew the ins and outs and predicted what could go wrong.

Devon wasn't Kip—far from it.

"You can look for the men and women in shelters or troll the internet for those thirsty men and women who want to be seen. Give 'em a few dollars to be somewhere at a certain time, or find people that don't have much to lose," The Kid said, bringing the details to light. It made sense to them.

"That's what I was gonna say, the homeless and other muthafuckas," Devon spat.

The girls looked at him doubtfully, with that *Uh-huh, okay—whatever* look. The Kid to the rescue—subtly, though.

"Okay, we listening," said Eshon.

Devon went on with the plan. It was to get five people that resembled them, get them cleaned up and dressed a certain way and bring them down to the club the night of the memorial party for Kip. The decoys had to completely fool Jessica.

Devon wanted everyone to wear red and white that night; it would make them stand out. The girls were in charge of doing the shopping. Papa John, Devon, and The Kid scavenged the hood for potential people that could become their decoys. They scurried around Harlem, then Manhattan, Midtown, the West Side, the East Side, and frantically searched for people that had the same features as them. There were homeless men everywhere, and not surprisingly, they found their first decoy to resemble Devon. The man had the same height, build, and complexion as Devon. He was a bit older, but he was perfect. They approached him in Washington Heights as he pushed a shopping cart of junk and dressed in tattered clothing. They asked him some questions. His name was Henry. He had been homeless for fifteen years. It was a long time.

"Listen Henry, how would you like to make some good money for one night?" The Kid asked him.

"How much money?" he asked The Kid.

The Kid smiled and replied, "Five hundred dollars."

It was a lot of cash. More than he'd seen in over twenty years.

"I'm listening," Henry replied.

"Good, come with us and let's talk. I'm a man of my word, Henry, and you'll get every penny."

"Young man, I got trust issues. If you got dat kinda cash, then lemme see whatchu workin' wit'." Henry wasn't raised by a fool. The Kid flashed a wad of cash and tossed Henry a twenty.

"Now let's walk."

They led Henry toward the minivan, leaving his shopping cart behind and took him somewhere private.

The decoys for Papa John and The Kid were found two days later—men named Jake and Cedar. One was a bartender and the other a wannabe actor. Both were desperate to make five hundred dollars apiece. The Kid had the gift of gab, and he had these men believing he was in the TV and music industry—that he was there to help solve their problems—savior talent scout of some sorts.

Finding girls for Eshon and Brandy proved to be a little more complicated. The difficult part with Eshon and Brandy were the girls in the neighborhood came with questions. A girl named Mina who resembled Eshon came with question after question. What were they being paid to do? Why choose them? Who were they working for? What reality show? What was it about? Eshon tried to convince her that it was part of the reality show happening and she wanted Mina to be a part of it. They thought that flashing money would be enough to get these girls aboard, but it wasn't quite so simple. These girls wanted to know the full 411, and Eshon's I's had to be dotted and her T's crossed.

Though it took some strong convincing and a lot of talking, finally, Eshon got Mina and a girl named Mandy on board with the scheme. But they had to be careful and discreet with the ruse. Eshon told the girls that they had to sign a confidentiality agreement which meant to shut the fuck up about getting hired. If word leaked, then they would be fired. Mina and Mandy thought that they were about to be the next Cardi B and NeNe Leakes. To help sell the storyline, and just to see how stupid these dumb bitches were, Brandy had them act out an argument scene. Both girls got really into cursing each other out like they had years of beef.

Brandy and Eshon had to bite their tongues to keep from erupting in laughter. These girls were going for academy awards.

Eshon and Brandy went shopping in the city. With a lot of cash on hand, they went inside various clothing stores searching for the perfect outfits for themselves and their decoys for the approaching evening. Everything had to match up. They would have to buy two of everything, from the shoes down to the hairstyles. One mistake and everything could turn out to be deadly for them.

Eshon picked out a red and white form-fitting short-sleeve minidress for herself and Mina. It was classy and sexy. They picked out a red side-tie halter dress with red heels for Brandy and her decoy Mandy. The men would wear red T-shirts, white jeans, and white Air Force Ones. The event was three days away.

\*\*\*

Everything had been put into motion. Early morning on the day of the event, Eshon strutted into Jessica's building and took the elevator to the traitor's floor and knocked on her door with a counterfeit smile. Eshon had to put on a front for Jessica to make it appear that all was forgiven between them and there were no hard feelings. It was a hard task, knowing what Jessica had planned for all of them, but it was necessary for their survival. She held her evening dress in her hand, covered in plastic.

The apartment door opened, and Jessica appeared wearing a long T-shirt and curlers in her hair.

"Hey," Eshon greeted and gave Jessica a hug that repulsed her.

"Hey, what's good? Why you here so early, homes?" Jessica asked, sounding slightly defensive. "The party's tonight."

"I wanted to show you my new dress," Eshon said.

"Oh . . ."

Eshon held it up for Jessica to see. It was a lovely piece of fabric—stylishly designed, it stood out.

"We gonna wear all red tonight," said Eshon.

"Why red?"

"It was Kip's favorite color, and it's a celebration for him, right?"

Jessica nodded. "It is."

"And red is the color of love. We need to show our love for Kip tonight, so we all decided to become unified with red and white. Love and peace."

Jessica was listening, taking it all in.

Eshon continued with, "I just wanted to thank you, Jessica. I needed this. I miss him so much."

"I do too."

Eshon sighed faintly. "Despite what happened wit' us, I still got love for you, girl."

It was a vast lie.

"Eshon, you know you my number-one bitch, homes. I always got love for you, too," Jessica returned.

Another lie told.

The girls smiled in each other's faces and expressed their forgiveness, but rooted deep inside both of them was unadulterated hatred for each other. Eshon wanted to scratch that bitch's eyes out and throw her body off the rooftop and watch it fall apart. It took everything she had inside of her not to react violently. She needed to stick to the plan. Jessica would get hers.

Jessica was thirsting for their demise. She saw Eshon and everyone else as a gaping hindrance that needed to be eradicated from her life. Maserati Meek was the only person she cared about. Greed and love had gotten the best of her. Her friendship with Kip's crew had expired. Jessica felt that she had moved on to better things. And after tonight, there would be no more threats to her relationship with Maserati Meek. Her past would be behind her, her friends would be dead, and she would be free to concentrate on her future with Meek.

Eshon pivoted and made her exit. She had done her part. Jessica believed the lie about the dress code being red and white. Eshon made it emotional and explainable. Her love for Kip was never-ending.

Once the door closed and Eshon was out of sight, Jessica went into her bedroom and picked up her cell phone. She immediately called Maserati Meek. She had to tell him the news about the red and white outfits.

His phone rang several times before he picked up. "Meek, it's me, baby. I have something to tell you."

"I'm listening," he said.

"They all will be wearing red and white tonight, in honor of Kip."

"Red and white, eh," he replied nonchalantly.

"Yes, this will make it easier for you to spot them out in the crowd. Right, homes?"

"It will, but you have no need to worry. Relax, eh, because tonight everyone will die no matter what they wear. I can promise you that," he said coolly.

He hung up.

Jessica felt left in the dark, but she knew whatever Maserati Meek had planned was something sinister. Everyone was going to die. It was guaranteed.

# 4

The Kid, Devon, and Papa John drove through the Holland Tunnel and entered New Jersey. A few miles away, nestled on the outskirts of Newark, was a Motel 6 where their doppelgangers waited for them. Time was winding down. The men were well groomed, fed, and treated fairly until the day of reckoning. So far, The Kid had made good on his promises to them. He put two hundred and fifty dollars into each of their hands. They'd get the other half when the night was over—though he didn't expect them to live through tonight.

If Maserati Meek executed his plan, then Kid and his crew would be believed dead and out of harm's way from the crime boss. The Kid needed tonight's plan to work. It was a cruel thing, using innocent men as pawns for death so that he and his men could live. But in this world, there were no such things as half-measures. You went all the way—kill or be killed. You moved your queen fearlessly around the board and took what you wanted, or you didn't survive the game. In Kid's eyes, the decoys were simple pawns, meant to be sacrificed so the king could live on and rule.

He wheeled himself into the motel room and greeted the men with a smile and a hello. Papa John and Devon stood behind him; each showed friendliness, too. The three men were happy to be there—in a simple room with a bed and bathroom. They were being fed, they had cable TV, and they looked like decent human beings again. The bartender and starving artist had grand visions of making it to the big time, perhaps getting a movie deal. The homeless man was just grateful to have a good meal, warm bed, new clothes, and money to blow on drugs once these shenanigans were over.

"It's time to get dressed. Tonight is the night," The Kid said to them. "Y'all excited?"

"Yes," Henry replied. "After years of being hungry on the streets, this is like paradise to me. Thank you for this."

"That's good to know. I'm happy for you," The Kid replied.

The look in his eyes didn't change. He still felt nothing after the man's kind words. As they say in Hollywood, the show must go on. The Kid had changed overnight, becoming something that Kip desperately wanted to keep him away from. As the streets would say—he was 'bout that life. It was a life where one couldn't look weak. It was a life where your claws had to be the sharpest. And it was a life where you hoped for the best but prepared for the worst.

Devon lit a cigarette and smirked. *These fools think something good is coming their way,* he thought. He couldn't believe that The Kid's plan was coming to life. In a few hours, hopefully, these morons would be dead. Then they would have ample time to plot their revenge against Maserati Meek. It would be a sweet revenge because Meek wouldn't see it coming.

"We got one hour. I don't wanna be late there," The Kid said.

Each man got dressed in tonight's gear: red T-shirts, white denim jeans, and white Nikes. They were groomed to look exactly like The Kid and his men. The Kid nodded toward Devon, and he exited the room. Moments later, he brought in a wheelchair that was similar to Kid's. Everything had to be perfect—in uniform.

Before the men left the Motel 6, The Kid pulled out his cell phone and instructed Devon to dial Eshon. Once again, he couldn't look like he was in charge. Everything had to go through Devon. Eshon was across the river in a Brooklyn motel with the girls.

"Yo, what's it lookin' like on your end?" Devon asked.

"Copacetic, so far," she replied.

"A'ight. We gonna meet up around ten," he said.

The decoys were ready and looked right for tonight. From a distance, Jessica wouldn't be able to tell them apart. The timing had to be right. Until the plan was to be executed, the decoys had to stay out of sight. Like the game of chess, each piece had a purpose.

***

The VIP area at club Sane was decorated in floating red balloons, expensive champagne in ice buckets, and a black and silver banner with Kip's name etched into it. The place was decorated as a memorial for the late Kip. Jessica had gone all out for the bash, knowing it was going to be her friends' last night alive—like Custer's last stand.

Sane was the place to be tonight: large dance floor, circular bar, popular DJ, and classy VIP. The revelers danced to hip-hop music as Jessica waited for the victims to show up wearing a sexy black and gold Chanel dress. The event had cost a pretty penny, but secretly Meek had paid for it all.

Everyone showed up at different times—within ten minutes apart. Devon, Papa John, Eshon, Brandy, and The Kid all made their grand entrances, and all seemed normal. They were escorted to their private area inside the club where champagne bottles were burst open and bubbly was poured into short-stemmed wine glasses.

"Yo, yo, I gotta give a shout out to Harlem's E&J Brandy Bitches in the house," the DJ announced through the microphone. "They are looking stunning tonight, and representing Kip Kane tonight. Rest in peace, Kip. You are missed."

The announcement made Eshon smile, and it touched her heart that the DJ had recognized Kip tonight. She tried her best to hold back the tears. Eshon looked Jessica's way and raised her glass, saying thank you. Although the party was a scam for their demise, for that split second, it felt special and real.

The Kid felt the moment too, missing his brother a great deal. But regardless of how special tonight felt, it was still all a lie. Kid made Devon strategically place four triggermen outside the venue, lying in wait for the big bang. How and when it would come, no one knew; that was why the decoys were placed secretly in reserve, waiting to play their roles. Devon and Papa John were carrying pistols, an extra precaution inside just in case Maserati Meek was crazy enough to try something inside the club. Club security turned a blind eye for a few hundred dollars.

The mood was upbeat, and the dance floor was crowded as the DJ blared hip-hop and R&B. The Kid had his eyes on Jessica, watching her every movement. She was constantly on her phone, talking and texting someone. He had an idea who. She was shuffling her deck, trying to play her cards right. The duration of the night went smoothly—drinks and music, women and dancing. The Kid refused to drink. He had to stay focused, watching everyone and everything from his wheelchair.

The 2 a.m. hour approached, and the party was still going strong. The DJ continued to shout out Kip's and the girls' names. He was being paid handsomely to do so by Jessica. Devon threw back a bottle of champagne and ground his body against a big-booty woman in a short black dress, enjoying the scenery with pussy on the brain. The Kid was somewhat displeased by his behavior. He couldn't be the only one sharp tonight; their lives were on the line.

But Devon was going to be Devon—a horny thug. He wasn't looking like leadership at the moment.

Papa John, too, was into the moment, throwing back shots and flirting with beautiful women. Had they forgotten that tonight was a setup—that their lives were on the line?

The Kid couldn't expose himself by lifting himself from the wheelchair. A cripple he was, and a cripple he would remain as far as everyone knew.

The text from Jessica came to his phone out of the blue.

NOT FEELING TOO WELL, I NEED TO LEAVE. CATCH YOU LATER.

She stood up. He looked her way and nodded. She strutted away coolly from the VIP area in her red bottoms. The Kid watched her walk away. This was it—something was going down, and she was removing herself from the line of fire.

The Kid had plans of his own. He got Devon's attention; the man wasn't too distracted from his duties.

Jessica gave the girls a hug goodbye, thinking it was going to be their final hug, and Devon was right behind her. Before she took her steps from the area, Devon was on her like white on rice. He grabbed that bitch from behind and jerked her arm back, skillfully thrusting his gun into her lower back. Through a tightened jaw he growled, "Bitch, you move wrong, and I'm gonna blow ya fuckin' spine out."

She had no choice but to comply.

Devon was itching to kill her. His blood boiled with rage as he escorted her down the long, narrow hallway leading to the back exit. Papa John went and snatched up Eshon and Brandy; it was time to leave. They knew it was going down. The Kid wheeled himself away too. No one around was any wiser to what was going on. The music played, the club moved, and enough money had been spread around to the right people to make it look like they owned the place.

The decoys had been waiting in a nearby room. There was food for them, but they were separated from the club. The girls were sitting impatiently; the men were becoming anxious. Everyone was eager for their payday and to get things started. The girls wanted to join the party. The DJ was getting busy, playing everything from "Bodak Yellow" to Rihanna's "Wild Thoughts."

The Kid entered the room. It was time. The decoys' instructions were to mingle with the crowd, dance, and then start leaving between 4 a.m. and 5 a.m. They believed the cameras would be rolling for a new reality show. They were dressed for success, and the VIP area was theirs tonight, including the free champagne. Things were pushing forward as planned.

Papa John drove Eshon and Brandy to the hotel room in Jersey City they had reserved earlier. They'd made their exit covertly out the back door of the club. At the hotel, everyone was to lie low until The Kid and Devon arrived. No sudden moves; whatever Maserati Meek had planned for them, they would soon find out with the decoys planted inside the club.

Devon had also left with Jessica at gunpoint. Devon smacked her repeatedly and threatened her life. She was in tears. He threw her into the back of the van around the corner from the club and thrust the gun into her face. "You fuckin' rat bitch! You fuckin' traitor! You gonna die tonight!"

The Kid knocked on the back door and made his way inside via the small ramp. Jessica was in tears, but she didn't panic. Everything had suddenly backfired on her. How did they know? What did they have planned for her? The Kid didn't say a word to her. He snatched away her cell phone and went scrolling through her call list and her text messages. The last one read: DID YOU LEAVE YET?

No doubt it was from Maserati Meek, though the contact read: *Heart*. He was securing his woman's safety. The Kid frowned and gritted his teeth. The man had Jessica's heart. She loved him—was in love with him.

Out of the blue, The Kid smacked Jessica so hard his hand stung. She sat there blank and took the hit from him. She didn't cry out or show any emotions. She did nothing. However, her eyes told them everything—especially Kid. She hated him with a passion.

"So, he moves you better than me, huh?" The Kid said.

"He does everything better than you! Fuck you!" she coldly replied.

He started to type on her phone, replying to Maserati Meek: YEA, HOMES, I'M ALREADY GONE. YOU CAN DO YA THANG. SEE U SOON.

A reply came back to her cell phone immediately: JULY 4TH CAME EARLY, EH? BOOM!

The Kid was confused by the text. July 4th was two weeks away. Boom? What did it mean? He figured it meant their deaths. They would be riddled with bullets from many guns. The Kid felt that he was one up on Maserati Meek. Soon, it would be checkmate.

Devon called one of his triggermen positioned outside the club. He wanted to know the 411.

"Yo, what y'all niggas see out there?" he asked him.

"Nothing. It's quiet," the gunman replied.

"When you see that bitch-ass nigga Maserati Meek or anyone connected to him, y'all niggas lay them muthafuckas out."

"A'ight, we on—"

Before the man could finish his sentence, there was a sudden explosion, and the sky was lit up with fire and billowing smoke. The sound was deafening, and the van felt like it had been caught up in an earthquake. It rattled from side to side like a giant had the vehicle in its grip.

"What the fuck!" The Kid cursed.

Instantaneously, pandemonium broke out on the streets of New York. People ran from the club in different directions—some were severely injured, bleeding and distraught. There was frantic screaming and yelling, and cars were speeding away from the scene, flying through red lights with horns blowing and phones frantically dialing 911. It was too early to say what had happened, but it felt like 9/11 all over again. The club had been blown up. The entire structure was in shambles. Whatever had been used, it brought the foundation down—there was nothing but rubble.

The realization finally sank in for Kid. He turned toward Jessica and punched her in the face. Her nose bled. He hit her again.

"You were going to blow us up!"

Jessica had no idea what just happened. She was as clueless as everyone else. The blood trickled from her face onto the floor of the van. She was in pain. Devon too was angry—hyped and amped. He glared at Jessica and hollered, "Yo, we should just kill this bitch right here, right fuckin' now!"

"I didn't know," she exclaimed.

"Bullshit!" Devon hollered.

"I swear to you, I didn't know what he was goin' to do," she said.

The Kid scowled. He hadn't seen it coming. He'd been thinking guns, but obviously Maserati Meek was a bit more extreme. A bomb—a fuckin' terrorist attack. He was flabbergasted.

"Kid, what we gonna do wit' this bitch?" Devon asked, hoping The Kid would say death.

"Drive to the hotel," The Kid said. "We gonna take care of her in New Jersey. It's too hot out here right now."

Devon nodded, climbed into the driver's seat, and floored the gas pedal.

Jessica was thrown to the floor. Her body was wracked with pain. She knew it was the end for her. There was no way she would survive this ordeal. The Kid and Devon were pissed. Maserati Meek had tried to blow them up, but it had failed. Now she was going to suffer the aftermath of that failure.

The Kid tried calling Papa John and the girls, but to no avail. The lines were busy and jammed. The bombing had created chaos on the streets. Several police sirens blared from a distance. Tonight would be another night that the city would forever remember. Though it wasn't on the same scale as 9/11, another bombing in NYC was a horrible reminder. When they thought things were somewhat safe again, so easily they were thrust back into the nightmarish reality of how unsafe their world was.

# 5

Papa John parked at the DoubleTree hotel in Jersey City, and the trio strode into the lobby. So far there was no news from The Kid or Devon. Papa John and the girls figured they were safe. Things appeared to be going according to plan. Papa John checked his cell phone for any missed calls, but there weren't any. He reattached it to his hip and followed behind Eshon and Brandy to the elevators. The lobby was quiet with a few guests scattered in the entrance of the hotel with late check-in and early checkout. Within a couple of minutes of them entering the place, the atmosphere changed. People were glued to their cell phones and had a look of shock on their faces. The hotel clerks and night staff were fixed on the Breaking News flashing across the flatscreen hanging above the lobby. People were freaking out.

"What's goin' on?" Eshon asked someone close by.

"You didn't hear?" the lady replied.

"Hear what?"

"There was a bombing in the city . . . some club in Lower Manhattan."

They had just come from a club in Lower Manhattan. Was it a coincidence or not? Papa John and the girls were taken aback by the news. They hurried to their hotel room and turned on the television. The nightclub bombing was being broadcast on almost every channel. Several text news alerts came chiming into their cell phones. It was big. Several journalists confirmed it—there was an earth-shattering explosion at an unknown nightclub. News cameras were everywhere. The details were sketchy; no one knew anything because it was too early. Was it a gas leak? They didn't know, but what they did know was that the death toll would be staggering.

Papa John started to worry. He tried calling The Kid, with no success. He tried calling Devon; it was the same. Where were they?

"It wasn't a fuckin' gas leak. It was a bomb—a fuckin' bomb," Papa John said, knowing a lot more than the reporters and police who were scrambling for information and details.

"We don't know yet," Eshon said.

"Think, Eshon. We just left that area. It's the same fuckin' block they're showing on TV. Maserati Meek had sumthin' to do wit' this. We were supposed to die in that explosion."

The girls couldn't deny it. It made sense.

"Try calling them again," Brandy said.

Papa John tried repeatedly, but his calls weren't going through. It was nerve-wracking not being able to get in contact with Kid or Devon. They didn't want to think the worst—but could it be that they had been killed in the explosion?

Eshon sat on the bed looking lost and concerned. To lose Kip was heart-wrenching, but to lose Kid and Devon too—it would take her pain to the point of no return. Papa John walked to the window and looked outside. His mind was flooded with worries and concerns, too. What if he was the only one left? Then what? How would he go on with his friends gone? What would he do? It was a frightening thought.

*∗∗∗*

Miles away from the hotel, lower Manhattan was swarming with police sirens, ambulances, and fire trucks rushing to the explosion. City blocks were shut down in a large perimeter around the incident. It was a horrendous thing to see, so many bodies battered and crushed under tons of concrete and steel. They didn't know how many dead there were yet, but most likely it would be in the hundreds. The smell of smoke and death permeated the night air, and officials of all kinds from the city police to the FBI plagued the area that quickly became ground zero. So many people were around. So many people wanted to know what had happened—and they were scared. The smoke was still heavy, and the rubble was high.

\*\*\*

Maserati Meek sat on the couch, shirtless and smoking a cigar, and watched the news footage of the bombing in the city. The explosion was destructive, and from what he saw on TV, it was effective. He grinned and puffed his cigar, then said to his men in the room, "Allah is good."

Maserati Meek's enemies messed with the wrong man. He assumed they were all dead—no more of Kip's cronies. He had squashed them all like bugs. He assumed Jessica was alive, since she had texted him earlier to let him know she had left the building. He couldn't wait to see her again. She had been very effective with the plan, and he had something special for her.

He stayed in a plush, nine-million-dollar brownstone in Brooklyn in an affluent neighborhood a block away from celebrities such as actress Michelle Williams and the late Heath Ledger. Life was good. Allah truly was the one God. He gave Maserati Meek success in destroying his enemies.

Meek and his remaining goons—eight Egyptian men—watched their handiwork unfold for the world to see. The tragic event would be front-page news for weeks. And there hadn't been a successful terrorist bombing in New York City since September 11th. Maserati Meek was a proud man. His men stood proudly too and shouted out, "Praise to Allah."

Meek smoked his cigar and walked toward the window. He looked outside. Brooklyn was the perfect neighborhood for him. He hid in clear sight. He didn't fret about anything. With one threat gone, now he could refocus his attention on Panamanian Pete. Maserati Meek wanted him dead, but in due time. Now, he wanted to have some fun.

He turned toward his men and hollered, "Now, we celebrate!"

They cheered and smiled.

Maserati Meek turned and looked back out the window. He was looking for Jessica. He texted her for her location, hoping she was close, but he didn't get a reply. He wasn't too worried. If he didn't see her tonight, there was always tomorrow. The bomb had the police everywhere, and the destruction in Manhattan made things hot.

Meek called some high-end escorts for his goons' entertainment, and an hour later, several beautiful ladies of various ethnicities came walking into the plush brownstone dressed sexy. They had all the right curves and long hair and long legs in erotic stilettos. For a high price, they came with promiscuous conduct and an appetite for sex. Maserati Meek had dropped twenty thousand dollars for the girls. It wasn't seventy-two virgins in heaven, but it came close.

It didn't take long for the party to get started. The girls undressed, and the men had their pick. Blow jobs and hardcore sex happened throughout the place, along with drinking and celebrating.

Maserati Meek sparked up another cigar and watched it play out. His eight Egyptian men had no shame in their actions, leaving their religious beliefs at the door. They were horny goons who took full advantage of Meek's kindness.

*Allahu Akbar!*

Yes, Allah was good, and Maserati Meek knew Allah was going to continue to be good to them. Their enemies were falling, and Meek would continue to show them what hell on earth truly felt like. Next up was Panamanian Pete.

# 6

Traffic toward the Holland Tunnel was unexpectedly gridlocked in the wee hours of the morning. There was a sea of cars that stretched for miles. Horns blew, drivers grew impatient, and what was expected to be a quick trip through the tunnel and into New Jersey was turning out to be a long process and a perpetual nightmare. The reason for the sudden traffic was the police checkpoint before tunnel entry. Several uniformed officers were slowing down vehicles, doing random inspection and searches of cars and trucks going in and out of the city. The bombing earlier created a ripple effect of police activity throughout the city.

At the site of the club explosion, bomb-sniffing dogs and first responders were indicating a bomb had gone off, but it was still too early to tell. The police commissioner had put the alert on orange until the cause of the blast was confirmed. If it was indeed a terrorist attack, then it would immediately jump to red. Bridges, tunnels, and landmarks were on high alert. Extra cops and security were placed strategically from downtown to uptown and from Brooklyn to Queens. NYC wasn't taking any chances.

"Fuck!" Devon cursed as he and Kid sat in the middle of the gridlock.

Jessica was detained in the back. Her face was slightly bruised and swollen. She lay there still and quiet, biding her time and waiting for an opportunity. Her captors weren't focused on her at the moment. She closed her eyes, thinking about a possible escape—if there was one—while feeling the van inching closer and closer toward the tunnel.

"This traffic is too much. Time we get out of this, it's gonna be the next fuckin' day," Devon griped.

The Kid sighed. From his position, he could see the flashing police lights, and cops were waving a few cars through and telling other vehicles to pull over for either questioning or a search. They started to sweat bullets. They were in a van, and it was mostly vans and SUVs being pulled over. There wasn't a reasonable explanation for that bitch in restraints, her bruised face, or the guns they were carrying. Unable to reroute, they were creeping toward shit creek nice and slow.

"Fuck, we can't turn off anywhere?" The Kid knew the answer to his question.

It was too late. Like being caught in a whirlpool—they were going down no matter how hard they tried to resist.

The Kid needed to think, and think fast. He wasn't going down like this. There had to be a way out. Jail wasn't for him.

Suddenly, a reaction happened, and it didn't come from them. Jessica was the culprit. Seeing her opportunity, she jumped up, hastily kicked Kid in his face, knocking off his glasses, and she lunged for the back door. It opened easily, being unlocked, and she threw herself out of the van, tumbling slightly. She sprung to her feet, her adrenaline on high, and took off running in her red bottoms. She moved like a track star in her heels. Other drivers nearby were flabbergasted by the sudden event.

What just happened? Who was the woman?

The fact that Jessica was running so hard in the traffic jam quickly caught the attention of nearby police officers. It was highly suspicious, and they gave chase her way.

The Kid cursed loudly. Jessica hadn't injured him, but he had fucked up. He wanted to punch a hole through the windshield. He quickly reacted, closing the door she had escaped from and planting his ass back into the wheelchair. He spotted several cops coming their way and looking at every car as they approached, trying to figure out which vehicle the woman had come from.

"Just chill and be cool," he told Devon.

Devon wiped away the sweat from his brow and found it hard to be cool, but he was trying. Four cops approached them; one shined the flashlight at Devon and instructed him to roll down the window. He complied. The officer took one look at Devon and told him to pull over. Both men cursed silently; their situation had gone from bad to worse.

While Devon pulled to the side of the checkpoint, The Kid could see Jessica and the police officers in a conflict. She was quickly detained and handcuffed, then shoved into the backseat of a police cruiser.

The Kid thought, *What is she gonna say? What is she gonna do?* But right now, he had to worry about his own predicament.

Two cops came to the van from both sides, and one shined a light into The Kid's face. He narrowed his eyes from the bright light and coolly asked, "Can I help you, officers?"

Right away, they noticed that he was handicapped. The Kid looked unassuming in his wheelchair and his wire-rimmed glasses, and there was a tinge of guilt from them. They were initially going to drill them, have the dogs sniff the vehicle, and ask to search their van. However, their attitudes became a little more amicable.

"Where are you two coming from?" the cop near Devon asked.

Devon spoke up. "Today's my cousin's birthday and I took him out to eat in the city, officer. We were having a great time until all hell broke loose. What's going on?"

"There was an explosion," the cop said.

"Oh my god," Devon uttered, looking shocked. "Terrorist?"

"We don't know," said the cop.

The Kid remained silent and still. He was extremely nervous. Usually, he would be the one doing all of the talking, but shockingly, Devon stepped up and took charge, becoming cool and quick-witted in a sticky situation.

The officers had a lot on their plate tonight, and dealing with a cripple and his cousin wasn't their top priority. They backed off and apologized for troubling them and told them to drive safe.

Devon steered the van back toward the tunnel, and he and Kid sighed with relief. They couldn't believe the cops had let them go. Still, Jessica's escape and her arrest were a major problem. The Kid couldn't do anything about it now. She was in the hands of the NYPD, and he didn't know for how long. He had no idea what she was going to be charged with, if there was a charge. And would she talk? One thing was for sure; he needed to eradicate the problem before it got out of hand. Jessica was a liability, and the fact that her man tried to blow them up tonight pissed The Kid the fuck off!

***

It was 5 a.m. when Devon and The Kid arrived at the DoubleTree in Jersey City. From the parking lot, through the lobby, and the elevator up to the sixth floor, things were tense. The hotel staff and a few guests were discussing the recent bombing. The news was calling the event a suspected terrorist attack although no group had come forth to take credit for it. Everyone seemed a mixture of shocked, confused, and utterly scared.

Devon pushed Kid toward the room. Both men were quiet. The plan tonight had gone somewhat well. They would be presumed dead. However, with Jessica still alive their plan blew up in smoke just like the building they were supposed to be in. All that planning and all those innocent lives lost were in vain all because The Kid was sweet on Jessica.

They entered the room to find everyone asleep. Eshon and Brandy were sharing a bed, and Papa John was stretched out across the other. Kid was annoyed. How the fuck could they sleep at a time like this? It was fucking Baghdad outside.

Devon was upset too. He looked at Kid and knew what to do. "Wake up!" he shouted. "Wake the fuck up!"

Everyone was startled. Papa John even pulled out his gun and was ready to react. Seeing The Kid and Devon alive was a relief. Devon picked up the remote control to the flatscreen and clicked on the news. The city and the world were devastated—on pause with shock and concern. As the sun was rising, more news rose about the club explosion. It was a fact that it was a bombing—a suicide bombing. A man walked into the Manhattan club last night and detonated himself, killing over two hundred people inside. It was an extreme act of violence that they weren't ready for.

The Kid sat silently. His eyes were fixed on the TV. The destruction and violence were palpable. Was this the world they lived in now? What troubled The Kid was that they were playing on a whole new level—a deadlier one. It was no longer the Wild, Wild West. It felt like the apocalypse. Maserati Meek chillingly blew up an entire nightclub to kill five people.

"Jessica got away," Devon told the group.

"What? How?" Eshon asked.

Devon frowned. "She got arrested."

Eshon's mouth dropped open, and Papa John said, "What the fuck you mean arrested?"

"Arrested?" Brandy blurted out.

"We fucked up!" Devon told them. "It was doomed from the start."

"Doomed?" Eshon asked. "How you figure that?"

Devon was tight. He could have been blown to bits or arrested for kidnapping all because The Kid had some kiddie crush on a whore who didn't give two fucks about any of them. "Jessica should have never had a chance to get away cuz that bitch shouldn't have been kidnapped in the first place. We didn't need her. She should have either thought we were dead like Meek or we should have killed her a long time ago. All these fuckin' mind games got a nigga's head about to pop."

Kid sat quietly for a moment and drank in Devon's frustration. Calmly, he readjusted his wire-rimmed nerd glasses and said, "You're right, Devon. So why did you let her live? I thought your plan was good, but now that you've broken it down, it seems you didn't really think it through."

Devon was incredulous. "My plan? *My* fuckin' plan?!"

Papa John intervened. "I think it was more me wanting to use Jessica and Devon was against it, Kid. Dee, next time I will listen when you say we need to dead someone. My bad."

Papa John had to jump in to keep the ruse. The girls had no idea what was going on. All they knew was that bitch Jessica would live another day.

It all felt like it was falling apart. With Jessica alive and now in custody, their chances of staying dead to Maserati Meek were looking slim. It seemed the hard work was for nothing.

They didn't get much sleep that night. The drama was still on full throttle, and the explosion was plastered across the television. The hotel room became a hub for The Kid and his crew. With Jessica alive and locked up, Kid had to come up with a game plan to get to Jessica before she was able to reach Maserati Meek. She would get one phone call, and he had no doubt who she would call.

As The Kid listened to everyone complain about almost being blown up and Jessica's betrayal and escape, he sat in silent contemplation. He said, "We need to call the precinct," in a meek and humble tone, one different from what Papa John and Devon were used to hearing.

"Call the precinct?" Eshon asked.

"Yes, to see if she was arrested, and if so, when her arraignment is," The Kid said.

He was right. It was a good idea. The more information they had about Jessica's arrest, the better. The clock was ticking. The Kid figured Jessica was detained at a precinct near the tunnel. He got online and searched, but there wasn't much information for them to go on. Things were hectic when Eshon called the precinct. For hours no one picked up. She figured things were crazy in the city.

"We won't get anywhere just sitting in this hotel; we need to be out there. You should take a cab to the precinct and see what you can find out," The Kid said to Eshon.

Eshon looked skeptical. "Honest, I don't wanna fuck wit' the city."

"I'll go wit' her," Brandy said.

"That probably won't be a good idea, Brandy. It would probably look less threatening and less suspicious if one person went," said Kid.

They felt he was right.

Eshon sighed and nodded. "I'll play her cousin, just in case she's there and they let her know."

"Look concerned and let them know that her whole family is worried about her because she was supposed to be at that club and she hasn't returned home yet. Play the worried family member," The Kid said. "We need to find her and keep track of her."

Eshon nodded.

With so many bodies under the rubble, it could be days until an exact death toll was announced and the dead were identified. The NYPD and the feds had a lot on their hands. There was so much to do, and everyone was watching.

For a split second, Eshon and Brandy noticed how Kid was giving them good ideas, and how at certain moments he sounded like his brother. It was strange. He was the same, but they couldn't help but think that there was something slightly different about him.

The Kid had to catch himself from giving out orders. It was supposed to be Devon's job. But he couldn't help himself; things were critical. He also noticed how Eshon and Brandy were looking at him. Maybe he had said too much.

# 7

The cab inched through the Holland tunnel. Going into the city from New Jersey was nothing but continuous brake lights and bumper-to-bumper traffic. There was a checkpoint at the exit, and Eshon sighed heavily and cursed.

The driver, a bushy-haired Caucasian foreigner, sighed too and glanced at Eshon through his rearview mirror. "The city is a mess today. There was some bombing last night at a nightclub. It's all over the news. I tell you, these damn terrorists, they just need to strap them all to a nuclear missile and send them off into space and blow them up. Show these idiots what a real explosion looks like."

Eshon wasn't in the mood for a conversation. The faster she got things over with, the better. She rolled her eyes at him because the last thing she wanted was a talkative cab driver while they sat in heavy traffic. She had a lot on her mind. Eshon had no idea what would transpire. What if Jessica was already with Maserati Meek and telling him everything? The last thing Eshon wanted was to be in the crosshairs of a ruthless terrorist. And with Kip dead, their leadership was shaky. She'd believed in Kip, but Devon was a different story.

It took nearly two hours to arrive at the 1st Precinct on Ericsson Place. It was a madhouse outside the precinct; cops, including Emergency Service Units, were everywhere. Security had been beefed up. With the city on red alert, paranoia had set in, and downtown looked like almost like a warzone with the military-like police vehicles parked everywhere. Eshon paid the driver and climbed out of the cab into a sea of chaos. She was in the same red and white dress she had worn to the nightclub, but she looked disheveled—it had been a very long night. She wanted to look inconspicuous, but her outfit stood out to some extent.

She walked into the building where everyone was uptight, angry, rude, and scared. It was crowded—lots of arrests and people wanting answers on whether it was a bomb or gas leak. The media said it was a suicide bombing, but there were some people saying that it wasn't. Everything was scrambled. The mayor would address the tragic situation this afternoon. He would stand in front of City Hall and try to appease the panic ensuing in his city. He would also state if it was a terrorist attack or not. His city needed answers.

Eshon walked toward the desk sergeant, and she wasn't the only one. His area was swamped with folks. People were talking over each other, and question after question was thrown his way. Eshon made her way toward the sergeant with a question of her own.

"I'm lookin' for my cousin. Is she here?" she shouted.

Numerous folks were searching for someone, and they were waiting for answers. Who was responsible for last night's explosion? Would there be more deaths? What were the police doing about it? Were they safe?

"People look, not now!" the sergeant screamed.

"But I'm lookin' for my cousin, she was—" Eshon didn't get to finish.

The sergeant glared at her and shouted, "I can't help you right now! You need to wait like everyone else! And I'm a sergeant, not an officer! You see the gotdamn stripes, lady?"

She frowned. She would have to wait patiently like the others. Cops made her nervous, but she remained unruffled. She found a long bench near a narrow hallway and planted her behind into a seat, next to other civilians at the precinct for similar reasons. She had one task to do, and she was determined to do it. Her life was on the line.

As Eshon sat and waited, looking at the comings and goings of cops and people in such a cramped area, she pulled out her cell phone to text Devon.

I'm here. Shit is crazy right now.

Looking around, Eshon knew it was going to be a long day for her. It was also an emotional one. She had no breakfast, she was alone, and the precinct reeked badly of every odor imaginable. An hour went by, then another hour, and she still sat there waiting. Eshon wasn't about to see the third hour go by without any results.

It was getting ugly in the atrium of the 1st Precinct. An altercation broke out between the sergeant and an irritated citizen. A man was angry because they had arrested his brother, and he wanted to know why. The sergeant lashed out at the man, but this person wasn't taking no for an answer. He didn't want to be shooed like some pesky pigeon in a park.

"Where is my fuckin' brother?" he had cursed.

"Sir, you need to calm down and have a seat," the sergeant replied.

"Don't tell me to calm down! Y'all muthafuckas arrested my brother for no fuckin' reason! He ain't do shit! We ain't fuckin' Muslim, muthafucka. We gonna sue this fuckin' place! Racial discrimination, nigga!"

"I'm not gonna tell you again. Have a seat," the sergeant warned.

"Fuck you!"

His harsh reply angered the sergeant and a few other cops in the area. They approached with caution, but with a fiery attitude. The NYPD was dealing with enough today, and they weren't about to take any disrespect inside their building.

"Calm the fuck down or leave the building," said another cop.

"Fuck you too, cracker-ass muthafucka!"

The cop was raring to go with his hand on his holstered weapon, legs spread. A reaction was his next action. He wasn't alone; several other officers had surrounded the disgruntled man and ordered him, "Get on the ground now! Get on the ground!"

The man wasn't complying at all. He was ready for a fight. When they tried to restrain him with force, he fought back. He punched two officers in the face with a wallop that echoed like thunder, and he wrestled with the others. They struggled with him. Although he was slim, he was strong and feisty. He screamed. Eshon minded her business on the sidelines as she watched eight cops crash against the man to bring him down and handcuff him.

It was an eventful morning.

After the melee, things started to get back to normal, if they could call anything about this morning normal.

Impatience bubbled inside Eshon; this wasn't about to be her entire day, sitting inside a precinct and seeking a cop's attention. She stood up and looked for a cop who would most likely talk to her. But she would have to change her story. She soon spotted a female officer entering the building. She was a black woman, about Eshon's own height and not looking sleep-deprived like the other cops. She looked refreshed and charged up. Eshon approached her, and uttered, "Officer! Officer! Please, I need your help."

The woman turned and looked at her. Her nametag read Miles. Officer Miles. Eshon had gotten her attention; now she needed to keep it.

"I was there!" Eshon uttered fretfully.

"You were where?" replied the cop.

"My friend and I were at the club when we got separated. I left the club, and then the building blew up suddenly. I just need to know, is she on that list? Is she dead?"

"No list has been put together yet; it's still too early. Did you try contacting the hospitals in the area?"

"I did, and she's not in any one of them. She's not home, and her family is really worried. I need to find her, officer."

"You'll find her."

"Has she been arrested?" asked Eshon.

"Arrested? Why would you think she's been arrested?"

"I just see that it's a madhouse here and in the city. Lots of people are being arrested since the explosion last night. And I'm just worried about her. It's my paranoia talking, that's all," Eshon proclaimed.

Eshon's outburst piqued Officer Miles' interest. She was trained to spot suspicious behavior, and there was something suspicious about Eshon.

"What is your friend's name?" she asked.

"Jessica Hernandez," Eshon answered.

Officer Miles said, "Wait here, I'll go check."

The officer pivoted and walked toward the front desk to access the nearest computer. Eshon stood there with butterflies swimming around in her stomach and watched her from a short distance. She thought about everything that could go wrong. *Shit—why am I here in the first place?* she screamed to herself. She felt too vulnerable. She feared being arrested herself. She wasn't a law abiding citizen, but a criminal herself. What if she had warrants? What if they came for her?

*Keep cool! Keep cool. Chill,* she told herself repeatedly.

Officer Miles approached Eshon and told her, "I have good news and bad news."

Eshon puffed out and said, "What is it?"

"We found your friend, and she's here. She has been arrested."

Eshon lied and replied, "I'm just happy to know that she's alive."

"Wait here and I'll find the arresting officer."

Ten minutes later, the arresting officer came walking Eshon's way. He was a tall, well built white boy with short-cropped hair, blue eyes, and a clean shave. He was looking fine in his NYPD uniform. Eshon fixed her eyes on him, and he fixed his eyes on her.

"Officer Spielberg. You're the one asking about Jessica?" he said.

She nodded.

"And you were at the club last night?"

"Yes."

"Let's talk then. Follow me," he said.

Eshon felt a lot more nervous now. She didn't like the way he looked at her, and the tone of his voice made it feel like there was something wrong. She followed the cop through the reception area, into the heart of the precinct and amid a sea of blue uniforms, phones ringing, and everyone busy with something. She followed him down a brick hallway and into a small, windowless room. He gestured for her to take a seat at the metal table. She did. He sat opposite of her.

"Your friend was arrested last night, early morning. She was running full speed away from an NYPD checkpoint, and when she was confronted, she put up a fight, kicking and punching a few officers in the scuffle. She's being charged with assault and resisting arrest. She's being processed now and will be transferred to Central Booking. But the way this day is going, no time soon," the officer stated.

Eshon fought to remain expressionless.

He continued. "Your friend is also unruly and disruptive, and if she keeps it up, we'll add more charges on her."

*Fuckin' dumb bitch!* Eshon thought. If Maserati Meek weren't such a threat to them, Eshon would have left her trifling ass to rot in jail. But Jessica being locked up was a threat to them, and they had to find some way to get to her or bail her out.

Officer Spielberg had his attention transfixed on Eshon. He noticed something about her—something a little off. "Can I question you?"

Eshon didn't want to be questioned, but she had to play nice. "Yes."

"You were at the nightclub last night, right?"

She nodded.

"What is your name?"

"Stephanie Brown," she lied.

"Date of birth."

"January first, nineteen ninety-five."

It was stupid to lie because she had no I.D. indicating that she was that person. And if he suddenly asked for proof of identification, then she was fucked! But surprisingly, he believed her, for now.

"What time did you leave the club?"

"I think an hour before the explosion. I'm not exactly sure."

"Did you notice anyone suspicious inside?"

She shook her head no.

"Were there any bags left unattended, that you noticed somewhere?"

"I didn't see anything. We were all having a good time."

"When did you become concerned with your friend's whereabouts?"

She had to play things out and keep her cool, even though she felt like a suspect all of a sudden. The way he was looking at her was disturbing. She had nothing for him, but she had to play along.

"Like I told the female officer, I left before her and was on my way home. We got separated. I got wind of the terrible incident. I called Jessica's phone repeatedly, but no answer. I checked the hospitals, but they said she wasn't there. I came here as a last resort."

"And why did you decide to leave the club?"

"I was tired. I had a long day, and I recently lost my fiancé . . . he was murdered. So Jessica wanted to take me out to have a good time and make me forget about my worries."

"My condolences," he said.

She didn't give a flying fuck about his condolences—like he cared about her fiancé and her well-being.

Officer Spielberg continued to ask more questions. He wanted to get to the bottom of the terrorist attack and arrest every culprit behind it. So far, this girl was their only lead.

A half-hour later, he was done with his questions. He received nothing useful, but because Eshon was so cooperative, he told her he would try to get Jessica to Central Booking earlier than originally planned and that he would let her know that her friend was worried about her.

"Please, don't let her know that I was here," she said.

With a raised eyebrow, he asked, "Why not?"

"I just wanted to know if she was safe. Honestly, we had an argument at the club . . . and we both said some nasty things to each other. Being truthful, I was tired, and it was getting late, and she was my ride. So I left without her. Then I hear about the explosion. I felt so guilty leaving her behind. And Jessica has an anger problem."

"I agree," he said.

"And I just want to get her to see that her anger is a problem." Eshon tried to sell her story to the officer. So far, there was no reason to have any doubts about her. In his eyes, he simply saw a concerned friend.

He removed himself from the table and handed Eshon his card before exiting the room. She took it. She was free to go, not that she had been detained in the first place. Everything seemed to check out, and, besides, he had more serious matters to deal with than a lone club patron who was worried about a friend. He figured that she was lucky to be alive.

The moment Eshon stepped out of the precinct, she dialed Devon's number. He answered, and she said, "She's here, at the 1st precinct being booked on assault and resisting arrest charges. But they're not sure exactly when they'll transfer her to Central Booking."

"A'ight, that's what's up. We on it," Devon replied.

She hung up.

Now it was their turn to do something—and do it fast. Jessica needed to be dealt with before Maserati Meek dealt with them.

# 8

"Fuck the NYPD, fo' real, homes! Y'all ain't nuthin' but some racist-ass muthafuckas. Fuckin' stupid pigs! Oink, oink assholes! This is bullshit, homes! Y'all got me locked up when there's fuckin' terrorists out there blowing shit up! Fuck y'all!" Jessica shouted.

She marched around the bullpen angrily looking like she was hopped up on drugs. She was the best dressed in the bullpen with her black and gold dress and red bottoms. Her adrenaline was on twenty and climbing. She wouldn't shut up and the cops couldn't make her, although they were tired of her reckless mouth and insults.

She gripped the rusted bars and glared at the cop reclined in a nearby chair, reading today's newspaper. "Officer, where's my fuckin' phone call? Don't I get a phone call, homes? Y'all gonna deny me my rights, too, *pendejo*?"

He ignored her. She was definitely hood, and her slang was becoming irritating. Jessica frowned and continued to march around the bullpen that was occupied with several other ladies waiting for their day in court and their one phone call. Things had been so hectic since the nightclub bombing, that everything was out of whack.

Jessica finally took a seat on the cold, hard bench in the middle of the bullpen and sighed heavily. She was itching to be released. She felt that they couldn't hold her for long. She would have to see a judge soon—within forty-eight hours. However, she was desperate to make her phone call. She'd just escaped being murdered, and Kid and his goons were still out there, plotting against her, and perhaps going after Maserati Meek, her sugar daddy. Also, the bombing had her in awe. She had never been that close to an explosion. Though she was held captive inside the van almost a block away when the blast happened, Jessica literally felt the ground shake underneath her. It felt like the van was going to tip over. The blast made everything tremble like a giant was stomping up and down the block.

What if she hadn't made it out in time? Would Maserati Meek still have detonated the device? He did love her, and he did care for her safety and well-being, right? The twist of killing people with bombs instead of guns was a whole new world for Jessica, and she was officially linked to a deadly terrorist. She was smart enough not to speak his name or say anything about last night. She was in enough trouble as is. While jailed, she had lost track of the time and the world felt still. She didn't know about anything on the outside and was nervous about what could be lurking once she was freed. She had underestimated Kid. He was much smarter than she predicted.

A few hours later, she was finally granted her phone call. Her arresting officer, Spielberg, called her name and Jessica hurried to leave the large jail cell to make her phone call. It had taken damn near all day, and she wanted to spit in the man's face. It was six in the evening. She had been awake for over twenty-four hours.

She picked up the receiver and her first call, of course, was to Maserati Meek. He was the only one that mattered. His phone rang and rang, but his voicemail picked up. She wanted to leave him a message, but what could she say with a cop in her face?

That asshole cop, Spielberg.

She hung up and she tried to redial his number. But Officer Spielberg suddenly stopped her, exclaiming, "You only get one phone call in here."

"But no one answered."

"That's not my problem."

Jessica wanted to scratch his eyes out. She swallowed her smart remark, and with sad eyes and a change of attitude, replied, "I don't know how things work here. Please, can I try another phone call?" That bitch she was earlier had faded away. Now she was much more desperate.

Spielberg exhaled, and said, "Just one more." Maybe he wasn't a dick.

Jessica managed to smile. Now she debated on whether to call Maserati Meek again or her family. She figured it was best to call her family since Meek wasn't answering his damn phone, probably because she was calling from an unknown number. It also wasn't smart to be calling him from a police precinct after a bombing.

She dialed home, the phone rang several times, and she prayed that someone answered. Finally, her cousin Jalissa picked up, and Jessica was thankful. To throw the cop off guard, she started speaking in Spanish, saying to her cousin that she was in jail.

"*La cárcel, lo que pasó?*"

"I don't have long to talk," she continued in Spanish. "But I need you to call this number for me. It's my boyfriend's number."

Her cousin was listening. Jessica was speaking with a sense of urgency. She gave Jalissa Maserati Meek's number and added, "Call now; don't wait!" Then she said, "Tell him this: 'Everyone in red left early.'"

It was a cryptic message, but Jessica felt a sense of relief once she hung up. She could trust her cousin. Jalissa had always been responsible and on point.

Jalissa had no idea what Jessica was talking about. She had every intention of making the call immediately, but she got distracted by some infuriating texts from her ex.

Right after Jessica's phone call, it was business as usual. Back to her nasty attitude, Jessica began cursing Spielberg out once again for arresting her. He just smirked. She was escorted back into the bullpen. Now her only option was to wait. Hopefully the judge would release her on her own recognizance or set a low bail.

*＊＊

Unbeknownst to Jessica, Officer Spielberg was fluent in Spanish. Though he appeared Caucasian, his mother was Puerto Rican and his father was Jewish. He understood everything that was said on the phone. Her saying that everyone in red left early bewildered him. What did it mean? He knew it had to mean something dealing with the explosion. The girl who'd come looking for Jessica earlier, a Stephanie Brown, had on red. Second, why was Jessica running like a track star at the police checkpoint not long after the bombing? When she was arrested, it wasn't a run that said "I need to get home," but "I'm guilty." Something had happened. She was involved in something—if not the bombing, then something criminal.

Spielberg remembered the phone number she gave over the phone and he jotted it down into his notepad. His gut instinct told him to look into it. There was something there. It was too early to put his finger on it, but it was a major case, and he wanted a piece of it.

He found a computer and started his investigation. Quickly, he ran the ladies' names, Stephanie and Jessica. Within minutes, he realized that he couldn't find anything on Stephanie Brown's information. Jessica had a previous arrest record with a Harlem precinct. Officer Spielberg knew that these two ladies were linked to the bombing somehow—if not directly, then indirectly.

With his newfound information, he went to speak to his sergeant with his gut suspicion. It was eating at him. He was definitely on to something.

However, Sergeant Harrison let Spielberg know that the cryptic line a young woman gave over the phone about people in red hardly made them terrorists, or linked to terrorists. He was dismissive of Spielberg because it had been a long night, and a longer day. Calls were coming in from everywhere, people were edgy, and the commissioner and the mayor were up everyone's asses to solve the confirmed terrorist attack on New York City soil. The death toll so far was 189 dead, with 75 still missing. It was a huge and popular club.

But why a nightclub? The attack had many high-end officials baffled.

Spielberg didn't want to give up. He knew he was on top of something big. Before he departed the sergeant's sight, he requested one last thing.

"Could we get Jessica's dress and have forensics swab her hands for any residue?"

The sergeant sighed, but he relented.

***

Exhaustion finally caught up to Jessica, and before she knew it, she was fast asleep on the hard bench in the bullpen. The officers knocking their batons against the iron bars suddenly woke her up from the bench, and the annoying and cruel sound echoed, waking other sleeping inmates.

"Ladies, let's get up and go!" a cop shouted.

It was time to move. It was time for her to be transferred to Central Booking—then it was to The Tombs, as some called the place if they were unlucky in front of the judge. The Tombs was a colloquial name for the Manhattan Detention Complex—a municipal jail in lower Manhattan at 125 White Street.

Legally, Jessica had to be processed within a certain amount of time. But before she went anywhere, two female officers approached her and asked her to follow them. Jessica was taken aback. Why was she the only one singled out of the group? What was going on? In a small room, she was asked to remove her dress.

"Fuck no!" Jessica cursed at them. She wasn't about to remove anything.

The officers anticipated this. They wore latex gloves and carried batons. The order had come in from high above and as a precaution, the sergeant had to alert federal authorities. Jessica was under suspicion, and the feds wanted to follow every lead, no matter how small or ridiculous it seemed.

"Y'all stupid bitches touch me, homes, and it's on!" Jessica threatened them. "Fuck y'all!"

The officers, both black and both from troubled neighborhoods, were no strangers to friction. Jessica continued to curse at them and scowled and scrunched her hands into fists. They stepped closer to her and Jessica swung at them. She went pound-for-pound with one cop, before the second officer intervened and attacked Jessica from the back with her baton. The blow to her lower back made her stagger.

"Ouch!" she screamed.

"Get down, bitch! Get the fuck down!" one of the officers barked at her.

Jessica relented. She had bitten off more than she could chew. She fell to her knees as the two cops wrestled with her and beat the shit out of her. Someone grabbed her long hair tightly and slammed her head against the floor. It was a hard and dizzying blow, and blood gushed from her forehead. Everything the lady cops had done was against protocol, but they wanted to hurt that disrespectful little bitch.

Jessica was forced to undress. The dress was taken from her, and she was given scrubs. Looking terrible and humiliated, Jessica threatened a lawsuit against the NYPD and the two female cops. She screamed out, "Police brutality!"

The captain and sergeant wanted Jessica out of their precinct now. They shipped her to Central Booking in her scrubs and sent both female officers home on a paid suspension. It was an unfortunate incident, but with a bombing on their hands, the last thing they needed was a police brutality lawsuit, even though the prisoner had provoked the fight.

# 9

Police lights still lit up downtown Manhattan, as the FBI searched through tons of rubble from the explosion, removed dozens of bodies, and asked many, many questions. Surveillance footage from dozens of cameras in the area had been confiscated, and the feds were meticulously analyzing every second of it, trying to pinpoint any suspicious behavior before the bombing. They questioned everyone, from young to old. Time wasn't on their side, and they were springing into action, already flagging passports at airports, train stations, and bus depots.

It was a balmy night with a bright, full moon above. Papa John walked out of the hotel lobby alone with a cigarette in his hand, a lighter in the other. He needed some fresh air, and he needed to think. Papa John lit his smoke and took a few needed pulls, then exhaled. Weed would have been better—preferably some Purple Kush. Unfortunately, he had to settle for the Newport to calm his nerves.

He missed his kids. He thought about his son, John Jr., who'd recently been diagnosed with autism. John Jr. was still staying with one of Papa John's other baby mothers, Tina. His son was in good hands with Tina. Papa John was getting his son the best treatment possible.

His thoughts involuntarily drifted back to the club incident. Every time he thought about it, it made him edgy. If they had stayed any longer at Sane nightclub, then they would have been crushed underneath all that rubble.

Papa John took another drag and a sweeping view of the Hudson Lake. The waters were dark, but calm, and on the other side was a place where he didn't want to be at the moment. There was too much going on in Manhattan, and although Jersey City wasn't exactly a haven, it was safe enough until they figured out what to do next. And that "what next" was dealing with Jessica.

The edginess refused to subside, so Papa John went for a walk. He traveled closer to the long pier that protruded out over the Hudson. With it being such a lovely night, there were scatterings of people seated on the benches and others leaning against the iron railing, looking out at the sea. Otherwise, activity was sparse since it was creeping toward midnight.

Papa John flicked his dwindling cigarette into the waters and released the last of the nicotine smoke from his jaws. His .9mm pistol was fully loaded and tucked snugly in his waistband, concealed by a long T-shirt and green jacket. He gripped the railing and looked at nothing in particular.

His autistic son and the club bombing weren't the only two things occupying his mind. He also thought about *her*—Dina, his father's fiancée. It had been weeks since they had last seen each other, but he wanted to see her again. He liked her. Though it was wrong, Papa John had a strong appetite for the forbidden that he couldn't shake off. Everything about Dina was almost perfect. She was smart and cool. She was sexy and well put together from head to toe. She was also a freak, and thinking about that pussy was creating an arousal in his pants at a not so appropriate place.

Papa John needed an escape from being locked away at a Jersey hotel, bored and paranoid. He wanted to see her, no matter the risk. They had started something that day in his father's home that the two couldn't deny. Though she was still engaged to his father, she had her fun with Papa John by sneaking around. It was a blissful fun that felt like it could continue forever.

Papa John removed his cell phone. He wanted to call her, but thought otherwise—most likely a text message would be safer.

You good, beautiful? I wanna see u, he texted.

Papa John started to walk away from the pier when he received a text back from her.

When, tonight? she texted him back.

Yes, tonight. Where my pops?

At work. The bombing in the city is keeping him busy, she replied.

If only she knew that the bombing was meant to kill him. Everyone thought the suicide bombing was a political statement against the city and the country. Little did they know, it was simply over some street shit.

I'm comin over, he texted.

What time?

Papa John thought how long it would take him to travel to Whitestone from New Jersey and replied, About an hour.

She sent him a smiley face.

It was the ultimate offense, having an affair with his father's fiancée. But Papa John couldn't help himself. Dina was different, and his father was lucky to have her—and so was he. Her skin, her smile, the way she wrapped her legs around him when they fucked, and the way she made her pussy contract, it made him come like a geyser. Papa John had to see her tonight.

He went back to the hotel. While he was on his way up, he was met with Devon at the elevators on his way down. Devon looked mentally insane with a cigarette behind his ear, his eyes bloodshot red and cloudy, his lips black, and hair nappy. He looked at Papa John and asked, "Where you been?"

"Outside takin' a smoke. What's up?"

"Kid wants us to make our move tomorrow," Devon said.

"On who?"

"Jessica."

"She's locked down."

"I know, but we need to be there just in case she don't remain locked down, which is possible. That bitch need to get got."

They had said too much in a public area, and Papa John needed to be somewhere. Devon had that look in his eyes—that satanic gape itching for payback and yearning for violence. Though they were both killers, Devon always looked like he ate, shit, and breathed for murder, while Papa John needed some time off from it and needed to indulge himself with the ladies, his kids, and a normal life. Kip's death was a wakeup call that tomorrow wasn't promised to anyone, and last night's chaos might have been an epiphany to him that this game wasn't for him anymore. He was in too deep to dig himself out right now, and he needed to finish what he started before he could begin whatever transition he was thinking about.

"Yo, tell Kid I'll be back," Papa John said.

"Back?" Devon replied with a frown and puzzled face, "where you off to, nigga?"

"I got someplace to be."

"At a time like this?"

"Nigga, I'll be back before morning."

"That ain't the point. We at war and you chasin' some pussy."

"My business is my business, nigga . . . you know that."

"Your business should be being on point, not goin' to see some bitch."

Papa John didn't like how Devon was coming at him. He stepped closer to his friend with something to say. "What, I'm supposed to hide out here all night with my tail between my legs? Nah, I'm still gonna do me. I still got my kids and my priorities out there. This ain't gonna shake me up."

"We need to stick together."

"And we are stickin' together. But right now, I need to stick to something else." No matter what was happening, there was still a slice of humor inside of him.

He had nothing else to say. Papa John didn't want to be controlled or told what to do. His life was his life. He wasn't about to live it being scared—though he did feel edgy. He turned and left.

Devon frowned. He lit his cigarette in the hotel lobby where there was no smoking allowed. If Kip were still alive, Papa John wouldn't be pulling this shit. But things done changed.

***

Papa John parked the truck around the corner from his father's place and killed the engine. Whitestone was a tranquil and serene place, especially at night. It looked like a ghost town in the suburbs. Everything in the surrounding area shut down, unlike Harlem, where it was busy twenty-four/seven. This was the way Papa John liked it. He didn't want to be seen while he crept into his father's house. He picked up his cell phone and dialed Dina this time.

"Hello."

"I'm here, baby."

"Okay, I'll open the back door for you."

He hung up. With his gun still concealed in his waistband, he climbed out of the vehicle and coolly walked toward the house. He entered the yard, slid down the driveway, and proceeded toward the backyard under the cover of night. He didn't see his father's Benz in sight. It was a good thing. Dina was waiting for him in the doorway. Dressed in a sexy silk and lace robe with a matching thong, she smiled at him. He smiled back. He was excited. She was too.

"Hey you," she greeted sweetly.

"Hey," he said, entering the house and wrapping his arms around her petite figure. They kissed passionately and welcomed each other's embrace.

He pulled away from her. "You sure he's gone for the night?"

She nodded. "Yes. That city bombing has every cop on duty."

It was all he needed to hear. He lifted Dina up into his arms, her legs straddling him, and carried her upstairs to the master bedroom. He wanted the fun to begin. But first things first, she had what he needed—what he'd been craving—a dime bag of Kush and two cigars.

"Damn, you my favorite girl. I think I'm falling in love wit' you," he teased.

She giggled. "Which dessert you want first?"

They smoked one of the blunts and got down to business. Now this was where Papa John wanted to be, deep inside of her as she rode him in the cowgirl position. She knelt astride him as she leaned forward on her arms with Papa John laid back—her dripping pussy swallowing his hard erection. She had much more control over him in this position—depth and angle of penetration. He caressed her hips and her tits. He lifted his torso on his elbows to suck her nipples. They both moaned, drowning in gratification. Her back and forth movement started to speed up. Her moaning grew louder as he thrust up into her, while she licked and sucked his nipples and kissed his neck.

"Ooooh, so good . . . you feel so good," he moaned.

They stared in each other's eyes and saw the intensity. Dina paused for a few seconds, letting the dick simmer inside of her. She released a naughty grin as Papa John lay underneath her, breathing in anticipation. Everything about her felt so good—and so right. He no longer thought about his troubles with Jessica and Maserati Meek. He was high from the sex she was giving him.

She started to grind against him again and again. He held her hips. She rode and rode until she squirted in an intense orgasm from the passionate friction. She got hers and continued to ride Papa John's dick until he soon got his too—squirting his semen into the condom as his orgasm induced a powerful shudder. It was so good that he cooed like a pigeon as his toes curled up and he fidgeted underneath her like he was an epileptic having seizures. He quickly became spent after a good nut. She collapsed on the bed beside him.

The two had pillow talk as they lay nestled against each other. Dina's head was against his chest, and she heard his heart beating. Her body was soft like silk, and her long legs were warm around him like a campfire.

"I so needed this," said Papa John.

They smoked another blunt. The time was moving into the early morning, two hours before sunrise. He looked into her eyes and though she wasn't truly his, he felt he could tell her anything.

"I was there," he suddenly uttered.

"You were where?"

"I was at the club the night it blew up."

"What?"

"That suicide bombing at club Sane, it had nothing to do with politics. It had something to do wit' me," he said.

Dina was baffled.

"They want to kill us, Dina. They were willing to blow up an entire club to kill me and my crew."

It wasn't the type of pillow talk that she had been looking forward to, but it was startling news. Dina couldn't help but wonder what kind of nigga she had in her bed that someone would bomb an entire nightclub to kill him.

# 10

Eshon lit her cigarette, inhaled, and then exhaled. She took comfort in the passenger seat of The Kid's van in the hotel parking lot. It was going to be another beautiful day, but her days were being spent watching her back, carrying a pistol for her protection, and plotting revenge on the people who had tried to kill her. Never again would she sit inside a city precinct and allow herself to be questioned unless she was under arrest. Her time there was a nightmare, but it was useful. She had come back with the information they needed. Now Devon was ready to make his move—and he was crazy enough to do something stupid.

Sitting there alone and thinking about everything that had transpired over the past weeks, Eshon sighed heavily, and a few tears trickled from her eyes. She thought about Kip, like she always did. Everything was different without him. Devon was a lunatic who probably would get them all killed. She missed Kip's leadership. She missed his strong eyes and his voice, and his assertive demeanor. She always felt secure around him. But now what would tomorrow have in store for her?

She took another puff from the cancer stick and had more thoughts about her future without Kip. She blew out the smoke and felt an uneasiness that she'd never felt before. When Kip was running things, everything had gone smoothly, or close to it. Yes, there had been a few hiccups down the road, but Kip had always had a way of smoothing it out. Now, these hiccups were becoming nonstop, and a lot more dangerous.

The sudden knock on the passenger window startled Eshon. She almost jumped out of her seat and reached for the .380 she had on her. But there was nothing to worry about. It was Brandy coming to join her.

"Damn bitch, don't be sneaking up on me like that," Eshon shouted.

"I'm sorry. You okay?"

"No, I'm not okay."

"Open the door let me inside."

Eshon pressed the switch and the doors unlocked. Brandy walked around to the driver's side and slid into the seat. The past twenty-four hours had been rough. Their hair was becoming undone, edginess had consumed them, and they hadn't had a good night's sleep yet.

"Can I get some of that?" Brandy asked.

Eshon passed the cigarette to her friend. Brandy took a few pulls herself and released. They were silent for a moment, looking despondent. The parking lot was swelled with cars on a clear and warm day. Brandy had her own issues and worries. Like everyone, she put on a brave face, but this bombing—and so many dead—knocked her off guard and made her feel guilty. Her hardcore attitude had been altered into fault and remorse. She was with the plan to have five innocent people killed for what seemed like the greater good, but now hundreds of people were dead. Would everything be traced back to them? They'd had nothing to do with the bombing—not directly—but now with the FBI involved and sniffing around, what would the consequences be for them? Would they all get blamed too? Would they look like terrorists in the eyes of America?

Brandy passed the cigarette back to her friend. She breathed out and looked her friend's way. "Let's just go."

"What?" Eshon didn't know what she was talking about. "Go where?"

"I'm sayin', we have no ties to anyone here, so let's get our shit and leave the city. This is not our fight; it's the boys'. We can just walk away and start over somewhere else."

Eshon leaned forward in the seat. "Start over? Start over with what? And where, Brandy? My life is here. All I know is this city. Harlem is home and it will always be home."

"It doesn't have to be. Kip is gone!"

Eshon didn't need to be reminded of that. "I know that."

"You think we can go back to Harlem after this, if we survive this shit? What our lives used to be, it all changed the night at that club. We at war, Eshon, and it's gonna get even uglier. I don't think I'm ready to see how ugly it's gonna get."

"What about Jessica, huh? I'm supposed to give her a pass after what she did?"

"She'll get dealt wit'."

"I want her to pay for everything she did. We had her back since day one, and she betrays us by tryin' to have us killed."

"I want that bitch dead, too. But she's locked up right now. And who's to know if she'll get out soon? And if she do, what makes you think Maserati Meek won't be there waiting for her wit' an army of his own?"

Eshon frowned. She never thought she would see the day that Brandy wanted to back down from a fight—no matter what kind of fight it was. The disrespect from Jessica was blatant. How could she let it go? How could she forgive that bitch? Eshon couldn't rest until she saw that bitch dead. Jessica was a terrorist too. She was responsible for all the lives lost that night at the club. She arranged everything. She knew what was going to happen. There was no way Eshon was going to allow her to live and breathe the same air on earth as her. She needed to pay for her sins.

She needed to die.

"Brandy, if you wanna leave, then leave. I'm not running. I'm staying!" Eshon said with conviction. "You don't understand the hate I got inside for this ho. She's fuckin' the weird nigga that killed Kip and then tried to kill me—to kill us. All of us! And over what? Some dick?"

There was no changing Eshon's mind. Brandy saw it on her face. Eshon had that look that said she would rather die trying to implement justice for Kip than run like a coward to a different state. It almost felt like she had Kip inside of her.

Brandy sighed. "Fuck it, if you staying, then I'm staying."

Hearing that made Eshon smile. She needed Brandy around. She needed a true friend in her life, and Brandy was it. Where would she be without her?

"Thanks," Eshon said.

"Fuck it, I'd rather die side-by-side with a friend than live separate and die alone," Brandy said.

The two ladies continued to share a cigarette and talk. They were scared, not knowing what tomorrow held for them. But they had each other's back. They were going to succeed in vengeance or die trying. Brandy's nerves were still rattled—going up against men with the knowledge and mindset to blow up buildings and kill anyone that got in their way was daunting. They were up against something a lot more evil than they'd ever seen. Brandy prepared herself for the worst—saying, fuck it, they couldn't live forever.

***

There were two hard knocks at the hotel door. Devon recoiled from the bed and grabbed his pistol and cocked it back. He glanced at The Kid, Eshon, and Brandy. They looked nervous. Papa John was still MIA, no doubt laid up with some bitch somewhere. If it had been him at the door, he would have called first to let them know he was on the way back.

Devon took the initiative to approach the door and see who'd come knocking—friend or foe. With his silver Berretta in hand and by his side, he cautiously stood at the door, looked through the peephole, and asked, "Yo, who is it?"

"It's Twitter," the knocker said.

Hearing the name, Devon relaxed and his uneasiness faded. He opened the door and allowed the man inside. Eshon, Brandy, and The Kid were clueless as to who he was. Twitter? What kind of character was he? The Kid hated being clueless, but he had to remain quiet and allow Devon to take charge like he was told to do.

Twitter glided into the room with a natural smile looking lost in time—a Blaxploitation character from the '70s. He was a black man of average height and had a neat Afro with larger-than-life sideburns. He was impeccably dressed in a light leather jacket in the month of June and a black silk shirt with the collar wide open, showing off a thin gold chain bearing a gold cross. There was a gold tooth in the upper right corner of his mouth, diamond earrings in both ears, a gold Rolex around his wrist, and pinky rings on both hands. He looked cheesy and sharp at the same time. He carried a large black duffel bag.

Twitter greeted Devon with dap and placed the duffel bag on the bed. The Kid looked at Devon, and Devon said, "He's a good friend. I gave him a call earlier. I forgot about it."

"Yeah, me and Devon go way back," Twitter said. "And I'm sorry about Kip. He was a good dude—my nigga fo' sure. I'm gonna miss him."

Eshon and Brandy were on the sidelines thinking, *What part of the game is this?* Kip had never mentioned him. Twitter saw the confusion on their faces and made it his personal business to introduce himself.

He shook the ladies' hands gently and considerately said, "Like Devon said, my name is Twitter. Why they call me Twitter? Because I got many followers for my business, baby. I'm everywhere, and now I'm here, at your service. I trend faster than the strike of lightning, and once I strike, like J.J., I'm dynamite."

The ladies found him charming and amusing. But why was he there? He spoke in riddles about himself—and though it was cute, they didn't have time to laugh and find it cute.

"And still, y'all look at me like I'm a calculus problem, so let me further explain myself, because show and tell is better than chatting and explaining," Twitter coolly proclaimed.

He went to the duffel bag and unzipped it. He reached inside and immediately started pulling out guns and placing them on the bed for everyone to see.

"I sell guns, ladies . . . and gentleman. But not just any guns. The best ones—military upgrades. The guns that do not come cheap, you feel me?"

Before they knew it, there was an assortment of handguns and several submachine guns on the bed. It was the type of firepower that they needed; the ones that could put holes through Kevlar and pierce through steel.

"I got the Smith and Wesson XVR 460 Magnum—highest claimed velocity in a big-bore production gun. I got the Desert Eagle .50 caliber, my personal favorite. It's a fuckin' predator out there, the most powerful handgun out there," Twitter proclaimed.

He pointed to the third handgun and said, "And then there's this baby here, the Ruger Super Redhawk. Bullets fly at just under 1,200 feet per second. This baby right here, it has speed and power, and it will stop just about anything in its tracks. Now the few machine guns I do have, we talking about Miami Vice type of hardware: Uzis and the Heckler and Koch."

"You definitely know your guns," The Kid said.

"A man has to know his business, his merchandise. You know it, you love it, and you buy it. The rules of business."

Everything on the bed was impressive, and if they were going up against a terrorist like Meek, they would need the best money could buy.

"How much for the entire lot?" Devon asked.

"Now you're speaking my math. For you and the memory of Kip, I'll let it all go for fifteen thousand."

It was a big number.

"Do we need it all?" Eshon asked.

"When it comes to survival, sweetheart, you never know what you may need," Twitter replied.

Devon agreed completely. But the streets were hot with confusion and madness, and the money wasn't coming in fast enough. They had to cut back on a few things, including guns.

"How about half then?" The Kid said. "We'll take seven thousand worth of your best weapons."

"Half, huh?" Twitter replied.

"Yes, seven thousand dollars."

Twitter thought about it, and then smiled The Kid's way and said, "You know what, I'm cool with it. Like I said, Kip was a good friend of mines, and I honor his memory by doing good business with his peoples."

Devon picked out the guns they would need. He reached for the Desert Eagle and the Smith and Wesson, and also grabbed several Uzis. For him, it was game time. He loved his guns. He was eager to try them out on his enemies.

Twitter smiled once more, his gold tooth shining, and said to Devon and the group, "Once again, it's always good doing business with you, Devon. You continue to make me money like always. Ladies, until we meet again, hopefully under better circumstances. I gotta sign out now, and on to the next venue."

He kissed the backs of the girls' hands, and his charm was flowing like Niagara Falls. With his duffel bag of guns in hand, Twitter made his exit from the room with his pockets filled with a wad of hundred- and fifty-dollar bills. Devon was already loading bullets into the .50 cal. He said to the group, "We got a bitch to kill out there and a terrorist to slaughter, and I'm not tryin' to see either one of them live another fuckin' day. They wanna blow shit up, then we gonna fuck them up!"

# 11

Maserati Meek was somewhat concerned about Jessica as he sat naked in the bedroom alone and puffed on his cigar. The television was on, and the nightclub bombing was the chief subject matter in the news. It had been twenty-four hours since the deadly incident, and the death toll was still climbing. Now it was officially 205 confirmed dead. An impromptu memorial for the dead had been arranged near the bombing site—lit candles, dozens of flowers, teddy bears, pictures, and sympathy cards were steadily multiplying on the city sidewalk. Dozens of concerned citizens and mourners gathered near the location now called "ground zero." The careful removal of rubble and debris would turn up bodies, and sometimes body parts—a leg here, an arm there, torsos, and numerous limbs. Poor souls, they never saw it coming. A night out of fun and partying transitioned into another disastrous nightmare in NYC—one that the city would never forget.

Meek stared at his work with apathy. He cared nothing for the dead Americans. What was tragic in America's eyes was a recurring thing in his part of the world. The American government committed mass murders in the Islamic world daily. Innocent men, women, and children were slaughtered by their continuous drone attacks from above—indirectly striking a town or city from afar like cowards. Or implementing havoc and fear with their ground troops and their assault rifles—snipers picking off whoever they assumed was a threat to their military. Where was justice?

The bloodshed in the Middle East was a common thing—like a car accident in the states, they were expected. But in the States, two-hundred or more souls are killed, and the Americans cry out like children and vow for justice and retribution. They wanted punishment—but who would punish the Americans for their crimes against his people? Though the bombing was an action against his enemies, not a direct act of terrorism against their society, Maserati Meek felt vindicated. So, let the Americans cry out and mourn their dead. His people were in mourning every day.

Meek doused the cigar in the ashtray nearby and stood up. His penis was flaccid, but still impressive. He muted the TV. He had heard enough. There was no doubt the FBI would be vigorously hunting for terrorists—waiting for some foreign group to claim responsibility for the bombing—most likely ISIS. But there would be no group claiming the glory. Though it was tempting to take the glory—to become the light and envy of others—Meek was no fool. He was about money, revenge, and business. With one set of his enemies dead, now he could focus on eradicating Panamanian Pete, and from there on, expanding his wealth and empire.

He walked to the bedroom window naked and peered out into the street. Things were quiet in his part of town. No sirens, no cops, no destruction—wealth had provided him a slice of paradise. The affluent Brooklyn neighborhood provided some of the best and most expensive homes in the city, as well as privacy.

He thought about Jessica. Twenty-four hours and still no word from her. She wasn't answering her phone or replying to his text messages. Was she blown to bits? Maserati Meek deemed that impossible. She had contacted him and informed him of her departure from the club. But could she have forgotten something, gone back, and then *boom*—too late?

There was a part of him that felt he should have included her in his plan. Told her about the bomb—the suicide bomber. Warned her about the mass destruction that was about to come. It would have been fair, right? But would she have been willing to accept it? Would she have been able to deal with the death of hundreds on her conscience? Jessica wasn't one of them. She hadn't given her allegiance to Allah. Most likely, she would have never shown up at the club had she known.

Below the bedroom, as Meek chose to be alone, his men were celebrating their accomplishment in the great room. Abdul had been successful, and now he would be rewarded in paradise—taking delight in the seventy-two virgins promised to him. His name meant "servant of the powerful," and Abdul was that until his end. Covertly, he had entered the nightclub through the rear with the help of a bribed employee. The explosive belt weighed twenty kilograms on his person, underneath a thick jacket. It consisted of several cylinders filled with explosive—de facto pipe bombs. Detonator in his hand, he had pushed his way through the revelers, positioning himself in the center of the dance floor, and hollered, "*Allahu Akbar!*" He didn't hesitate to press the detonator, igniting the device and blowing himself up with many others. The explosion resembled a shotgun blast; it shook and it was extremely powerful—so powerful it left a large crater where Abdul once stood.

Maserati Meek had deceived his men; they all believed that they were in the United States for a political cause. They were frustrated and desperate, and they all felt that everything they had tried to do to make the world a better place according to their value system had failed them tremendously. They saw no alternative. They would be heard. Their voices would travel and tremble through the air. America was a place of sin and lies, and it was believed that Muslims hated the country's policies. The world's greatest superpower—they wanted to see it crumble.

What Maserati Meek's men didn't know was that his motives weren't for Allah, or to move their cause further. It was all over him feeling disrespected by Kip's renegotiation of a price for a murder. Things escalated out of control. The fire continued to rage on.

Maserati Meek presented another lie to his foreign killers. He had them believing that the kaffirs, which is a racial slur for a black man, wanted to kill him because they didn't want him sending money to support ISIS and all they represented. It was a no-no. He told them that a kaffir cartel wanted to stop their movement.

No one would stop their movement, not even a kaffir cartel!

Maserati Meek removed himself from the window. It was time for his nightly prayer. Still naked, he needed to cover himself, and he did so with a towel, where the nakedness of a man is considered to be between the navel and the knees. He stood tall in the bedroom and silent. Communication with Allah would bring life to the prayerful and bring them courage. Allah was talking to them.

Maserati Meek ensured that his area was clean, and then he placed a mat on the floor. He then faced the Qibla. He rose in hands up to his ears and said in a modest tone, "*Allahu Akbar.*" Subsequently, his right hand went over his left hand on his navel and he kept his eyes focused on the place where he was standing.

The prayer took him five minutes to complete, and once done, he ended the prayer by turning his head to the right and saying, "*As Salam Alaykum wa Rahmatullahi wa Barakatuhu'.*" He turned his head to the left and repeated the same phrase.

Allah was good, and He would always be good.

*** 

The next morning, Maserati Meek lingered in the shower. The cool, cascading water was refreshing and it made him relax and think. Still, no word from Jessica. She had gone MIA. He couldn't worry about her. If she was alive, then he'd see her soon, but if she was dead—killed in the club explosion—then she was a simple casualty of war. He was good to her and she was good to him, but there would be others.

He stepped out of the shower and toweled off. He secured the towel around his nakedness, wiped the mirror clean of its haze and looked at his Middle Eastern appearance. Clean shaven, lean, and with his long hair, it was no secret why the ladies loved him. He spent a moment primping his hair in the mirror. His hair was his pride and joy. He combed it while admiring his own physique in the mirror.

"You're a handsome devil, eh," he said to his reflection in the mirror.

To Meek, it was just another normal day for him. Yesterday was yesterday. He didn't think about the bombing or his enemies. His heart didn't harbor regrets or empathy. He was a powerful man on the top, and what it took for him to get there was to become soulless and heartless. He had to become the worst of the worst, and he had to be daring and smart. Where he came from, there was no such thing as weakness. The weak were the first ones to be devoured.

He wanted to look handsome and suave, and to enjoy being himself. Since it was a beautiful morning, Maserati Meek thought about having lunch in the city—someplace nice—maybe Gramercy Tavern on East 20th Street. But no, he thought against going into the city. It was a bad idea. Things were still hectic. He thought about Traif in Brooklyn, on South 4th Street. Their Asian dishes were some of the best food around. But then he thought of a better place: the River Café on Water Street. It was a landmark place, newly renovated, with stunning views of Manhattan. It would be perfect.

Meek continued to groom himself inside the swanky bathroom. Surrounding and protecting his comfort in his lavish Brooklyn lair were eight lethal and heavily armed men who spoke in their native tongue. They had a strong arsenal and ammunition that could take on a small army and homemade bombs that could take out an entire city block.

Maserati Meek moved from the bathroom to the adjacent master bedroom. He swung open the closet door and stepped into the walk-in closet. So many clothes and shoes to choose from. His choices appeared endless, and it all was very expensive. Meek wore nothing but the best.

What to wear?

Today would be something simple and comfortable. He put together white shorts, a white T-shirt, and a pair of crystal leather slide sandals that cost six hundred. Although his look appeared simple, the shorts and T-shirt collectively cost eight hundred dollars. While he dressed, his cell phone vibrated against the dresser in the room. He walked to the phone and looked at the caller I.D. It was a 718 number he didn't recognize. He answered anyway, believing it to be Jessica calling from a different number.

"Hello? Hello, Jessica, is this you? Can you hear me, eh?" Meek said.

There was a lot of noise and commotion in the background.

"Yes, this is Domino's Pizza and I'm on my way with your order. Ten minutes until delivery, sir," the caller said.

"Pizza?" Meek replied, baffled. His mind started to race. "I didn't order any pizza. Wrong number."

He hung up. It was a strange call that got the gears in his head turning. He stood there with the cell phone in his hand, trying to analyze the call. It was unusual, and a man in his position couldn't afford to overlook the slightest thing. There was something not right with that phone call. He waited a beat and then he called the number back. The call hadn't come from a cell phone; it came from a pay phone that didn't accept any incoming calls, the recording indicated.

Now that didn't add up—a delivery person calling from a pay phone. Also, there was earlier missed call on his cell phone—a call that he had overlooked—a mistake on his end. His instincts told him to call it back and be cautious. He dialed, it rang twice until he heard, "1st precinct, how may I…"

Meek had heard enough. He quickly ended the call. His heart started to race. The first ones he suspected were the alphabet boys—DEA, FBI.

Were they on to him? How? Paranoia set in and he figured that at any given moment, they were going to kick in his door and raid the place. One could never underestimate the FBI. But if they connected him to the bombing, how had they done it so fast? Then it dawned on him. Jessica. She had to have snitched. She was talking to the police. It was the reason she wasn't answering her phone or replying to any of his text messages. The feds had somehow turned her. There was no other way. She was talking and giving law enforcement everything.

Now he definitely wanted to find that grimy, two-faced bitch!

The 1st precinct was all over the news, being one of the police stations closest to the explosion. There was no time to linger in panic and go to pieces. It was time to go—retreat. Meek hurried and got dressed, and darted out of the room to inform his men of the situation.

"It's time to go!" he shouted. "Pack everything up. We've been breached."

Reaction in the room was prompt and sharp-witted. Everyone scrambled. Guns and bombing paraphernalia were hurriedly packed into bags and small wooden crates. Documents were shredded and hard drives were destroyed. The entire place was stripped clean, and anything important was loaded into two SUVs parked in the driveway. Each man fled in haste from the brownstone. There was no time to wipe the place clean in case the FBI was en route. Maserati Meek had only one option left—to burn it.

Two of his men lit Molotov cocktails and smashed them against the walls of the place. Immediately a fire erupted and spread intensely, heat and flames rising. Next were the cell phones. He and his men removed the SIM cards from the burner phones and tossed them into the blaze. Meek climbed into the passenger seat of one of the vehicles and they sped off, on the move to the next location. He had locations all across the city. He and his men moved like a ball in a pinball machine—fast and everywhere.

# 12

Officer Spielberg's gut suspicion was right. He knew it! The minute the receiver answered the phone with a Middle Eastern accent, he strongly felt these were the people responsible for the club explosion. There was no way he could let it go. It had been eating at him. Off duty and on his way home, he decided to call the number on a whim—not knowing who was going to answer, or if there would be an answer at all.

Spielberg stood by the pay phone contemplating. What to do? His gut instincts told him he was on the right track, but a phone number he overheard an arrestee saying and a man answering with a Middle Eastern accent wasn't exactly concrete evidence. He couldn't go back to his sergeant on a whim. He needed something more. How would he get more? Whoever these people were, they needed to pay for their actions. They'd killed hundreds of people.

Then the light bulb went off in his head—the feds. They would surely pursue this new lead. They had the manpower and the technology to investigate further. Yes, the FBI would listen to him.

Officer Spielberg walked toward his Ford Fusion and climbed inside. He felt anxious. What was next? Hopefully the feds would listen to what he had to say.

He drove to the bomb site on Spring Street. Everything in the surrounding area had been shut down during the investigation. It was going on forty-eight hours since the explosion, and lower Manhattan was still active with police and the media. Heavy vehicular traffic plagued blocks because of numerous street closings, bodies were still being pulled from the rubble, and the FBI was swarming about everywhere.

It was a zoo. And the animals behind this, they were still out there, maybe plotting another bombing. Though New York City had suffered from the largest terrorist attack known to man—9/11—this still didn't happen in his city. People were safe. They went on with their lives and American citizens didn't have to worry about this kind of attack on the regular. But once in a while, they were reminded of what kind of world they lived in. That people still hated their country and wanted to destroy it. With fanatic groups like ISIS and Boko Haram, terrorist threats lurked everywhere. These organizations had men who would go to extreme lengths, even committing suicide to spread their message loud and clear— they weren't going away, and they wanted people to die and suffer. They wanted to see organizations and democracy collapse, and to instill fear in America and all their allies.

Officer Spielberg climbed out of his Ford and approached the devastation as close as he could get. He flashed his NYPD badge and was allowed closer to the scene. What the media blasted across millions of television sets, he was seeing himself, up close and personal. Bloodshed spewed across Spring Street. The smell was horrendous. There were people everywhere, mostly law enforcement and FBI jackets milling around the area. Everything was investigated—no matter how small or big, it was scrutinized.

He could feel his eyes welling up with tears, feeling the emotions swarming inside of him although he had no connection to any of the victims. This was his city and his home, and someone had the audacity to strike it. He vowed to uphold the law and take action if a crime was happening. Spielberg wiped away a few tears and frowned. *Jessica,* he thought. That feisty little bitch had something to do with this, or she knew the men behind this attack.

He had seen enough. He turned away from the destruction and walked back to his car in sadness. He sat for a moment, thinking. Having been a police officer for eight years, he had seen it all—well almost. This was his first suicide bombing, and it would be something forever seared into his mind.

***

The following day, Officer Spielberg marched himself into 26 Federal Plaza—the Jacob K. Javits Federal Building. He was ready to meet with whomever possible and present the evidence he had attained. He had a phone number, a name, and a hunch. It might not be much, but Spielberg was sure that the FBI had solved cases with less than that.

He wanted justice for the lives lost that night, even if he had to implement it himself.

# 13

It was four in the morning, but the Harlem projects on 133rd Street were never fully asleep—never silent. On a June day, in the early morning before sunrise, there was still life inside the lobby of one of the towering project buildings. Several black men with their sagging jeans and jewelry showing stood around a craps game with a few hundred dollars up for grabs. They were in their own world, smoking weed and drinking alcohol, all while nestled around the corner from the elevators. There was no foot traffic and no police presence, and that was exactly how they liked it. They were loud and tipsy, and there were arguments between them, but nothing escalated into anything serious.

Nearby, a BMW X5 came to a stop on Old Broadway. The passenger door opened and a man stepped out. Dressed in a green cargo jacket zipped up to his neck and a pair of combat boots, the man coolly walked toward the project building with his hands stuffed into his jacket pockets. He was expressionless. Though he wasn't an African American male, he walked into the ghetto unworried and fearless. He marched toward a certain building. The X5 drove off, and now the stranger was completely alone. He never looked back. His eyes were on the alert. He trekked up the pavement leading into the nineteen-story project building and entered the dilapidated lobby, immediately catching the attention of the local thugs gambling close by. He immediately stood out in his coat and boots.

"Yo, what the fuck is this? Who the fuck is this clown-lookin' nigga?" one of the thugs uttered.

"Yo, Arab! You lost, muthafucka?" another thug exclaimed his way.

The stranger didn't pay them any attention. He was there for a reason. Ignoring the harsh comments, he proceeded toward the stairway. There was no time for the elevators. He moved opposite from the thuggish looking men. They took insult from his silence, and their dice game no longer became their priority.

"Yo muthafucka! You hear us talkin' to you? What's your business in this fuckin' building, nigga?"

Still in silence and disregard, he entered the stairwell. This angered the men, and they followed behind him, ready to teach the Arab a hard lesson about disrespect. A few of them were armed with guns. They didn't want to kill him, but they wanted to beat him down for his disrespect. This was their building—their territory, and no strangers were welcome.

The stranger made it up one flight before he was suddenly being chased. They were coming for him, charging up the stairs two at a time. But before they could dig their claws into him to teach him a lesson, he pulled out a gun and opened fire at them without any hesitation while ascending to the third floor.

*Pow! Pow!*

One thug took a bullet to his chest and tumbled down the concrete stairs. He was dead. The gunshot echoed through the stairwell. And now it was war. The thugs pulled out their guns and returned fire. A shootout ensued. This stranger was still undaunted. He struck another goon in the arm and moved forward. The chase continued.

"Yo, get that muthafucka!"

The man hurried with his purpose. He didn't have much time to carry out what was right—what he was instructed to do. Although he wanted to die, now wasn't the moment, and he had to fight to live until it was. He hurried toward the eighth floor as bullets whizzed by his head. They wanted to kill him. He thrust himself from the stairwell with the remaining thugs not far behind him. On the eighth floor, he quickly unzipped his jacket and his true intentions were revealed. Strapped to him was enough dynamite and C4 to create total destruction. He removed his left hand from the coat pocket and positioned his thumb against the detonator. All it took was one simple push of the button. He rushed to a certain apartment while the building thugs came flying out of the stairway, scowling like rabid dogs and taking aim at the sudden threat. Now was his time to die.

He raised his left hand into the air, clutching the detonator, and shouted, *"Allahu Akbar!"* and then squeezed. The consequence was immediate—*BOOOOOM!*

The building shook violently, causing smoke and fire to bellow everywhere, and the thugs were blown to pieces. It was total destruction from floor to floor. Although the project building was still standing, a raging fire erupted and hell took over.

The suicide bomber's name was Muhammad. He had succeeded in furthering the cause and dying for his beliefs—for Maserati Meek. He had no remorse and ordered another attack, and this place was unsuspecting.

The surviving residents were shocked. What just happened? The explosion was so loud and violent, that some were thrown from their beds while asleep. It didn't take long for the entire neighborhood to see what had happened. They had been awakened to disaster and turmoil. Raging flames and debris were pouring from the sixth, seventh, eighth, ninth, and tenth floor. Fire trucks and police sirens blared in the early morning.

The reason for the bombing and the destruction—Jessica. Maserati Meek was on a warpath.

# 14

They herded the criminals through like cattle at an auction. Central Booking was a busy place, and today wasn't any different. It was early in the morning, and for dozens of criminals, it was arraignment day—bail or no bail, released or remanded. Some arrestees were dressed in orange overalls while others were in their civilian clothing. The daily routine for many court officials had legitimately started. The judge—an aging African American with salt-and-pepper hair, a clean-shaven face, and hard eyes—presided over the courtroom in his long, flowing black robe. To his left, the prosecution and the authorities gathered, and to his right, the court-appointed lawyers sat on the front bench with their economical suits, worn shoes, and tired eyes. They came and went, depending on the defendant they represented.

The bailiff started to call out each case by its document number, followed by the defendant's name, and the judge rattled off drug charges, misdemeanors, robberies, armed robberies, assaults, parole violations, and some ambiguous sexual attacks. The defendants' names were called and they were led forward to the bench for their prompt judgment day. Many stood in silence and awaited their fate. Paperwork was shuffled around, and some were denied bail while some were released on their own recognizance.

Among those waiting to see the judge was Jessica. She had seen better days. She was fatigued and her long hair was in disarray. She yearned to be a free woman again. Though it had been less than forty-eight hours, it felt like an eternity behind bars. She wanted to go home. She needed a long, hot shower, some decent food, sleep, and some dick. It took a lot of flirting with the guards and the gift of gab to have her case brought forward in the early morning, or else it might have taken her the entire day to see the judge.

She was escorted into the courtroom. Her charges were read for the judge to hear. Jessica stood still and silent. Her angry attitude was gone. It was replaced with a humbled and tired-looking young woman. She stared at the judge and he stared back. Her court-appointed lawyer flanked her. He was a middle-aged white male with a dark mustache, curly blonde hair, and blue eyes. He looked like he had never stepped foot in the ghetto. His clientele was mostly blacks and Hispanics.

The judge asked, "How do you plead, young lady?"

"Not guilty," she replied.

He read over her case and her history: no serious priors, et cetera. Then there was the incident with the two female cops at the 1st precinct. The NYPD was at fault. Jessica had the right to file a suit. The prosecution wanted to throw the book at Jessica, but the judge had a lenient look in his eyes. Within two minutes of her appearance, he released her on her own recognizance. The judge gave her another court date two months from now. Jessica smiled. Finally, she could go home and meet up with Maserati Meek and tell him about everything.

Unbeknownst to her, the wheels of her demise had already started to turn; parked outside of the court building were Devon, The Kid, and Papa John. They were waiting patiently for her dismissal from the building. An informant on the inside had already given them the details, and now it was only a matter of time before they ran into her. The men were heavily armed—and cautious, too. Who else was waiting for the girl? There was tension inside the van. The men didn't know what to expect. Maserati

Meek had caught them off guard with his last stunt. What next? Would he try to blow up a city block too?

"Everyone be careful and watch your back," The Kid said.

Devon nodded. He looked undaunted. The only thing he was concerned about at the moment was Jessica's death. Papa John sat in the back looking cool as a cucumber, but on the inside it felt like he was falling apart with apprehension. The Kid sat with a poker-faced appearance, still portraying a cripple and hoping that he survived this ordeal.

While they waited on the Manhattan street, camouflaged amongst the morning traffic, their cell phones started to ring simultaneously. They looked at each other. Something was going on. What?

Eshon was calling Kid. He answered his phone. "What's up?"

"Ohmygod, Ohmygod!" Eshon cried out frantically.

"Eshon, what happened?"

"You didn't hear?"

"Hear what?"

"It's all over the news…Jessica's building exploded early this morning."

"What the fuck?" The Kid uttered in awe.

Devon and Papa John were receiving the same news. Each man was also stunned by what they'd just heard.

"What you mean, exploded?" The Kid asked.

"They sayin' it was another bomb! People are dying, Kid." Eshon was clearly shaken up and upset.

The Kid sat there taking it all in. Maserati Meek was becoming more destructive. But why Jessica's building? She was still in the courts. Something was going on, but what was it?

"What the fuck is goin' on?" Papa John said.

"We can't let this shake us up," The Kid said.

"Nigga, he blew up a fuckin' project building! What kind of crazy shit is that?"

The Kid sighed. Yeah, what kind of crazy shit was that? They had never seen anything like this. Muthafuckas were really crazy. Even Kip wouldn't have been ready for this shit.

Devon had no words. There was some trepidation inside of him, too, but the anger he felt was even stronger. He gripped the .50 cal tighter while seated behind the steering wheel. He kept his eyes fixed on the entrance to the courtroom. Today's date would be etched on Jessica's tombstone!

\*\*\*

Jessica came trudging out of Central Booking at a little after ten that morning. The sun was bright and the day warm, but her mood was dreary. It had been a long morning, and she looked like hell. Her dress was gone, replaced by the atrocious set of prison scrubs, and she still had on her high heels. Everything about her was unmatched and a mess. She had broken a few nails, her hair felt dirty, and she had the stench of jail all over her.

Standing at the top of the long court stairs, Jessica looked around cautiously. No Maserati Meek—nobody was there to greet her. Her cousin Jalissa hadn't relayed the message to her man. She'd thought she could trust her, but it was obvious that Jessica was on her own. No Meek—also, no Kid, she assumed. So far no trouble. The area was busy with people and traffic.

The first thing she thought about was going home, then yearning to see Meek. She had no idea what had happened just a few hours ago—that there was no more home for her. Her entire family was dead.

With her cell phone in hand, she jogged down the stairs and stopped on the sidewalk. She looked at her phone and cursed. "Fuck!" It went dead. She had no way of contacting anyone. What a mess. *What to do?* she thought. It was a long way back to Harlem from downtown. She had little cash on her. Pay phone, yes—a pay phone would help her out. Although they were obsolete in the age of the cell phone, Jessica was sure she could find at least one still around. She started to walk and looked around for the nearest one.

Following her from a distance and trying to fight the morning traffic were The Kid and his crew. They watched Jessica's every move, including her cursing her dead phone.

"Follow that bitch," The Kid said.

"Not a problem," Devon said.

Jessica stood out from the downtown crowd in her prison scrubs and high heels. She received fleeting looks and probing gazes while roaming with the white-collared pedestrians in the downtown district. Despite her rough-looking appearance, her strut was still fierce. Muthafuckas could look at her any way they wanted, but she knew that with one phone call, her world would be back right—girl on top loving a boss nigga.

Devon rode at a snail's pace three cars back as he rounded the corner toward Jessica. They couldn't snatch that bitch right in front of the court building; there were too many witnesses around and not much room for an escape. They had to wait until the perfect moment presented itself. With the morning crowd everywhere, the right moment was looking almost impossible. But they were determined. If they lost sight of her and let her get away, then there was no telling the ripple effect that could come.

The waiting was the difficult and nervous part. She walked two blocks, then three—and finally, she turned left from the busy street onto a side street. Beekman Street was a narrow block, a one-way with few people and little traffic. Jessica fumbled with her cell phone a bit and looked around for a pay phone and became unaware of her surroundings. A bad mistake. She continued to walk while cursing her situation while Devon slowed the van down almost to a crawl, riding parallel to the curb.

Papa John slowly slid the door back with his eyes on the prize. The foot traffic was sparse, and it gave him a window of opportunity. When they were close to her, Papa John leaped out from the back and grabbed her from behind. His hand covered her mouth to prevent her from screaming for help. There was a struggle. Jessica wasn't going down without a fight. She elbowed Papa John in his stomach. It was a hard enough blow for him to loosen his grip around her. She attempted to run, but Papa John maintained his hold on her.

"Get the fuck off me! Help! Help!"

He grabbed her in a chokehold. She resisted by biting his flesh and squirming madly while in his clutches. She was feisty. The Kid had to intervene. He leaped from the van and smashed the butt of his pistol against her head. The blow hard enough to make her dizzy and her knees buckle. They quickly dragged her into the van and closed the door. Finally, they had that bitch in their possession again.

"Drive, nigga!" The Kid instructed Devon.

Devon drove away as quickly as he could, but downtown Manhattan wasn't the perfect place to execute the Indy 500. The blocks were inundated with traffic, construction, and people walking. He did the best he could, at the same time trying to remain inconspicuous. Jessica was on the floor of the van in pain with blood on the side of her forehead. Her blurry vision was coming back. The Kid held her hostage at gunpoint. He smirked when she looked up at him.

"Your boyfriend can't save you, and there's no miracle escapes for you anymore, bitch. We on point now," The Kid said.

Once again, Jessica found herself in a sticky situation. How had she gotten here again? How could she have been so sloppy? This time, there was definitely no escape. Her fate was sealed. All she could do was lock eyes with Kid and frown. The Kid wouldn't try to kill her while they were in the city. He'd have to wait until they were someplace secure and remote—and then she would try to make yet another escape.

Twenty-five miles away from New York City, on a remote and shrouded road called Helmetta Boulevard in East Brunswick, New Jersey, Devon pulled the van onto the shoulder of the road and put the vehicle in park. Now was the time. Jessica stared at Kid, trying to keep her cool, but on the inside she was falling apart with fear. The Kid pointed a .9mm with a silencer on the end at her dome. He glared at her with pure hatred. He'd been waiting for this moment.

"All your family is dead," he said to her.

"You're lying!"

The Kid smiled. "You'll see the truth shortly."

He put the gun to her head and she looked at him with a fierce look. She refused to close her eyes—so be it. Her luck had run out A few tears trickled from her eyes. The Kid squeezed the trigger—*Bak!* Her blood splattered, and Jessica's body crumbled backwards to the floor, her blood pooling underneath her. They removed the prison scrubs and red bottoms, leaving her stripped down to her bra and panties. They'd destroy her clothes and shoes later. The van door opened, and her body was dumped on the side of the road. Let the wildlife have at it.

"Y'all niggas hungry?" The Kid asked.

They drove off.

# 15

A sea of flashing lights from all types of emergency vehicles flooded the Harlem block. Fire trucks, police cars, ambulances, the bomb squad with their bomb-sniffing dogs and, of course, the FBI crowded 133rd Street and Old Broadway from corner to corner. It was a circus of law enforcement. Several news helicopters circled the area, catching a glimpse of the project building that had been bombed.

The area residents were in awe. Their homes had been transformed into a spectacle for the world to see. Many people had suddenly become homeless, some were forced out of their apartments by the authorities for safety reasons, and every building was warily inspected. The city wasn't taking any chances. Harlem now had the world's attention, and the city would remain on red. This was an act of terrorism. But the location had many scratching their heads. They were baffled. Why Harlem? Why suddenly this location? What did these terrorists have to gain by attacking the ghetto? These were nothing but average folks: no political ties, no power, no money. It didn't make any sense.

The ripple effect from the bombing had already started. How many were dead? They didn't know yet, but people were growing mad. They had lost family, children, and friends. It was the Muslims' fault. The audacity of terrorists attacking their ghetto. Discrimination started to escalate, and a fight broke out at the bodega two blocks away from the bombing. Several black men attacked the owner. His name was Abdul, and he was a man the people had seen every day for years, but now he suddenly had become public enemy number one. A scuffle broke out, and Abdul had a bottle smashed against his head. They jumped him—kicking and stomping him—and shouted obscenities at him. They were angry. Somebody had to pay, and the people didn't care who it was.

The cops had to break up the brawl. They were going to kill Abdul. But that wasn't the end of it. If someone looked Middle Eastern, they became a sudden target for the growing lynch mob. The authorities, especially the FBI, were hauling everyone into custody for questioning, and their targeted groups were Muslims, Middle Eastern, or South Asian men. The city was falling apart with fear and racism. No one thought that Harlem would ever be under attack, but now certain folks took it upon themselves to take the law into their own hands. The police suddenly found themselves overwhelmed with hate crimes expanding across all five boroughs.

\*\*\*

Officer Spielberg heard about the Harlem bombing through his police radio. He had just walked into the 1st precinct to start his shift when it was all over the radios, and on the news. He couldn't believe it himself. It seemed so unreal. What was happening to his city?

Everyone was uneasy and on high alert. If they could attack Harlem, then what was to stop these people from attacking cops and police stations? Every cop in the city was on edge. At roll call, every cop was briefed on current terrorism intelligence and tactics. They were told to keep a keen eye out for anything suspicious, to not overlook anything no matter how small or simple it appeared to be. If there was anything left unattended, packages or bags, they were to contact the bomb squad.

Cops were gathered at certain locations and deployed to various soft-target locations. The Financial District was under intense twenty-four-hour coverage. NYPD was on constant watch everywhere. They didn't need a full-blown panic from New Yorkers. They needed to keep the peace and keep people calm.

"Keep an eye out there for anything suspicious, and be safe out there, too. I want everyone to come back safely to their families," their sergeant said to the uniformed cops at roll call.

The sergeant dismissed roll call. Officer Spielberg stood there in his police uniform and clenched his fists. He wanted to do something about the bombings. He felt he wasn't doing enough. He gave the feds what he had on Jessica, and the phone number that was most likely linked to the terrorists. He wondered if the feds had followed through on the evidence he'd presented to them. He didn't want to be played for a fool.

"You okay, Spielberg?" the sergeant asked him.

"Yeah, I'm okay."

The sergeant tapped his right arm and said, "You're a good cop out there. Keep your head up. We'll find these assholes."

He nodded.

The sergeant left the room with Officer Spielberg right behind him. When they entered the hallway, they saw the feds swarming their precinct like busy bees in their dark suits and badges. The man they asked for was Officer Spielberg.

"I'm right here," said Spielberg.

"The director wants to have a word with you," said an agent.

Officer Spielberg was ready to talk and share everything he knew so far. He figured he had given the feds their only good lead in these bombings. The club Sane bombing didn't have any reliable footage, there were only a handful of survivors, and so far there were no groups out there taking credit for it—no witnesses, no suspects. For all the feds knew, it might be homegrown terrorism instead of ISIS or Al Qaeda.

Officer Spielberg felt a tinge of nervousness as he rode to the federal building with the agents. The feds were the big league, and now he had their attention. He wanted to impress them. Spielberg had always been smart and observant. His mother always told him to look, listen, and learn. He always felt that he was born to be a cop, maybe something higher, and he always wanted to do the right thing. He had been considered a Boy Scout since he was ten years old.

Officer Spielberg did his best not to look nervous as he took a seat in one of the many rooms at the federal building. The room was windowless, carpeted, and closed-circuit. It was similar to the typical interrogation room at his precinct, but a lot nicer looking. He sat proudly at the table waiting to speak with someone. He had been told it would be the director himself. He took a deep breath and waited.

Moments later, the door opened and the director stepped into the room with a few of his subordinates. The man was sharply dressed in a dark blue suit with a bright red tie, polished wingtip shoes, and his credentials showing. He had black hair, strong blue eyes, and was clean shaven with a refined stature.

"Officer Spielberg, it's a pleasure to meet you."

They shook hands and the director sat opposite him.

The situation was growing serious in New York. They wanted to have a chat with him. The first thing they wanted to know was, who Jessica was and how she was involved with terrorists. Spielberg gave them his intel. He wanted to help out the best he could. They'd had investigated the cell phone number he had given them, but it was no longer in service. It was a burner phone. It was hard to track, but they were working on it. The investigating team was already putting together a warrant, ready to have a judge sign off on it to find out whose names and numbers were on the phone. They ran Jessica's name and pulled up a DMV photo of Jessica and her license. An agent entered the room and quickly whispered something into the director's ear. It was an update. He nodded.

"What's going on?" Officer Spielberg asked.

"The information on Jessica's license was just matched to the project building that was bombed earlier this morning," he said.

It definitely wasn't a coincidence.

They needed to speak to her ASAP. Office Spielberg informed them that last he checked, she was being arraigned in Central Booking today. They needed to pull her out of Central Booking and question her immediately. The call was made to Central Booking, and authority there was overruled by the feds—whatever the FBI wanted or needed, they got. They wanted to put a hold on Jessica's arraignment. She was too much of a risk to be let go. A team was heading down there to pick her up.

Fifteen minutes later, several agents arrived at the building with their badges and authority and stormed inside to detain Jessica. But to their dismay, she had already been cut loose on her own recognizance. There had been some mix-up in their system and she had been released.

Word of this reached Officer Spielberg and he couldn't contain his frustration. He shouted, "Fuck!" and banged his fist against the table.

Where was she? She needed to be found.

# 16

Eshon found herself butt-naked on her stomach and sprawled across the king-size bed. She closed her eyes and felt him slowly climb on top of her. His touch was riveting against her skin and sent sensual chills all through her flesh. He parted her legs and positioned himself between them. She could feel his strong erection against her body, ready for rear entry. She panted in anticipation to feel him inside of her. Her body quivered slightly as he penetrated her—her pink pussy walls folding in around his hard dick. She pushed her ass into the air a little, like a small hump, allowing the best stimulation for her G-spot. He thrust and pumped inside of her. She was so wet—wetter than any river running on the planet. She could feel her juices splashing as he fucked her with a sense of purpose. He kissed her backside, clutched her ample ass cheeks, and made her moan out like the wind blowing. She felt protected by him. Their lovemaking became wicked, and she couldn't help but to call out his name. "Oh God, Kip . . . don't, baby—please don't stop. You feel so good." She didn't want this thing with Kip to end. He was fiercer in spirit than before. He turned her over slowly and they locked eyes. His smile was real, but his passion felt so unreal.

"I love you, baby. And I miss you," she said to him.

Eshon received nothing but silence. She felt him inside of her again. He was lifting her higher the more passionate their lovemaking became. It almost felt like she was touching the sky. She closed her eyes and felt herself being carried away. Her pussy was throbbing like it'd never throbbed before. Her nipples were firm, and it felt like her soul was about to have an orgasm and then take off like a rocket—to where, she didn't care. Wherever Kip took her, it didn't matter, even if it was in the middle of space—as long as she was with him, she felt secure.

She wrapped her arms around Kip and held him close. She didn't want to let him go. She was afraid that if she did, then she would fall away from his grasp and she would never see him again. They danced on air with their intense lovemaking and scribbled their passion across the sky. It was the perfect night. And it was beginning to feel like the perfect orgasm. Eshon huffed and puffed as he caressed her body and entwined her soul with his. He made her clitoris tingle and dance with excitement and gratification. She howled in his grasp.

He still remained silent, speaking with his body and his touch. He had never looked so handsome—so fine. His eyes continued to smile at Eshon. Wherever he kissed her, she wanted to cherish.

"Oh, Kip, I miss you so much. Ohmygod, I'm gonna . . ."

Then suddenly, she was thrust awake from her dream. There was no more Kip. She opened her eyes and found herself back in her reality. Between her thighs, she was soaking wet. It had been a deep wet dream. Not seeing him around and not being able to hold him, Eshon started to tear up.

It had seemed and felt so real. Waking up and not seeing Kip there next to her was like losing him all over again. She quickly removed herself from the bed and went into the bathroom. Brandy was asleep on the next bed. She closed the door and locked it. Alone, she fell to her knees and quietly started to cry. The sorrow was plastered across her face like thick makeup.

After a few minutes, she took a deep breath and did her best to regain her composure. The dream she had took her to a place where it felt harder to move on from. She took a seat on the toilet and chilled. The good news was that Jessica was finally dead. They got that bitch and left her on the side of a road where she belonged. But it wasn't over yet. People were dying and Eshon felt somewhat responsible for it.

She finally gathered herself and walked out the bathroom. Her face was free of the tears. She had to see him. It had been too long since her last visit.

*** 

The cab came to a stop on 155th Street, right at the front entrance of the Trinity Cemetery. It was a costly trip coming from New Jersey, but to Eshon it was worth it. She wanted to come despite the risk of being exposed, and regardless of everything that was happening in the city. Not too far from the cemetery was pandemonium. Her home, the neighborhood she had grown up in, was in absolute disarray from the bombing.

She paid the fee and climbed out of the cab holding a bouquet of flowers. Dressed for the warm, sunny weather in a green tank flare dress and a pair of embellished thong sandals she'd picked up in Jersey, she somberly entered the cemetery. She traveled toward Kip's grave. His plot was grassy and clean, and etched on his tombstone were the words *Kip Kane—Forever Loved and Always Missed.*

Eshon crouched closer to his manicured plot and placed the flowers against his tombstone. Silence overcame her for a moment. A few tears trickled down her cheek. She then sat against the tombstone and embraced it, saying, "I wore this for you, Kip. You always liked me in green or blue."

A deep sigh escaped from her lips. It felt good being close to him. Where he was buried was the perfect location—near a large oak tree and shaded from the sun at times. The caretakers did maintenance around the area twice a week. With what they'd paid for the gravesite, Eshon wasn't accepting any slack from them. Everything had to be perfect. She wanted Kip to have the best upkeep.

She sat there and conversed with him. She told him everything that was going on, and mentioned how frightened she was. "If you were alive, what would you do, Kip? You always knew what to do somehow. Devon, he's tryin', but he's not you. He will never be you. He will never take your place. You were the best leader anyone could follow," she proclaimed.

The afternoon sun was in her face, and she felt at home and secure by his grave. It was peaceful. She could hear the nearby traffic. She could hear Harlem alive while she was among the dead.

"Kid, he's doing fine. He's changed a little, but he's still into his chess, and like me, trying to cope with not having you around. I miss you so much, Kip." A heavy sigh followed.

She sat and conversed for over an hour with Kip. She reminisced with him, laughed and cried with him, and gave him an update. Each day without him already felt like an eternity.

It was soon time to go. The afternoon was fading, and she had to travel back to New Jersey and remain low-key at their new hub. Her life was no longer the same. In a year, where would she be? Would she still be alive? Out of the blue, she thought about the conversation she'd had with Brandy earlier, about leaving the city and starting over someplace different—someplace new. Could it be possible? Would she be able to uproot herself and become someone new in a different state?

Before her departure from the gravesite, she leaned forward and kissed the tombstone. She unloaded a few more tears and heaved another sigh before she pivoted and walked away. It was always hard for her to leave. Her walk toward the exit was a sad and lonely one. She wiped away the tears and closed her eyes briefly. It didn't make sense to ask why—why out of everyone that night, was he the one that had to die? It was a question she would never know the answer to.

\*\*\*

Devon stopped the van on Amsterdam and West 129th Street in Harlem. He couldn't travel any further. The Kid sat in his wheelchair and saw it for himself. The police and the FBI had the entire area shut down. The streets were blocked with cop cars and emergency vehicles. Several helicopters hovered over the Manhattanville projects. They were still finding bodies from the bombing—families were wiped out overnight, and many residents were in awe and terrified. The K-9 unit, mostly cadaver and bomb sniffing dogs was in full force, working tirelessly to try and find survivors or bodies, and making sure there weren't any more threats in the area. The media was camped out everywhere capturing footage of the destruction and interviewing many residents. No one would have thought terrorists would strike Harlem. There had to be some reasonable explanation for it. It wasn't downtown Manhattan, the Financial District, or Midtown. What did the projects have that these people felt they needed to attack?

"Let me out," The Kid told Devon.

"You sure? It's crazy out there," Devon said.

"This is our home, Devon. I wanna get out."

Devon didn't argue with him. He stepped out of the van, walked around to the side door, slid it open, and released the access ramp, allowing The Kid to wheel himself from the van and onto the sidewalk. The area was a madhouse.

The Kid was brokenhearted. This was his home? This is what he knew, where he lived his life every day, and now it looked like a scene from overseas in places where there was civil war and shattered foundations.

Devon tried to wheel Kid closer to the destruction, but they were like pawns on the street; their movement was limited because of newfound restrictions in the area. The entire projects had to be evacuated for safety reasons, and in doing so, there were hundreds and hundreds of folks scattered around looking despondent. Some cursed the police. Some cried in each other's arms, and some were at a loss for words. They were angry. They had never seen anything like it. What were the police and the FBI doing to make their lives better?

A few local people quickly recognized Devon and Kid. They had been gone for a while now. Some took the time out to give their condolences about Kid's brother although they were in a crisis of their own. The brothers were missed in the neighborhood, and things didn't seem the same without them. Devon wheeled Kid around while armed with his pistol. The Kid knew he was taking a huge risk by being back in the old neighborhood. He and Devon were supposed to be dead. But who would snitch him out to Maserati Meek? The people were going through hardship of their own, but still, Kid knew it was a careless mistake on his end. He didn't stay in the area long. He felt it was time to go.

# 17

The police and the FBI put out a BOLO alert for Jessica. Her picture was given to the media, and every news station plastered it across millions of TV screens in the city and beyond. She was a person of interest in two potential bombings. Unfortunately, she was nowhere to be found. The manhunt for her was extensive—and the feds chased lead after lead, but they still were coming up short.

The Manhattanville projects became even more in uproar once the news had gotten out about Jessica possibly being linked to a terrorist group. Nah, it couldn't be, not one of their own! For so many residents, it was a hard pill to swallow. Jessica didn't look like a towelhead—but then again, what did a terrorist really look like? She was linked to Eshon and Brandy—the E&J Brandy bitches, and they were linked to robberies and stickups. It was no secret. But to attack her home—the thought of it was too farfetched. Her family was dead, too. What the fuck was the world coming to?

"Yo, I used to fuck that bitch, real talk," a corner thug bragged to the cameras filming—of course his statement was censored for TV. "She ain't no fuckin' joke though, fo' real!"

"Nah, not Jessica. That bitch is too sexy to be a fuckin' terrorist," another thug spewed his two cents.

"I don't put anything past anyone nowadays, ya know what I mean? Bitch or nigga, I don't trust anyone out this bitch, ya know what I mean?

Shit is real out here, like crazy 'n' shit, ya know what I mean? And that bitch is MIA too, some conspiracy shit, feel me. . . ya know what I mean?"

"I haven't seen her around lately," a girl mentioned.

"She used to hang wit' these real serious bitches around here, robbing people, and then I heard she got wit' some baller," another female proclaimed.

It was 9/11 all over again, many felt, and people wondered why the any terrorist group would want to blow up a nightclub and then attack a New York City housing project. There were some raw emotions for the group responsible for the bombing.

"Yo, fo' real, it's like Baghdad out here! Now muthafuckas wanna act all concerned. Fuck those Taliban niggas! Yo, we here all day, nigga. Fo' real! Try that shit now!" an angry resident barked into the news camera.

"Yeah, we ain't scared to shoot back. Fuck them towelhead niggas! That's some cowardly shit to blow up shit. Bring the guns, nigga, and see how we do out here," another man chimed.

The pot was boiling, ready to spill over into downright madness, and tempers were flaring. Some felt that Jessica was another American brainwashed by ISIS somehow—becoming sympathetic to their cause and wanting to bring destruction to her own country. It was a disgrace, they felt, and many didn't want anything to do with her. It was the gossip through Harlem—Jessica and terrorists. It was all anyone wanted to talk about.

Jessica—where was Jessica and what was her involvement with these bombings?

\*\*\*

An hour before sunrise Early morning in East Brunswick, Mrs. Patrick went for her daily jog through Jamesburg Park in her tank top and tights. She was a runner, loved every bit of it—it gave her life. She'd competed in several marathons and could do six miles in under an hour. Her favorite time to run was early in the morning, before the sun became visible in the sky. The air was better and crisp.

This particular morning, she jogged down Helmetta Boulevard, jogging on the shoulder of the road. The traffic was sparse. Sweat covered her brow as she pushed her Nikes to the limit. She glanced at her watch, timing herself—three miles in twenty minutes, not bad. She huffed and moved her arms while listening to Coldplay on her iPhone.

She was focused until something from her peripheral vision caught her eye. She slowed her pace and then stopped, noticing something bizarre peeking from the trees nearby. Her heart dropped. It was a foot. Her eyes followed the length of the foot until she saw the limp body on the grass. It was a woman, dead. Shocked, Mrs. Patrick became wide-eyed and screeched in terror. She had stumbled across a dead body, most likely a homicide. Immediately she pulled out her cell phone and frantically dialed 911.

East Brunswick PD showed up shortly to investigate the dead body. Helmetta Boulevard was closed for the time being, inconveniencing drivers. It was a homicide, and detectives and forensics were on location— crime scene photos were taken of the body and the area. CSI thoroughly scoped the scene. Plainclothes detectives scoured the surrounding area, but it was pointless. Unfortunately, there were no witnesses; the area was secluded. It was obvious to them that the woman had been dumped there. She was shot in the head and wearing only her bra and panties. She had no I.D., but they made her out to be in her early twenties. Who was she? And where had she come from?

Two hours later, Jane Doe was bagged and tagged and placed inside the coroner's van for autopsy. First the detectives needed a name. To further their investigation, they had to find out who she was. Somebody had to be looking for her. Was there a missing persons report filed on her? For now, she was just a body—a young girl who had come to an unfortunate fate. Was she raped? There were so many questions, but nothing to go on. The primary detective on this case knew it wasn't going to be a slam-dunk. He sighed heavily from receiving a case that titled who did it? Not a clue, not a name.

Unbeknownst to the East Brunswick PD, the body they'd stumbled onto was a wanted woman in New York City.

# 18

It was best to keep moving, shuffle all around the Tri-state area, and keep a low profile at the same time. They didn't want to get too comfortable and too familiar with one location, so Kid and his crew relocated their headquarters from New Jersey to New Rochelle. New Rochelle proved to be better for the group; they didn't have to travel through tunnels or cross over bridges and deal with traffic, police checkpoints, and toll booths. New Rochelle was a straight shot into the Bronx, and into Harlem. It was closer too.

The group checked into a Days Inn and rented two rooms, one for the men and one for the ladies. The hotel was near a park with a large baseball field and middle-class homes with manicured front yards and people living their mundane lives.

Everyone got settled into the rooms. The girls showered and rested, while Papa John lingered outside the motel with a cigarette. His phone was keeping him busy, texting back and forth with Dina.

Devon laid his arsenal out on the bed and prepped his weaponry like a Boy Scout shining his medals. He wanted to put the gun Kid used to kill Jessica up on his wall as a trophy, but The Kid wanted him to get rid of it. He had big plans for the gun they would use to kill Maserati Meek—maybe get it dipped in gold and keep it as a souvenir.

The Kid sat in his wheelchair in the room with Devon and looked out the window. There were a lot of things he couldn't forget. What Maserati

Meek did to his home—the Manhattanville projects—and the innocents that lost their lives that night, he couldn't let it go. Then there was Jessica. He couldn't get her out of his head. It was haunting him to some extent. For years he had liked her, loved her even. He thought she was someone special. Now this—he had taken her life. There was some regret inside of him, but he knew that he had to do what he had to do. He had to bury that regret and become someone else. It wasn't back in the day anymore—they'd all done changed. He had to live with that nightmare.

As The Kid lingered by the window, staring off into space, a knock at the door brought him back to reality. Always cautious, Devon picked up a .45 and moved toward the door. He glanced through the peephole and then relaxed, realizing that it was Eshon. He opened the door and she walked in.

She looked at Devon with the gun by his side and then stared at Kid. "How long is this gonna last?"

"Until Meek is dead and rotting in the fuckin' ground," Devon replied.

"Where's Brandy?" The Kid asked.

"Sleep," she said.

"What's up?"

"I can't sleep," she said.

Devon went back to tending to his guns. His guns were like his children, and he inspected them like they were his little soldiers ready to go to war and he was the general. He sat on the bed and took apart an M-16 with ease, and Eshon was somewhat stunned to see him do it.

"Where'd you learn to do shit like that? You were never in the Army."

"I got my ways."

"You're starting to really scare me."

He smirked. "Fear is what I'm lookin' for."

"Well, I'm tired of living in fear. I just want things to be normal again," she said.

"When was shit ever normal in our neck of the woods? This is what we do and who we fuckin' are— fuckin' criminals and dangerous people. We robbed and killed niggas for profit. It was like that with Kip, and it's gonna be like that after Kip," he proclaimed.

"It's why Kip is dead," she retorted.

"Kip knew the risk, Eshon. He was the main nigga that got us into this shit. Shit, my nigga being dead don't make him a Boy Scout now."

"But all this death—"

"What, you scared now? I'm not! A nigga can blow up a thousand fuckin' buildings, and my heart still won't be timid. He came for us and missed. Now we go for him and fuck his shit up!" Devon growled.

The madness in Devon's eyes and in his soul was swelling like a tumor. He was a man on a mission, and there was no deterring him. He was going to avenge Kip's death or die trying.

"I need to go for a walk. I need some air," Eshon said.

"You strapped?" Devon asked.

She shook her head.

Devon picked up a .9mm and handed it to her. "Take it. Better safe than sorry."

"I don't think I'm gonna need it right now."

"Take the pistol and watch your back out there. I don't care if we are in New Rochelle, death is everywhere, Eshon. You should understand that."

She was reluctant to take the pistol, feeling that it was not needed. Besides, where was she going to hide the gun? It was a balmy summer night with a full moon in the sky. The Days Inn was nestled in the gentleness of the New Rochelle suburbs. Who would recognize them in the area? Eshon turned and went to exit the room.

The Kid wheeled himself closer. "Wait, I'll join you."

He needed some fresh air, too. She welcomed the company. They passed through the hallway, into the elevator, and breezed through the

116

quiet lobby. Stepping out into the summer air felt energizing.

Eshon lit a cigarette and then pushed Kid down the quiet boulevard. It was just the two of them—friends out on a walk. For a moment they were silent, taking in the calmness of the area. Few cars passed by, and the twenty-four-hour McDonald's was starting to form a long line going through their drive thru. They traveled half a block.

They wanted to forget about their troubles behind them and the quandary ahead of them, but it was difficult. They were at war with a terrorist group, something completely unexpected—and these suicide bombers weren't just a threat to them, but to their country. What would they attack next? And how long would it go on? It was a question that had crossed both of their minds, but now didn't feel like the appropriate time to talk about it.

The Kid held the keys to the legacy his brother had left behind—a vessel floating aimlessly at sea and armed with lots of guns. He was steering the ship, but to where? So far he seemed to be doing a good job keeping everyone alive and pushing forward against very dangerous enemies, but could he completely fill his brother's shoes? Was he a thug like them? Could he carry on with this lifestyle and die for it like Kip had died for it? He had already proven himself to be a killer. It had to be in his blood like it had been in Kip's. His kills were increasing, Jessica being his latest coldhearted act. But how soon until he found himself on the other side of the gun or blown to pieces by one of Maserati Meek's suicide bombers? Was he smarter than them, or was it just luck on his side?

"Kip didn't want this life for you," Eshon said, out of the blue.

"Who knew what my brother wanted?"

"He didn't want this for you, Kid. He always thought you were smarter than this. I did too. He did him out there only to try to give you a better life."

"A life without him isn't a better life," he said.

She sighed. "I agree. But Kid, you always had something the rest of us didn't. You have talent, and you're smart. And even though you can't walk, your intelligence can take you places none of us can even dream of. You never allowed your handicap to defeat you. You found a way to defeat it."

It was a motivational speech. Kid kind of felt bad for deceiving her.

"What do I have to go back to, Eshon? Our home looks like Syria, Kip is dead, and Nana's dead, though I couldn't stand her . . . and yeah, I'm smart, but my intelligence didn't help my brother much. He looked out for me, but I couldn't look out for him."

"You think hanging around Devon and Papa John will bring some kind of closure in your life—that they gonna make things better for you? Devon is a monster on a violent warpath. They're killers, Kid, and you're not. Those niggas are about that life—they got nothing to lose, but you're one of the best chess players this city has ever seen. When I watch you play, it's like watching Michael Jordan on the basketball court. You're just as unstoppable. I would hate to see something happen to you because of you hanging around with them two fools and their wild crew."

Her words made him smile. If only she knew the truth about him, what would her thoughts be then? He was exactly like Devon and Papa John—maybe a lot worse.

"Right now I don't know what I want, Eshon. I know I need to be around familiar faces right now. I don't wanna be alone."

"You're not alone. I'm here for you and I will always be here for you. You're my friend, Kid, and you'll always be my friend."

"And you'll always be my friend, too."

Eshon continued to push him down the street. The heart-to-heart talk they were having was a bit therapeutic. Eshon felt that Kid was the only one she could talk to. She could tell him anything. Even when his brother was alive, she could confess her feelings about Kip to him, whether they were good or bad, and he wouldn't overreact. Kid was never an emotional person, and he didn't judge people. He had always been reasonable and understanding.

"You know, Brandy came to me not too long ago about leaving town—packing our bags and starting a new life somewhere else," she mentioned. "I damn near cursed her out for bringing it up."

"Why?" he asked.

"I always felt that my life is here, in Harlem and in this city."

"Is it still here?"

A heavy sigh escaped her lips as they crossed the intersection. She looked ahead of him, transfixed on a thought. "My heart was filled with rage. I wanted Jessica dead with a passion. I couldn't leave New York while that bitch was still alive. But now that she's dead . . . I don't know, I thought I would feel better, but I don't. It's like . . . I feel a lot sadder now. I just want things how they used to be."

"It will never be the same."

"I know, but what next? This fight with Maserati Meek, is it my fight?"

"He killed my brother."

"But I don't want him to kill you too, or us. What are we up against?"

"You can leave town with Brandy if you want, Eshon. If you're looking for my blessing, I give it to you. I can take care of myself," he proclaimed.

She didn't truly believe that. "I made a promise to Kip to look after you. It's a promise that I plan on keeping."

"I got my life and you got yours, Eshon. Just live it without feeling you have an obligation to me—because you don't."

"You're no burden on me, Kid. We're family."

"And I don't want you to feel like you owe me anything, because you don't. Like you said, this wheelchair doesn't make me a cripple. I'm smart enough to know how to take care of myself."

Eshon pushed him along the sidewalk. Their talk felt like it was becoming a lot more turbulent. He wanted to leap from the wheelchair and show the strength in his legs, but it would be stupid of him. If he did so, it would change everything between them. She would see him as a liar. True friends didn't keep secrets from each other.

They traveled three blocks with their conversation growing more and more. They continued to talk about Kip. It was one way she was able to find healing—by reminiscing and talking about Kip to someone who knew him too. It felt like he was still alive.

"If you were to leave the city, where would you go?" asked Kid.

"I don't know, maybe out west . . . California. I always wanted to see Cali. The way Jessica would always talk about it, it seemed an exotic and exciting place to see." The mention of her name made her teeth itch and feel rotten. "I never have been outside of New York."

"I haven't traveled much either."

"If you were to leave, where you would want to go?" she asked him.

He gave it some thought and replied, "I would leave the country, maybe Africa. I've been researching Ghana."

"Africa?" Eshon uttered, taken aback by his answer. "Why Africa?"

"It's a rich and thriving continent, despite what you hear about it from the media—the white man's media. Africa has a growing middle class, and its urbanization rate is already at thirty-seven percent. I wanna go back to my roots . . . to the Motherland. Like Kunta Kinte."

"See Kid, you're smart. You know shit that I probably can't even comprehend. Not too many people from Harlem would say they want to go back to Africa."

"Kip and I always talked about it."

His statement shocked Eshon. "What? Kip was talking about Africa?"

"He was. He would bring it up at times. My brother was many things, even a killer. But he did have some culture in him. He was smart, and he wanted to escape from who he was at times. He would always compare himself to Shaka Zulu—leading his people into battle against indifference and injustice. I remember when we first saw his story on TV as kids, my brother was captivated by the man. A half-naked black man with a spear and courage, having all this power over these people and putting fear in the white man's heart."

Eshon chuckled. "Kip was a warrior."

"He was. Sometimes I felt he was born in the wrong era."

"Harlem wasn't ready for a man like him," Eshon said.

"Harlem . . . New York City wasn't ready for him. Kip was ready to take on the world."

"And I was ready to be his ride-or-die queen right by his side."

They managed to laugh while talking about Kip. They felt some light in the dark. Eshon exhaled somewhat. The emotions started to flood inside of her. The memory of Kip was always welcome. There were so many things she still didn't know about him. Ghana. If he was willing to move to Ghana, Eshon would have been on the plane with him. If it took relocating to Africa to start a new and better life with him, there would have been no hesitation on her part. Thinking about it brought some sadness to her, though. She could see it, the two of them raising a family in the Motherland.

"If he was alive you think he would have taken me with him . . . to Africa?"

"He did love you. I just think he had difficulty showing it."

"He used to break my heart a lot, and yet, I always managed to forgive him and let him back into my life. I wanted to give him kids. Sometimes I felt so stupid when it came to him."

"You were a woman in love. It's not a crime," said Kid.

"No, it's not a crime, but it sometimes felt like I was on death row with him," she said faintly.

"Hey, we were brothers and sometimes I felt like the invisible man when he was around. Kip had this way of bringing you up so high that you felt you would never come back down, and he knew how to bring you down so low, that you could feel the fires of hell at the heels of your feet."

"He did. Shit, I still carry the scars in my soul because of our ups and downs. But you couldn't help but to love that man."

"Yeah, we did. But you were the only one he truly cared about. He never talked about anyone else with me. And you knew how to push his buttons too, Eshon."

She laughed. "I definitely had my moments with him."

"Quite a few, if I recall."

Before they knew it, they had walked six blocks while engrossed in conversation. Their talk was needed, and the laughter was needed between them a lot more. But then the present came up.

Eshon looked fretful. "Where do we go from here? I'm scared, Kid."

"I wish I knew. I'm just along for the ride like everyone else."

"I know you are, Kid. Devon worries me though. He has this look about him, it's almost satanic."

"He's always been like that, Eshon."

"I know, but it's a lot scarier since Kip died. He's the type of nigga to give the devil the chills," she said.

"He is a scary guy."

"Too scary. They was Kip's peoples, not yours. You should just part from them and rebuild somewhere else."

"And you need to stop telling me what I need to do. I'm a grown man, Eshon. I may not be Kip, but I'm still able to take care of myself."

"I know you can. I guess I worry about you because you're the only brother I have."

"I'll be all right, Eshon."

"You promise?"

"I promise," he replied.

They turned around and headed back to the motel. It was getting late.

# 19

The cigarette smoke danced around the SUV as Papa John worked on his third cigarette. He was sitting in the driver's seat parked on the still and quiet street, and keeping a keen eye on his father's place. A .9mm sat on passenger seat, but Papa John had nothing to worry about in Whitestone. The only threat he saw was his father. Having an affair with Dina was risky, but it was worth it. She gave him pleasures and an escape from his turbulent lifestyle. He ached to see her again. He took another drag from the cancer stick and exhaled. Finally, he watched his father's Benz back out of the driveway and drive off. To be on the safe side, he continued to sit in the vehicle for a few minutes. He dialed Dina and she answered almost immediately.

"Hello?"

"He's gone for the night, right?" he asked.

"Yes."

"A'ight, I'm parked down the block. Give me ten minutes and I'll head that way."

"Okay."

He ended the call and finished his cigarette. Weed and pussy were the only two things that could cool his nerves. He was energized for another night with Dina, and he couldn't wait the full ten minutes. Papa John exited the SUV five minutes early and trekked toward the house with his head held low and a dark baseball cap pulled low over his brow. He entered the driveway and swiftly moved toward the backyard.

Dina already had the back door opened and was waiting for him in a black silk robe. He hugged her right away, which was followed by a passionate kiss. The door closed and the fondling began. But before things got too hot and heavy between them, Dina placed her hand against his chest and pushed him back. She stared at him.

"What's up? Something wrong?" he asked.

"I'm worried about you, Papa John."

"Worried about me? Why?"

"These bombings in the city—who's after you and why?"

Papa John sighed. He didn't come to talk about his troubles. He felt stupid for even mentioning it to her.

"Look, everything's gonna be all right," he said.

"How? Your father is working twelve-hour shifts because the NYPD is going crazy looking for these terrorists, and the man I'm having an affair with is involved somehow."

"I'm not involved, it's just a beef wit' this stupid muthafucka," he corrected.

"You need to tell your father about this," she suggested.

"Are you fuckin' crazy?"

"Papa John, you need to do something. What if these people who want to kill you track you here? Did you ever think about that?"

He hadn't. But Papa John was certain that he wasn't being followed. He made sure to cover his tracks and watch his back.

"I'm not being followed, Dina."

"How do you know that?"

"Because I know," he retorted.

She huffed and folded her arms across her chest. She didn't plan to argue with him, but the situation was becoming too real. She didn't want to bring his drama into her home—her fiancé and his father's home.

Looking into Papa John's eyes, she clearly saw that he was a dangerous man. The same thing that had turned her on was now turning her off somewhat. The last thing Dina needed was the feds or a threat encroaching on her fairly happy home with Darryl.

"Look, you don't have to worry. I'm not being followed, and nobody knows about you, Dina. Shit, my pops is this big-time detective and the muthafucka is clueless too. You think I'm gonna bring some drama to his crib and put you at risk? Nah, it ain't even gonna go down like that."

He wrapped his arms around her waist and fondled her body. He wanted to feel her close. He needed her loving. The softness of her body was bringing on an erection inside his jeans. Dina still looked hesitant. Papa John kissed the side of her neck and caressed her body.

"Baby, I didn't drive over here to argue wit' you; I came because I missed you, and I missed this." He reached between her thighs and embraced a handful of pussy.

She cooed a little. His tender kisses continued against the nape of her neck. His touch became more audacious against her flesh. He untied her robe and found she was naked underneath. He slipped his index finger inside her pussy and started to slowly finger her.

"I need you tonight, baby. I got a lot on my mind and I need this release. I need your loving," Papa John said.

Her robe slid from around her shoulders and dropped to her feet. Her naked body was always a pleasure to see. He cupped her breasts and groped her. Her back to his chest, his arms around her nude flesh, and his kisses started to create a serious wet leak between her knees.

What was it about Papa John that made her crumble with sin and infidelity? Darryl was one heck of a man—a strong man, and a good man—but Papa John carried that bad-boy persona flawlessly, and she always had a weakness for bad boys. Fucking a cop and his criminal son at the same time was daring and stimulating.

She felt herself being lifted off her feet. Her legs straddled him and he carried her into the master bedroom.

With Dina on her back with her legs spread, Papa John went in for the kill. He tasted her completely, tickling her clit with his mouth and tongue and kissing her thighs while parting her lips and fingering her gently. She moaned and squirmed. He ate her out until she came. The sex was always mind-blowing. Papa John made his escape from his plight as he twisted and knotted his father's fiancée into one sexual position after another, the big dick moving in and out of her repeatedly with strong friction ready to set flames to her pussy. Dina held on tight and was truly enjoying the ride of her life. When he came, she came too—and then came again three and four more times. Afterwards, they spooned on the bed with their bodies once again spent from all the sexual play. It was then that she decided to tell him the news, and it wasn't so good.

"I'm pregnant," she blurted out.

"Shit, I'm gonna have a baby brother?"

"Or a son."

"But I always bag up."

"And the condom has broken how many times?"

"Is it—"

"I don't know if it's yours or Darryl's," she said.

Shit. Papa John laid there with blankness in his eyes. If the baby was his, then this would make baby mama number seven for him. His numbers were climbing higher than a good day at the stock exchange.

"Damn," he simply uttered.

"That's all you have to say?"

"What else is there to say?"

She sighed heavily. What if it was Papa John's baby—then what? She was living a good life with Darryl. He provided for her and took care of her, and he treated her fairly. But she had fallen in love with his son.

Somewhat frustrated, Dina removed herself from Papa John's arms and went into the bathroom, slamming the door behind her. The attitude came quickly. She didn't want to hear "Damn" or "What else is there to say?" from him. She needed something more constructive coming from his mouth. She was risking everything by having an affair with him. Now things became critical. Papa John was the first to know about the pregnancy—even before her fiancé. Eventually, she would have to tell Darryl, but there was another option—an abortion. If she chose that road, then the money would have to come from Papa John, because Darryl would certainly want to keep the baby.

Papa John removed himself from the bed and started to get dressed. He had to go. The hours were flying by, and morning was imminent in a few hours. Dina was still locked in the bathroom. Papa John knocked on the door and said, "Dina, I gotta go. We'll talk about this later."

He received nothing but silence.

He left. Dina sat on the toilet in tears, wondering if she'd made the biggest mistake of her life. Papa John lived in a dangerous and deadly world. There was no telling if tomorrow was promised for him. And there was no telling if his world would come crashing into hers. If so, how would she explain it to Darryl?

# 20

The large flatscreen TV broadcasted the nightly news in the Far Rockaway beachfront property, and the core subject was the two deadly bombings in the city. Now the feds had a person of interest. Forty-five people were confirmed dead in the Harlem project building bombing, and another twenty residents were seriously injured. The bomb used was powerful with a strong kill radius—same as the nightclub. It almost felt nuclear. The blast took out several floors and shook the building's foundation. The feds were worried.

Maserati Meek perked up when he heard the anchorwoman mention Jessica's name. His eyes became fixed on the TV and he raised the volume to hear clearer. He was astounded to see her face on TV.

"What is this, eh?" Maserati Meek asked his men as they sat around in the plush decorated living room and watched the news.

Meek was confused. Why were they searching for Jessica? He assumed they already had her in custody. He assumed that she had snitched on him. She had betrayed him. She needed to be taught a lesson, so that's why her family and those closest to her had to die.

"It's a trick," Amir uttered.

"You think so?"

"The FBI will do anything to catch their man, even lie."

Maserati Meek wasn't so sure. There were a lot of questions he wanted answers to. Where was she? Was she truly on the run? How did the FBI find out about her? How did they track her down? He started to feel anxious. She wasn't answering her phone or texting him back.

"Yes, it must be a ruse. They want to confuse me," Meek said. "I must call her again. Bring me a burner phone."

Amir looked at him and said, "We must stay focused and continue on with the task. We are at war, my brother. And Allah has chosen us to relay His message. This girl, she's a distraction."

But she wasn't a distraction. She was some of the best sex that he ever had in his life. Too bad it had to end. Maserati Meek paced back and forth in the opulent beachfront home. He felt secure there with his dedicated and armed Muslim brothers. The place had marble flooring with an open living area, a modern eat-in kitchen, and a luxurious master bedroom. It had a sweeping view of the ocean, a granite wet bar, and a double-side wood fireplace for the cold winters.

Amir kept his eyes on Meek. He had noticed something different about Meek—whose true name was Akar Mudada. Amir was a die-hard extremist who wanted to strike terror into the lives of as many Americans, Israelis, and Europeans as he could. He believed that by killing those who did not serve their cause, he would make the world a much better place. They were fighting on behalf of all Muslims. And when his time came, Amir planned on taking out as many American lives as possible. He was bred for destruction. Allah was his calling, and violence was, most times, the only voice of reason—violence was the path to paradise.

"I need some air," Meek said.

Amir nodded.

Meek stepped onto the spacious brick-paved patio. He looked at the sea. It was time to get back to business. While Amir and the others cared about their religious cause, it was making money that Maserati Meek truly cared about. But there was one more obstacle in his way: Panamanian Pete. Pete was his true distraction. He was a man that could match his wealth and his power. With Panamanian Pete finally gone, Meek could fully corner the market and manipulate prices, from drugs and racketeering to having absolute power. He could become a god on the streets and beyond. It was something that he refused to tell his Muslim brothers—that he was a big-time drug dealer in business with the black man. He was selfish, and Amir and the others were killing themselves based on a lie. Swelled with megalomania, Meek was determined to have it all by any means necessary.

While Meek lingered on the patio, Amir looked at him with suspicion from the next room. He had many questions for Meek. First, why had he changed his name from Akar? Why was the girl Jessica on TV, and why was she the person of interest for their handiwork? Who was she really to Akar? Was their Muslim brother in love with this woman? Things were going awry, and he felt it needed to be fixed right away. He turned and moved away from Meek's line of view. In the following room, Amir removed his cell phone and dialed a number. It was a long-distance call, back home to Egypt, and Amir soon got in contact with Meek's dad, Shahib Abu Mudada.

# 21

The Bottom's Up was a seedy urban strip club in the heart of Bed-Stuy, four blocks from where the legendary Biggie Smalls grew up. It was a busy night at the club, swamped with thugs and pimps, locals and squares, perverts and first-timers. Overall, they were all there for the same things—pussy and drinks.

Inside the dim, loud club, a sultry dancer named Passion took to the stage butt-naked in a pair of clear stilettos with blaring rap music as her soundtrack. Her chocolate-covered body was curvy and flawless. Numerous tattoos decorated her skin, including one on her back of a large glistening diamond containing hundred dollar bills—a metaphor for being rich on the outside and in. Her tits sat up perfectly, her nipples were darker than coal, and between her thighs was the perfect shaved camel toe.

She grabbed the pole and skillfully swung herself around it a few times, moving to Drake's "Hotline Bling." She then hoisted herself up the pole, showing off her upper body strength, and contorted her body around it like a coiled snake. The muscles in her arms and legs worked together as she acrobatically worked her body down the pole, from the ceiling to the stage. It was just the beginning of her wild act tonight. The men crowded around the stage and tossed money at her like it was free, and a few were able to make it rain on her. Passion was everyone's favorite.

The club was saturated with sexily dressed and promiscuous women. The Bottom's Up was the place to be on a Friday night. The drinks weren't watered down, the women were sprightly, and for the right price, they were available for anyone's pleasure.

Panamanian Pete lingered in the back of the club near the office door, puffing on a cigar and keeping his eyes on everything. It was one of the many businesses he owned in the Tri-State area. Bedford-Stuyvesant was a neighborhood he controlled and where he always felt comfortable. He was a major player on the streets, with a reach that extended from the Brooklyn streets into NYPD corruption. He had money and power that only a few could dream of.

Wearing a dark Armani suit that highlighted his authority and a gold Rolex around his wrist, his eyes looked at Passion working her magic on the stage. She was special, and he knew just how special she was. She had platinum pussy and a mouth that could make any man come in minutes. Watching her twerk on stage and then spread her legs eagle style, exposing her pink cookies, Panamanian Pete stood there a little turned on. Passion had given him plenty of private performances in his office when the club was closed. A few of those nights led to three pregnancies and three abortions.

Panamanian Pete couldn't see a woman like Passion having his kids. She was only good for one thing, and that was having a good time. So the abortions were forced on her, no matter what she felt. She didn't have a choice.

Spending time in one of his strip clubs temporarily took his mind away from his conflict with Maserati Meek, along with the death of his brother and his missing $800,000. But he would never forget. Pete wasn't a forgiving man. He felt the urge to kill Meek and everyone associated with him. *In due time,* he told himself.

He took a few more pulls from the cigar. Passion was about to start one of her infamous acts. She began covering her tits with shaving cream from a can as the crowd waited in anticipation. She pulled out a match, lit it, and set fire to her chest. The flames raged against her skin and yet, Passion looked unharmed. She strutted around with her tits on fire for a few seconds, even twerking, and then easily snuffed it out. The crowd in the place went wild and applauded her risky trick. Panamanian Pete never got tired of seeing her do it. It was her signature move in The Bottom's Up.

During Passion's act, two of Pete's goons entered the club, Rodney and G-Dep. Both men looked ominous and unfriendly. Between the two of them, they had a combined body count of twenty-six victims. Murder was their forte. Security refused to search them, knowing that they were connected to the boss man. It was Pete's club and Pete always gave them the okay to come inside carrying their weapons. Both men knew better than to show out in his place of business.

Panamanian Pete locked eyes with Rodney and gave him a simple head nod, meaning they needed to talk. Rodney nodded back. The killers needed a drink first. It had been a long day. Pete gave them five minutes to step into his office. He didn't like to wait.

Panamanian Pete supervised his strip club, but Charles Ray was the manager. Charles Ray approached him with some urgent news. He stood six-five with a bald head and always wore a tracksuit. He leaned closer and said into Pete's ear, "Meek's bitch is on TV."

Pete looked at him in confusion. "What?"

"Feds are lookin' for her."

Panamanian Pete pivoted and headed into his office with Charles Ray right behind him. With the door closed, Pete snatched up the remote to the forty-inch flatscreen and turned on the nightly news. Lo and behold, Jessica was on the news—her face was splashed across his TV screen. He had heard about the bombing, but never in his wildest imagination did he think that Maserati Meek had anything to do with it. But there she was, Meek's bitch Jessica and the FBI. Somehow she was a suspect.

"Fuckin' crazy bitch," Pete said.

"Yeah, it caught me off guard too," said Charles Ray.

Pete was zoned in on the news. They mentioned terrorism. Once again, he was taken aback, but not fully shocked. If Maserati Meek was linked to terrorism, it fueled his rage more and gave him more of a reason to slaughter the man. He hated terrorists.

A knock at the door turned his attention away from the news. "Come in," he said.

Rodney and G-Dep walked into the office.

Panamanian Pete looked their way and asked, "So, what y'all two muthafuckas got for me? Is it done?"

Rodney spoke up. "They weren't at the location. When we showed up the fire department was putting out a fire in the building."

"Fire? What fuckin fire?" Pete asked.

"I think they knew we were coming and set the place on fire to cover their tracks."

It was news that Pete didn't want to hear. He had gotten the intel on one of Maserati Meek's hideouts and acted on it. Panamanian Pete had plenty of resources spread everywhere to gather information. His moles and snitches were working feverishly on the streets. If something was out of place, or there was an anomaly somewhere, he wanted to know about it. He hated surprises. However, Meek was a tricky and slippery bastard, and fortunately for him, he'd left the Brooklyn location just in time.

"What you want us to do next?" G-Dep asked.

"Y'all niggas chill for a moment. I'll find y'all some more work soon."

Rodney and G-Dep were two of his best killers, but they'd struck out. Pete walked around to his desk and took a seat in his high-back leather chair. He lit another cigar and leaned back. He looked up at the black-and-white security monitors. He was the eye in the sky, and nothing went down inside The Bottom's Up without him knowing about it. With Meek, his only option now was to wait.

\*\*\*

Panamanian Pete put out money on the streets for any solid information on his foes. He figured two hundred thousand dollars was a large enough sum to get people excited—to get people talking. For that kind of money, folks would sell out their own mothers.

It didn't take long before Pete got a nibble on the line. It was a strong bite, and he was ready to reel it in and finally skin this slippery fish and cut off his head.

\*\*\*

Panamanian Pete and his armed thugs sat parked in Canarsie across the street from upmarket two-story row homes looking like lions ready to pounce on a grazing deer. The nondescript blue minivan they sat inside was camouflaged among the other vehicles on the Brooklyn street. It was the location of their target—supposedly, Maserati Meek.

Everybody was quiet with anticipation, simply waiting for the right moment. Five men including Pete were ready for bloodshed. It was unusual for him to involve himself directly in a crime. He had spent years isolating himself from the day-to-day street life—the violence, the drugs, and his soldiers. He had generals and lieutenants who regularly reported to him. He was the cream that had risen to the top through hardcore violence and murders, and he had enough money to pay anyone to do his dirty work for him, including murder. But tonight was different. This was personal. The loss of $800,000 was huge, but the death of his brother Mike, and then Lance prompted him to personally get down and dirty. It wouldn't feel right to Pete if he wasn't there to kill Maserati Meek himself. He had high-priced lawyers on retainer and he had honorable sources spread everywhere if he ever found himself in a sticky situation.

Panamanian Pete understood that money was the core to everything. It got things done, it brought results, and without it, there was no life. If you had enough of it, life could be good. If you had tons of it, then you could become a god. And Pete felt that he was a god. He wanted to see Maserati Meek go down himself. At first he put Rodney and G-Dep on it, but changed his mind once one of his informants came to him with reliable information about a place in Canarsie that was very valuable to Meek. Now Pete wanted to pull the trigger himself.

Maserati Meek was known to move around a lot. He rarely stayed in the same location for more than a month, if that. He was like a nomad. He had real estate everywhere in and out of the city. It made him a slippery fish to find and to catch, and his money made him a man with the means to evaporate from society.

The middle-class and commercial neighborhood looked like a ghost town in the middle of the night—there was an echo of silence. Panamanian Pete puffed on his cigar. Seated in the passenger seat, he clutched a chrome Desert Eagle, the Bentley of handguns. The house they were watching sat huddled in the middle of the block. There was a small porch, but no lights were seen outside or inside, and no activity so far. But Panamanian Pete's stool pigeon was adamant that Meek would show at the address tonight. It was one of Meek's major money locations. On a good day, two to three million dollars would be smuggled out of the residence. Some of it went to help fund terrorism. Only a handful of Meek's people knew about the place, and most times Maserati Meek himself would show up to the address to supervise and make sure everything went as planned. When millions of dollars were to be moved, Meek was there. He trusted no one.

"If this nigga don't show tonight, I want y'all to put a bullet in Manny's fuckin' head. He assured me that tonight would be my night. I don't wanna be wasting my fuckin' time on bullshit," Panamanian Pete growled at his killers.

They nodded. It would be easy to do.

Another hour went by. Cigarette and cigar smoke lingered in the vehicle. Pete was known to be a patient man, sometimes—but after three hours of sitting and waiting, he was starting to become agitated. Pete wasn't the only one becoming agitated. The longer they waited, the more doubt started to fill their minds. Manny gave them false information. He told them 11 p.m., but it was nearing three in the morning. If there was a no show, Pete was ready to put four bullets into Manny's head and chop his fuckin' head off. His time was too valuable to waste.

Finally, there was activity on the block. A black Escalade pulled up and double-parked outside the row homes. The passenger and rear doors opened and Maserati Meek exited the SUV flanked by three men, all of them African American and looking serious. It didn't make any difference to Pete. A friend or associate of Meek's was an enemy of his. Black, white, Middle Eastern, South Asian, they were poison to the city if they did business with Maserati Meek.

Pete's blood boiled when he finally laid his eyes on Meek. "Fuckin' wigger," he snarled.

"You wanna go now?" one of Pete's goons asked.

"Nah, we wait for their exit. He comes out with the money, and then we kill two birds with one stone. I'm owed my eight hundred thousand plus interest," he said.

So far, they weren't spotted. One of Meek's men looked directly over at the minivan parked across the street and it didn't set any alarms off. To everyone, it was another normal pickup in the neighborhood and every car belonged on the street. Smart though, doing it in the middle of the night: less eyes and less attention.

Ten minutes went by. Panamanian Pete cocked back the Desert Eagle in his hand and readied himself for the carnage. He was the only one with a handgun. The others carried assault rifles. They were ready to implement overkill. The last cigarette was smoked and dowsed, and movement inside the van was limited. They wanted to keep the element of surprise.

Nimbly, the sliding door was opened nice and slow to not attract attention. The interior lights had been shut off, shrouding the van with darkness, and Panamanian Pete and his murderous hooligans filed out of the minivan while crouched low. Two men stood guard outside. No doubt they were the muscle, and no doubt they were armed. Including Maserati Meek, three went inside. The cars and SUVs on the street gave the encroaching threat the cover they needed. To Pete it felt like old times again. His adrenaline was on high. His goons could have the others; he was focused on killing one man—Maserati Meek. Like ninjas cloaked in darkness, they perched in the shadows and waited to execute death.

Meek was the second to exit the place. He walked between his two black thugs carrying two metal suitcases. Two, three million, it didn't matter to Pete, he was taking it all—the money and their lives. Maserati Meek walked down the porch stairs with his security locked around him, headed toward the double-parked Escalade. As far as he could see, nothing was off during the pickup of his money. The night was quiet and the neighbors most likely asleep.

Then it happened—abrupt and loud, gunfire started. Panamanian Pete and his bloodthirsty ruffians emerged from the darkness and opened fire on Meek and his men.

*Bratatat—Bratatat—Bratatat!*

*Rat-a-tat-tat-tat-tat-tat-tat!*

One man went down immediately—struck in the chest with multiple bullets that jerked him around violently. Maserati Meek and his men quickly took cover behind the nearest solid object.

"Fuck! Fuck!" Meek screamed in panic.

A barrage of bullets shattered car windows and slammed into cars, houses, and trees. Machine-gunfire lit up the night. The shooters were reckless. They didn't care about anything but killing. Pete's Desert Eagle exploded at Meek It missed him, but Pete was determined to kill the man.

It didn't take long for Meek to realize that his men were outgunned. Bullets whizzed by his head, splintering the tree he hid behind. His .9mm was no match for the machine guns. He noticed that his driver was still alive. He was about eight feet away from the SUV. If he didn't move now, then he was a dead man. Another of his men went down swiftly; his brains were on the sidewalk. Meek huffed. He outstretched his arm around the tree and desperately returned gunfire.

*Bak! Bak! Bak . . . Bak! Bak!*

Hit or miss, he didn't know. It was his feeble attempt at cover fire, trying to distract the shooters long enough to run for it. And he did. He took off running toward the truck like a bat out of hell with its wings on fire. He ran like he was Jessie Owens in the 1936 Olympics. Everything exploded around him; windshields and car material were being shredded. He was not going to die tonight.

Panamanian Pete saw Meek fleeing frantically. He raised himself from behind the car, took sniper's aim, and cut loose with the Desert Eagle—*Boom! Boom! Boom! Boom!*

He saw Maserati Meek drop suddenly to the ground. It was a direct hit. There was blood, and Pete was sure that it was head shot. He wanted to run across the street and finish what he had started, but he heard the police sirens blaring from a distance. The police were coming. He couldn't stick around. Maserati Meek had gone down, and Panamanian Pete presumed him dead. They all retreated to the minivan and sped away.

Panamanian Pete felt he'd just closed his chapter of revenge. Maserati Meek was dead, right?

# 22

"heckmate!" Kid exclaimed, easily beating Eshon in seven moves.

"Damn, again?" Eshon said, but it wasn't shocking. She didn't expect to beat him at chess. She was still learning the game from him, and he was a chess master.

The Kid laughed. "Some advice when playing chess—when you see a good move, look for a better one."

"I don't know how y'all play this game. It's just so hard."

"It just takes time to learn the game, and it takes patience and a third eye to master it."

"You damn sure mastered it, Kid. You're unbeatable," she proclaimed.

"When you love something, then you believe in it, and once you believe in it, then you become the best at it."

Eshon stared at the chess pieces, looking transfixed by a sudden thought. Without looking at Kid, she said, "The only thing I've been good at was loving your brother and helping him rob people."

"You're smart, Eshon."

"I'm not smart like you."

"Everybody's born with an individual talent."

"And I never found mine. I'm just a cute girl from the projects now caught up in some crazy shit."

"You need to stop beating yourself up and stay focused, Eshon. This isn't going to be your end—our end."

"But what next?" she said.

"I don't know what's next. We just have to take things one day at a time. We have enough money to live comfortably for now, so we stay in New Rochelle and stay under the radar. Do you like the place?"

"It's nice. It's definitely not the projects."

Motel life was becoming too confined, so Kid set out to find them a rental place somewhere in the area. He went online and searched for something convenient, affordable, and comfortable. He found a location in Oakwood Heights, New Rochelle. There was an elderly widow looking to rent out her house for $2,000 a month. It was a modest house, three bedrooms and two bathrooms. The Kid jumped at it.

Mrs. Prestano was white and Italian. The Kid and Eshon met with the woman under the guise that they were a recently married couple looking for their first home. When the woman saw The Kid in a wheelchair, she was immediately sympathetic toward him. First impressions were lasting impressions, and The Kid and Eshon put on one hell of a show for the lady. She couldn't deny a couple the place when one of the pair was handicapped. Kid paid her three months' rent in advance.

With their new place, The Kid advised Papa John and Devon to move someplace safe as well, until the death of Maserati Meek. He knew they couldn't stay there with him and Eshon. They would bring too much attention to the place. It was a quiet and polite neighborhood. The last thing The Kid wanted was attention. Devon wasn't fit for suburban life, and Papa John wasn't either. So the two men continued to live out of motels.

And Brandy suddenly became homesick.

Eshon had always been good to The Kid, and he trusted her and was loyal to her. They had a special bond—a friendship that seemed unbending and unbreakable. Kip's death had made their friendship even stronger. Away from it all—the violence, the murders, the concrete jungle of Harlem—things seemed normal for them. But how long would things stay normal?

The Kid didn't mind it. He allowed Eshon to assume the role that his brother had filled. She made sure he ate and kept the place clean. She had become his impromptu caretaker. They talked every night, sometimes for hours, and most times it was about Kip and Harlem.

One night The Kid caught a glimpse of her bona fide outer beauty. She had just taken a shower, and the bathroom door to the lower floor was ajar. He happened to roll by and got a glimpse of her toweling off. He sat there mesmerized by her nudity. Her sexy curves and perky breasts were exceptional. *How could Kip mistreat her sometimes, when every man in Harlem chased her and wanted to cherish her?* he thought. She was definitely a man's dream girl. Eshon was a beautiful woman with so much to offer a man. She was caring by nature, and though she could be rough around the edges, there was something special about her.

She turned and caught his stare upon her. Eshon didn't become startled by his clear perversion, but she simply smiled and politely closed the bathroom door. The Kid smiled himself and wheeled himself into the next room. Once again, if only she knew the truth—who he really was—a mobile killer like the others. What would her reaction be? Would her smile still be there? He was a lie to her, but the lie felt so good. Their friendship was so real. But would their friendship be decapitated if one day he stood up in front of her and walked her way? If he told her about the killings he committed, even killing his own Nana, would Eshon see him as a cold-blooded monster like Devon?

They decided to play one more game of chess. The Kid wanted to teach her the game. He liked teaching others to play.

"I wanted to teach Kip the game, but he never had time to play with me. He didn't want to learn it," he said.

"He was always a busy man."

"He was. Always too busy for the two people that loved him the most."

Eshon tried to concentrate harder on this new game. She moved her knight recklessly. The Kid saw it was a damaging move and made her recant it. He explained why it was a reckless move. Every move she made, he criticized it.

He picked up a pawn piece, and then said to her, "I see this chessboard as the world. Every move we make, there's always someone or something trying to take us out—trying to knock us off the board. And you got to respect that some people were meant to be pawns and some meant to be kings and queens. But don't underestimate the pawns. Though they have one simple move, they're still able to take out higher opponents if they're moved just right. And when these little bitches somehow make it to the other side of the board without being taken out, then they're promoted. They can either become a queen, a rook, a knight, or a bishop. They just have to make it to the other side of the board, which most times, looks almost impossible with what they're up against, but it can happen."

She listened. His parables were interesting. Her next move on the board was more thought out.

The Kid smiled and said, "Nice one."

She smiled back.

They continued to play. She was improving. Her next move was a challenging one, but it was still inferior to The Kid's.

"I'm a good teacher, I see," he joked.

She chuckled.

Out of the blue, Kid's cell phone rang. The caller I.D. identified Devon. Kid looked at Eshon and said, "Excuse me for a minute."

He pushed himself back from the table and answered the call. "What's up?" he asked.

"We need to talk. Me and Papa John are outside," Devon said.

"A'ight, come inside."

Eshon wasn't too surprised to see Devon and Papa John come into the new house. Lately, they would come over to see Kid. They all would disappear into a room to talk. She would be left out. It was odd to her. Why were they meeting with Kid? What were they talking about? Were they chatting about capers? It was bewildering to her—two cold-hearted killers now socializing with a chess champion. Kid was a humble man—a good guy. She figured it was nothing. With Kip dead, hanging out with his two best friends was probably the only closure Kid had in his life. And besides Eshon, there was no one else to reminisce about Kip with but Devon and Papa John. They knew him best, too.

Devon closed the door to the bedroom. The Kid looked up at the two men, and by the look on their faces, something had gone down.

"What's up? What's going on?" The Kid asked.

Devon looked at Kid and said, "Maserati Meek was hit."

"What?"

"He was shot."

"Is he dead?" The Kid asked in anticipation.

"Don't know, but he got hit up the other night in Canarsie at one of his money houses. Word is, he had about two mill on him," Devon said.

"Shit!"

It was a lot of money. The Kid wished he had that nigga's money in his possession. But if Meek was coming out of one of his places with two million easy, there was no telling how much more money there was out there. The Kid wanted it all. It was owed to him since Meek took his brother's life.

"Who went after him?" The Kid asked.

"Not sure. It could be Panamanian Pete or some other niggas out there itching to blow his fuckin' head off, like me."

"First things first. We need to know if he survived the attack."

Devon and Papa John nodded.

"And second, find out who was responsible for the attack. Whoever got that close to Meek might be of value to us. You know what they say: The enemy of my enemy could be a friend to me."

"And what if it's Panamanian Pete? He will never be a friend. We robbed that nigga of eight hundred grand and killed his peoples," Papa John said.

"But to my understanding, he's blaming Maserati Meek for it all. That makes us clear of any wrongdoing toward him."

"It's still risky to reach out to that nigga," Papa John advised. "I don't trust him, and I never will."

The men talked for several minutes and then they left the room. The Kid wheeled himself out of the bedroom and noticed Eshon lingering in the hallway. Papa John and Devon said their goodbyes to her and left the house.

"Is everything okay?" she asked him.

"Everything's fine," he replied. "We were just talking."

*Yeah, about what?* she wondered.

"It's getting late. I'm going to bed," he said.

"You need any help?"

"Nah, I'm okay. I can handle it."

The Kid wheeled himself into the bedroom on the first floor. He closed the door behind him. Eshon was left with questions on her mind, but she retreated to her own bedroom to get some much-needed rest.

# 23

The Manhattanville projects looked like a dystopian society. So many were homeless because of the bombing—their normal lives were suddenly ripped away from them. Many others were being arrested for disorderly conduct. Folks were sick and tired of being mistreated and lied to. They felt dehumanized. They were the victims of a terrorist attack; however, the police were treating them like they were terrorists themselves. There was heated tension between the police and the people, and scuffles broke out on the streets multiple times a day.

It was a circus in their community. The news media, the FBI and city police had overrun their community. The media were exploiting their misfortune. The residents didn't have access to any information on the *who* and *why*. They were kept in the dark. There were a few who were allowed back into their homes, but there were plenty of other residents who were left in limbo. The unfair treatment in their community was spiraling out of control, and many voiced their upset and anger via social media and the news. Where was the Red Cross? Where was FEMA?

"If this had happened in a white neighborhood, it wouldn't be like this. White people always get help in a heartbeat. But the black community, we gotta wait and be patient, and hear the same lies day after day, 'Help is on the way.' Bullshit!" an angry black citizen voiced into the news camera.

"Damn right I'm mad," another resident spoke out. "We get attacked and we don't know why. But cops are out here trying to lock us up because we don't know what to do or where to go, and my friends are dead . . . and we want answers, and we want our homes and our lives back. But we're getting treated like criminals. I lived here all my life and never seen anything like this."

"Fuck them terrorist muthafuckas! Yo, fuckin' towelheads come see me, fo' real. I'm right here in Harlem all day wit' my fuckin' Glock and my nine, and I'm ready for these niggas. I hate them muthafuckas!" a young thug told the journalists. Of course, most of his segment was censored.

The tears and anguish were overwhelming. There were a lot of lost and broken souls between Old Broadway and Amsterdam Avenue. It was panic, trepidation, anger, and vengeance all rolled up into one cigar, and the smoke was spreading.

Stopping short of the swarming media and police cars that flooded the block was a black Charger. All four doors to the car opened and out stepped several FBI agents and Officer Spielberg. He had been temporarily assigned to work with the feds to assist with their investigation.

Officer Spielberg looked around at dystopia, and once again he was saddened by what he saw. The damage to the area was extensive, not just physically, but mentally. He knew that most of these people would never be the same again.

They were there to talk to anyone that knew Jessica. She had completely gone off the grid, and it was critical that they find her. Where was she? How could a young ghetto girl elude law enforcement for this long? The feds strongly felt that she'd had help, maybe from foreign terrorists. Their biggest fear was that she'd fled the country somehow.

They needed any kind of information they could piece together on her. Who was she? Was she a loner—an introverted person? Or was she an extrovert? Had her behavior changed suddenly?

Spielberg and the agents canvassed the area with questions, but no one was talking. There was so much disdain for anyone wearing a badge, and they particularly despised the FBI. But the agents and Spielberg were relentless. They showed Jessica's picture to everyone in the area. They knew who she was; it was obvious by their demeanor—and then came some unfortunate news. There was one woman willing to talk to them. She was a grandmother in her fifties, and she was now homeless because of the explosion.

"Yes, I know who she is. Jessica Hernandez," she said.

"Where can we find her or her family?" Spielberg asked.

"Her family's dead. They were all killed in the bombing," the woman told them.

The woman had nothing else to say. The men continued with their investigation, and although people were hostile toward law enforcement, there were some folks that wanted to help. They simply wanted justice. The agents soon learned about Eshon and Brandy.

"Who were they to Jessica?"

"They were all good friends. They used to hang out together," a man said to them.

Now they were getting somewhere. If they couldn't find Jessica, then they would search for Eshon or Brandy. Knowing all three had been good friends once, the feds strongly felt that these two girls were their only and strongest lead to finding Jessica. And when they found Jessica, she would lead them to the culprits behind both bombings.

It didn't take long to find an address for Eshon. Fortunately for the agents, her apartment was inside one of the buildings that were cleared for residents to return to. But their luck was short-lived. They knocked on her door and quickly found out via a neighbor lady that Eshon had moved away. Her mother had recently moved to Brooklyn with a boyfriend to be closer to where she worked. She wasn't sure about Eshon's dad. It was all she knew. The neighbor had no idea where Eshon had moved to— they didn't converse regularly, but the apartment had been vacant for a while. Still, they went inside to look around and didn't find much. The furnishing was sparse, and there were no pictures of Eshon anywhere. It was a skeleton of a place with not much to go on.

Lead two was Brandy. They had her address and made their way there to question her.

*** 

Brandy sat slouched on the couch and took a much-needed pull from the burning blunt. With chaos surrounding her, she needed a break from it, and smoking weed was her remedy. Next, she needed some good dick. Being back in the old neighborhood felt familiar to her, though it was chaotic with police, violence, prying journalists, and federal agents.

She was supposed to be dead. Kid advised her not to return, but it was hard not to. She missed it. She wanted to run away, but to where? Home was home, and her apartment was the same as she'd left it. She planned on keeping a low profile anyway, not showing her face much, chilling and smoking, and she had protection with her—a .45 ACP. It was loaded and readied for anything.

Brandy missed the old times with her friends. Now they were gone, and it all happened so quickly, it felt like her head was spinning. But she couldn't dwell on the nightmares that were happening. It was time to put her life back in order—and how was she going to do that? She had no idea yet. But it started with not running away anymore.

She didn't like New Rochelle or New Jersey, and Devon and Papa John started to make her feel really uncomfortable. She strongly felt that being around them would increase her chances of dying. They were both marked men—but what had she done to piss anyone off? Jessica was finally dead, so who else out there would want to harm her? Maserati Meek was a man she didn't know and had never met, and she doubted that she was on his radar.

Jessica had put herself in a bad situation and she lost her life because of it. Brandy did her dirt too, but that was when Kip was alive. She considered herself a small-time criminal with a customary life. After what she'd told Eshon that night in the car about not going back to Harlem because of the ugliness spreading, she had gone back on her word and returned. She had decided to chance things and gone back anyway.

It felt impossible for her to stay away.

Brandy took a few more pulls from the blunt, lounging in her panties and bra. The pistol was lying on the coffee table. It was twilight outside, and she could hear the madness from her open living room window—not too far from her it was ground zero with death and destruction. Her building was steady and secured though, and living on the second floor had it advantages.

She closed her eyes. But then she heard several hard knocks at the door. She jumped up and reached for the pistol on the table. There were only a handful of people who knew she was back home. Could it be danger? Brandy's heart started to race. Was it a friend or foe? She cautiously approached the apartment door and looked through the peephole. What she saw completely baffled her. It was the FBI at her damn door.

"Shit!" she uttered.

They continued knocking. They weren't going away. She knew someone told them that she was there. She scurried around the room, extinguishing the blunt and hiding the pistol underneath the couch cushions. She threw on a robe and quickly sprayed some air-freshener to smother the weed stench.

She was totally nervous and stunned. Why were the feds at her door? She would soon find out.

She opened the door and the agents identified themselves with their unmistakable insignias. They asked to come inside. How could she tell them no? She nodded yes, and they all marched into her apartment one-by-one like machines. The look on their faces was stern. They showed some politeness, but Brandy was so nervous that it felt like her heart was about to launch from her chest and explode. She tried to remain cool, but she immediately she regretted coming back to her old place. It was a stupid mistake.

Brandy was an odd one to the agents with her blonde weave, blue contacts, and dark chocolate skin. She had ghetto written all over her. The feds, including Officer Spielberg, remained standing in the living room. Her apartment was instantly under observation; nothing much so far.

"Do you mind if we look around?" an agent asked.

"What are y'all lookin' for?" she asked them.

"We like things to be safe for our comfort."

She shrugged, though she was screaming on the inside. "I have nothing to hide."

Two agents broke away from the room and went looking around the apartment. Officer Spielberg remained with the primary agent. He felt she knew something.

"Do you know an Eshon Williams and Jessica Hernandez?"

Brandy shook off the jitters that swam inside of her and knew it was game time. She didn't want to go to jail. She felt she did nothing wrong. But somehow, she was involved with the craziness happening in her projects by association with the wrong person. The feds tracked her down. The feds were a league she didn't want to get herself involved with.

The two agents who searched the apartment rejoined them in the living room, seeing that the place was clear: no Jessica and no threats.

"Yes, I know 'em. Me and Eshon were cool wit' Jessica until that fight."

"What fight?"

"That fuckin' bitch played herself. She's from Cali and she was cool. We looked out for her, and then that bitch started to change when she met some nigga in the club."

"What man did she meet?"

"I don't know his name. I don't even know what he looks like," she said.

"So you never met this individual?"

"Nah, Jessica kept him a secret from me and Eshon."

"Why did she keep him a secret?"

"I don't know. It was her business. We ain't sweat it," she said. "But we know he had money. She started coming around us with really nice and expensive things—clothing, jewelry, and shoes. He took her to Vegas once. And she was gone all the time, spending time wit' him, forgetting about her friends. He changed her."

"How did he change her?"

"She was just becoming different—you know, actin' more like a bitch. Like she was better than us. I think that fool got into her head; brainwashed her somehow."

The questions came right after another—like a continuous fastball in a major league game. Brandy was up to bat and she couldn't afford to strike out.

It was imperative to the feds that they found out who this mystery man was. They continued to pressure her. They wanted a name, but Brandy didn't give it to them. There was, of course, a name she did know—Maserati Meek—but she refused to tell it to the feds.

The FBI was relentless. Brandy was their first solid lead, and they were willing to drain her dry for anything leading to the whereabouts of Jessica and others that were involved with terrorists.

"When was the last time you spoke to or had contact with Jessica?" another agent asked her.

She sighed. "Honestly, it was at club Sane."

"So you were there the night of the bombing?"

She nodded.

Officer Spielberg felt this was it. She was about to come forward with some relevant information. She had to know something critical. She was there. She had been in contact with the suspect.

"Jessica picked the club and set up everything."

"The bombing?"

"No, we didn't know anything about the bombing. I swear. She set up a party for us. Actually it was supposed to be a memorial for a friend that was recently killed. And it was like a peace treaty between us because we were beefin' for a moment, so I guess she wanted to make things right wit' us, y'all feel me?"

They were listening.

Brandy continued with, "The party was expensive, so I knew her new man helped pay for it. We all were supposed to wear red and white, you know, to honor my nigga that died. The whole thing was strange to us."

"What time did you and your friends leave the party?" Officer Spielberg finally threw in a question.

"We left at different times. Eshon and I left first. We didn't see anything strange that night. We all were having fun."

"And this mystery man dating Jessica—he never showed up that night?"

"Nah, he didn't. He always kept himself away from us for some reason."

Brandy felt the urge to get high again. Her earlier high was wearing off because of the intense interrogation. Some potent Kush was needed right now. Dealing with the FBI was nerve-wracking. She felt at any moment, they were going to arrest her and drag her out the apartment and have her detained. She couldn't stop them. She was just some young ghetto bitch trying to survive in the world she was born into. She'd made some dangerous and poor choices in her life. Now it felt like those choices were finally catching up to her.

There were more questions. The agents observed her body language. They locked eyes with her several times and looked for any clues that she was lying to them. But so far they felt she had been truthful.

"When was the last time you spoke or were in contact with Eshon?" they asked.

"That night. We were all in shock about what had happened. I mean, we were just fuckin' there. It could have been us in that bombing too. We went to her cousin's crib in Brooklyn."

"Where in Brooklyn?"

"Bed-Stuy."

Everything she said was jotted down. Brandy was ready for them to disappear so she could smoke again and then breathe. Her body felt stifled by their presence alone.

Officer Spielberg had some questions for her. "Do you have any pictures of Eshon?"

"I don't."

Spielberg prodded more. "Really? No selfies on your phone? Nothing on social media?"

Brandy thought quick. "Naw, I don't really fuck with Facebook. Too much drama, ya feel me?"

"Well, can you describe her to us?"

"She's about five-three, short dark hair with black eyes, petite, and pretty. She's in her mid-twenties." It was an inaccurate description of her friend.

Spielberg took notes. He was disappointed. He wanted to find Jessica and her boyfriend. They handed Brandy their business cards and instructed her to get in contact with them if any new information came about. She lied, saying she would. The agents and Spielberg made their exit.

Brandy sighed with relief. But deep inside, she knew it was far from over.

# 24

Maserati Meek felt like he was on fire in the hot seat. The bullet in his shoulder hurt like hell. Another bullet grazed his head. The pain was searing. He bled profusely all over the backseat of the Escalade. The driver saved his life, though. His reaction time was on point when Meek dove headfirst into the backseat and screamed, "Go! Go!"

The driver slammed his foot against the accelerator and screeched tires, speeding away from the shootout. The front end of the Escalade smashed into a parked car, but they continued moving. Maserati Meek hollered from the pain and collapsed on his back against the leather. His breathing was frail. It felt like his arm was about to fall off. The right side of his body had gone numb, the hole in his flesh from the 50 cal was gaping, and there was blood on his head. Although the pain was agonizing, he was still alive. He had escaped death by the skin of his teeth.

"No hospitals!" Meek had told his driver.

He knew their policy was to contact the authorities when treating gunshot wounds. The last thing he needed was cops in his face.

"Oh, these sneaky muthafuckas," he said. "They come at me and miss, eh? I'm gonna kill their families."

He didn't get a good look the culprits that attempted to take his life. They'd killed two of his men, and his money—two million dollars—was left on the sidewalk for the vultures to pick apart. He had an idea who was behind the attack. Panamanian Pete. He was the only one with the money and reliable sources to track him down. Somehow, Pete had caught him slipping, but no more.

"Take me to Westchester. I already got a doctor on standby," he told the driver.

\*\*\*

Twenty-four hours later, Meek sat in the swanky doctor's home with thick bandages on his shoulder and head. The trusted doctor had stopped the major bleeding by applying a tourniquet to the wound and then cauterizing the injury by applying hot metal to it in two- to three-second bursts. It was extremely painful, but it was needed.

Meek had to stay calm, which he was. Allah wouldn't allow him to die. The doctor had removed the bullet from his body, cleaned his wounds, sewn him up, and applied a few gauze pads to the damage. Now he needed to rest. The doctor had a spare room in his home where Meek could recuperate—all for a generous price of course.

The only company Meek wanted around him was his Muslim brothers. He wanted to plan more attacks. He wanted to find Panamanian Pete and show him the true wrath of Allah. Two million dollars of his money was gone because of Pete, and it made Maserati Meek sick.

\*\*\*

The call came in to 26 Federal Plaza from the East Brunswick Police Department before noon. A detective asked to speak to an agent. It was urgent. Within five minutes of calling, Agent Seitz answered the call from New Jersey.

"Agent Seitz here, what's the reason for this phone call?"

"My name is Detective Hint from East Brunswick PD, and I'm calling because we have a body here—a Jane Doe—and I think she's the woman the FBI has been searching for. She might be Jessica Hernandez."

Immediately, the Jersey detective had Agent Seitz's ear. The news reached the primary detectives on the case and Spielberg, and within two hours of the phone call, they were arriving at the East Brunswick Municipal building. The FBI in the area was a big deal. They walked with certainty into the building, and Spielberg was right behind them, riding their coattails, watching and learning. He was critical to them because he was the arresting officer of Jessica at the tunnel. He'd had words with her. He knew what she looked like. He was there to identify her body—to make sure it was her in the morgue.

They soon met with Detective Hint, a tall, slim white male with piercing blue eyes and a sandy goatee. He was dressed sharply. The conversation between him and the agents was brief. They were guided to the city morgue, and inside the cold, gray room, the medical examiner pulled a body out of the freezer. She removed the white sheet and presented to them a naked Hispanic female that had been shot in the head, which left her face a little disfigured.

"We found her a few days ago on the side of the road—Helmetta Boulevard. It's a secluded place in the park. A jogger discovered her early in the morning. She had no I.D. on her, and her fingerprints weren't in AFIS," said Detective Hint.

Officer Spielberg instantly knew it was her. She was a pretty girl, but now she was cold and her face contorted with death. Despite that bitch that she was, he was sad to see her like this.

"Yes, it's the same girl I arrested the other day. It's Jessica," Officer Spielberg confirmed.

"Shit!" an agent uttered with frustration.

Someone had gotten to her before they could. It was a disappointment to them. Whoever these people were, they were definitely covering their tracks. Officer Spielberg couldn't help feeling accountable somewhat—if only they had gotten to her before her arraignment, maybe she would still be alive. But there was still someone else to track down—Eshon. Now it was essential that they find her before she was killed too.

The medical examiner covered the body and the men left the room. They smoked a cigarette outside the building, talked amongst themselves, and then piled back into the car to drive back to the city. Next move, find Eshon Williams. They barely had a description of her, and they couldn't put out an APB or go to the media. They typed her name into the computer, and nothing came back. Eshon Williams had no pictures, no warrants, and no priors—nothing. So far she was clean. It was frustrating, like hitting a brick wall, and there was no way around it.

They needed this girl alive. If she knew that they were looking for her, chances were she might run. So the feds had a few tricks up their sleeves, and one was tapping Brandy's cell phone. Trick number two? Surveillance. Eshon was out there, and maybe Brandy might lead them to her. It was one reason why they didn't detain her. They needed her free—she would be their trail of breadcrumbs.

While driving back to NYC, Officer Spielberg was quiet with his attention fixed on nothing in particular out the passenger window. His mind was spinning with thoughts. Then it dawned on him—the girl that came to the precinct looking for her friend—looking for Jessica. Though she'd said her name was Stephanie Brown, he believed the woman was actually Eshon.

In a way, it all started to add up to him. But something was wrong. He had to piece it all together—he had to, and he wouldn't rest until he had Eshon in his clutches and got to the bottom of everything. For terrorists to attack a nightclub, and then a project building in Harlem—it didn't make any sense to him. Why? Why these two locations, when the city had so many other prime targets that would make a stronger statement?

Maybe this was personal, he thought. It had to be. He had to look at things from a different angle, and Eshon was his starting point.

# 25

The black Tahoe stopped in front of an extravagant-looking brownstone on 88th Street, the Upper West Side of Manhattan. The home harmonized perfectly with the affluent area, which had a reputation of being the city's cultural and intellectual hub. Columbia University was located at the north end of the neighborhood. The residents there were upper-class and prestigious. What was happening in Harlem seemed like it was many miles away—a completely different world from theirs.

It was a beautiful sunny summer day with temperatures soaring to a blistering ninety-five degrees. Air conditioners ran rampantly throughout the neighborhood as people tried to beat the heat.

The city block was tranquil as Amir sat behind the steering wheel smoking a cigarette and waiting. Today, he would be an escort for a pretty girl. While Maserati Meek was healing in Westchester, Amir was his eyes and ears on the streets, and his errand boy too.

Ten minutes went by; she was taking forever to exit the home. Amir finished the cigarette and flicked it out the window. Shortly, the door to the brownstone opened and a lovely looking black woman named Cindy was making her exit.

Amir looked at her with admiration. She was a beautiful woman with long, silky black hair and hazel eyes. Dressed in a printed dress with her long, gleaming legs erect in a pair of studded gladiator wedges, she glided down the concrete stairs with class and style clutching her Gucci handbag.

She climbed into the backseat of the Tahoe. Amir greeted her, but she ignored him. He smirked. She was strikingly beautiful, but a bitch. Her only interest was Maserati Meek. She was yearning to see him again. Amir put the truck into drive and slowly drove away. Cindy sat back comfortably in the backseat and looked out the window.

Forty-five minutes later, they arrived in Westchester, where Maserati Meek was convalescing in the doctor's home. The doctor had left town, and Meek had the place all to himself. He trusted the location. It was unknown to many, and off the grid. He had no ties to the real estate and he felt it would be impossible for anyone to track him there. In the bedroom, he had just finished his prayer, saying, "*As Salamu Alaykum wa Rahmatullahi wa Barakatuhu.*" He turned his head to the left and repeated the same phrase.

Amir walked in with Cindy. She was overflowing with eagerness. She'd met Meek in an upscale lounge where he spoiled her with high-priced champagne and first-class conversation. Their chemistry was strong. Maserati Meek's infatuation for black women was potent and no secret, and Cindy was something to keep him occupied during his healing. She had all the ingredients that he liked: black, sexy, curvy and somewhat urban. Cindy smelled the money and power in him, and she didn't hesitate to give him the time of day, and soon, a piece of her.

With Jessica missing in action—and an assumed snitch—he needed a new and more loyal bitch in his life. And his body didn't just need physical healing; it needed some sexual healing too.

Maserati Meek emerged from the bedroom shirtless with his bandages exposed. He had in his hand a bottle of Grey Goose. He took a quick swig from it. The alcohol helped him cope with the pain, but sex would help him feel alive again.

"She's here, like you asked," Amir said.

"Thank you, Amir," Meek said.

Amir nodded. He was excused from the room. He pivoted and left.

Cindy smiled at her newfound friend. "I love the place . . . classy."

"It belongs to a friend of mine," said Meek.

"Well, your friend has some very nice taste."

"I would think I have good taste too," he said.

"You picked me, right?" she replied.

Meek approached closer.

Cindy couldn't help but notice the dressing wrapped around his arm and shoulder. "What happened?" she asked.

"A misunderstanding, eh. Nothing to worry about," he said. "Today, I have fun with you. You are my worry, eh."

Cindy continued to smile. "Well, let us both worry then."

It was unambiguous to her that she was there for sex—to keep him company. They locked eyes. Her beauty was enticing. She removed her dress and shoes, causing Meek to become fascinated by her beautiful flesh. Her nipples were dark and big like nickels. Her body was flawless with no tattoos.

"You are a very beautiful woman," he said. "Come closer. I can't experience paradise from where you stand."

She stepped closer to him, and Meek pulled her into his arms. The joy started. Their kissing was intense, with Meek tasting the softness of her lips, his tongue exploring further into her mouth. Their tongues danced together. He then kissed her body, her neck, her shoulders, and her stomach. He tasted every bit of her. He could smell her lust.

Her breathing became animated as he cupped her breast, pinched her nipple, and fingered her pussy. He continued to caress her body, feeling his manhood erecting harder than steel itself.

Cindy lowered herself in front of him, taking the dick into her hands, and started to stroke him nice and slow. She was no stranger to oral sex, including deep throat, and she was impressed by his package. He watched as she wrapped her lips around his dick, taking it all in gently—watching her lips slide back and forth over his dick, and seeing her suck on the tip like a lollipop. The action emitted a moan from Meek. He cooed. He enjoyed it. She was no Jessica, but she damn sure came close.

Soon, their action toured into the bedroom, where Meek was eager to perform one of his pastime pleasures on her. Cindy's juices were raining liberally. Her clit was exposed and Meek lapped her juices. The sexual deed made her moan and quiver witlessly as she was swiftly enveloped by pleasure. Cindy grabbed her legs and held them back, giving her man excessive access to her most private places. Meek licked her soft clit, sucked her pussy, and fingered her simultaneously.

"Oh shit! Please don't stop . . . oh God . . . oh God!"

Maserati Meek was the kind of man that liked to keep his woman on edge. He kept her aroused and horny, begging for more. With a glazed look in her eyes, she wanted to be fucked by him ASAP.

Maserati Meek positioned himself between her legs and thrust inside of her. Her legs wrapped around him and she pulled him closer to her by grabbing his hips. The pain no longer registered in Meek's body. Pussy and alcohol made any pain suddenly go numb. He crowded her pussy with his dick, as Cindy gasped and felt waves of pleasure consume her. Missionary, he pushed her legs back to her chest and drove his dick deeper into her. Cindy was as flexible as a rubber band. He fucked her deep, slow, and then hard. He could feel her pussy grabbing his dick tightly and the sensation of her wetness enveloping him.

"I'm gonna come!" she announced.

Their heated sex continued with them changing positions. She climbed on top of him and crashed her pussy down on his hard dick. She never knew a Middle Eastern man could fuck her like this. It felt like he was on something—was it Viagra, cocaine?—whatever it was, she didn't want him to come down from it anytime soon. Every moment he was inside of her was absolute bliss. She screamed out and rode him like a champion. He reached up and squeezed her tits, and again, pinched her nipples.

"Fuck me!" she cried out. "Fuck me! Fuck me!"

He looked up at her and for a split second he saw Jessica's face looking back down at him. It freaked him out for a minute, but he shook it off. Was it guilt? No, it was just a flashing moment. The thought was immediately eradicated from his mind.

"I'm gonna come," Cindy cried out again.

She milked his dick. She feverishly rocked her hips back and forth while on top of him and his dick pulled in and out of her with her pussy throbbing. Soon, they both reached the point of no return—exploding together.

She wasn't in any rush to leave. Maserati Meek welcomed her company. His goons were boring him and his wounds were barbing his skin. Sex with her also made him forget for the moment about the two million dollars he lost.

They lingered on the king size bed. The TV was on, and like regular, Maserati Meek watched the news. The update on the bombings became habitual. While watching TV, Cindy toyed with his nipples while nuzzled against his chest. Her body was completely satisfied. Meek turned from one news channel to another. There wasn't much news at first. But then breaking news—the girl the FBI had been desperately searching for was found dead in New Jersey.

"The FBI search for Jessica Hernandez has ended. She was found dead in a New Jersey park early Tuesday morning. A passing jogger discovered her body with a gunshot wound to her head. So far, the authorities have no suspects in custody, but the search continues for the people responsible for two city bombings in the past week," the anchorwoman proclaimed.

Maserati Meek was completely taken aback by the news. Jessica was dead? He removed himself from Cindy's tender grasp, sitting upright, and fixed his attention on the television. He turned up the volume. He listened intently to every word out of the anchorwoman's mouth.

Who shot her? Who had gotten to her? And what did this mean?

Meek was troubled by the news. He felt the man responsible for Jessica's murder was Panamanian Pete. What other enemies did he have out there? He believed Kid and his crew to be dead, killed in the club explosion.

Then a thought briefly crossed his mind. If she was dead, then it wasn't possible that she was snitching or avoiding him. He'd overreacted and killed her family along with dozens of people over nothing. He sat there in a minor trance.

Cindy noticed the change in his demeanor. "Did you know her?"

He didn't look at her, but kept staring at the TV and nonchalantly responded, "No. She was no one special."

He couldn't dwell on it. What was done was done. But it wouldn't be finally done until he tortured and murdered Panamanian Pete. And then it would be done.

# 26

The Kid moved his rook on the chessboard and hollered, "Checkmate!" He then smiled.

His opponent was shocked. He didn't see the move coming. He lost. How did he lose?

"Are you kidding me?"

"Hey, it was a good game," Kid said.

The old head stared at the move made by The Kid and scratched his head. Mr. Cots was one of the best players at the YMCA in New Rochelle, but Kid took him out like a gladiator in the arena, swords swinging, blood gushing, and heads being decapitated—no mercy. The Kid had applied the box mate move, having the side with the king and rook box in the bare king to the corner or edge of the board. It was a move The Kid knew well.

"You wanna play again?" The Kid asked.

"I don't know how you beat me."

"You leave your left side too open," said Kid.

"Now you gonna teach me how to play chess?"

"I'm just saying, a pro like me saw your moves coming a mile away."

"A pro . . . yeah, okay. You just a little nigga that got lucky," the old head griped.

The man subtly passed Kid a fifty-dollar bill. It was money well earned. The old heads always had a hard time with being beaten by a young kid in a wheelchair.

The Kid smiled. He felt like his old self again, playing chess and winning. Resuming his former life, or what was left of it, felt good. If he wasn't playing chess at the Y a few blocks from his new home, then he was playing video games at home. He was behaving more like a nerdy gamer than a man who killed people, ran drugs, and was at war with a major crime boss.

The Kid had made the YMCA his new hangout. He loved the company and there were some decent chess players there. He still held the title of being unbeaten, though. Playing again got his mind off his troubles, and it helped him heal from his brother's death.

The Kid sat in front of the chessboard. He was anxious to play again. Quickly, word was spreading through the YMCA that there was a chess prodigy in the place. It felt like St. Nicholas Park in Harlem all over again. The Kid spent hours at the Y, regularly playing chess and chatting. He got to meet new people, and soon found out who was who in the new neighborhood.

"I'll play with you," a young girl said, taking a seat opposite him.

"You know how to play?"

"I wouldn't be sitting here with you if I didn't," she replied smugly.

"Okay, you have a point. But to give you fair warning, I'm a beast."

She was unperturbed by his comment.

She was short, petite, and cute with high cheekbones, long lashes, long black hair, dark ebony skin, and brown eyes. Her outfit was simple—a white T-shirt and blue jeans with old Nikes, and it all looked like hand-me-downs.

"You have the honor, since you're unbeatable so far," she said.

"No, pretty ladies first," he replied.

No smile. The girl already seemed focused. She moved her pawn, and Kid moved his. Two more pawns were moved, then a knight by her and a knight by him. Kid moved his queen, and she maneuvered with her bishop. Their game was quick. It looked like they were both on a time limit. In her first five moves, Kid could already see that she could really play. In fact, she was challenging him.

They were prepared for each other. Pieces were being removed from the board and their style of play started to gain notice from other folks lingering nearby. A few people stood around the table watching the match. Finally, someone was giving Kid a run for his money.

Kid took her queen, but it didn't matter. Both her rooks were fierce, and her bishop was on the attack. They were locked in battle, their eyes fixed on the board and nothing else. She moved her knight, and Kid was taken aback by the move, but he didn't falter. He came stronger with a move of his own, and his queen was ruling the board.

Fifteen minutes into their match and the board was sparse with pieces—causalities of war. The Kid lost both his knights and his rook, all pawns were gone from both sides, and soon it was over.

The young girl quietly uttered, "Checkmate," and it was unbelievable. The Kid had finally lost a match. He was stunned. She had trapped him in a strategy called the Blackburne's mate, a rare method of checkmating.

Kid was in awe. He stared at the board, finally on the losing end, and realized where he went wrong. The girl's bishop had confined his king's movement by operating from a distance, while her knight and her other bishop were operating in close range.

The people looking on were stunned too.

"Wow, he lost. He's actually a mortal," someone joked about Kid.

"Damn, you're good. You were able to beat me, which is very rare."

"You wanna play again?" she asked nonchalantly.

The Kid smiled. "I had enough for today. It's getting late."

"What's the matter, you scared?"

The Kid chuckled. He was never scared. He'd spent six hours at the YMCA. He needed to rest his mind and body.

"Next time, I promise you," he said.

"Okay, fine with me."

"What's your name?"

"Jackie."

"Kidar. They call me Kid."

"I know," she said quickly.

"So, you heard about me and decided to take on the best?"

"I just wanted to play chess."

She was aloof. The Kid wanted to have a conversation with her. She was attractive, and she was different. She intrigued him.

Jackie stood up. The Kid wheeled himself away from the table. "Are you leaving?" he asked.

"Yeah. Besides you, there's no other competition here."

"Well, can I walk with you?"

She stared mockingly at his wheelchair.

"You know what I mean. If you wanna be literal, can I roll with you?"

"It's a free country. You can go anywhere you want," she said.

She rotated abruptly and walked off. Still no direct invitation from her, but Kid didn't care; he followed her to the exit.

They left the YMCA. It was dusk outside and still very warm. She went left and he followed behind her. She was five steps ahead of him, almost power walking, and Kid's arms worked tirelessly to catch up to her.

"You know you're a very pretty woman, Jackie," he hollered.

"Thank you," she replied dryly.

"How old are you?"

"I'm eighteen."

"I guess you live around here, huh?"

"You guess right. I'm walking, right?" she replied matter-of-factly.

The mouth and attitude on her was something else. But it turned The Kid on. He had to shout out his questions for her to hear because she didn't slow down to listen. She was an eighteen-year-old queen in his eyes. She was beautiful and he was desperate to get to know more about her. She continued to speed walk and Kid's arms were losing their fuel. He so badly wanted to leap from his wheelchair and take her by her arm and slow her down. She was rude, but it wasn't a deal breaker.

"Listen, beautiful, can you just slow down a bit so I can talk to you normally?"

"I have somewhere important to be," she shouted.

"So tomorrow, are you gonna be at the Y?"

"Maybe . . . maybe not," she answered with mystery.

The Kid sighed. Jackie was half a block from him and kept moving hurriedly. The Kid finally stopped pursuing her. He was defeated in chess and now he was defeated in romance. He hoped to see her again. He sat there watching Jackie walk like she had fire to her feet, and then she faded from his view. He figured she lived close by, and he was determined to see her again. Though she was young, she had caught his eye. With Jessica gone, The Kid found a new love interest. It didn't help that he was horny too—and living with Eshon. Though they were friends, the presence of a woman had his heart thumping loudly.

The Kid wheeled himself home and thought about Jackie. What was it she didn't like about him? It had to be the wheelchair—most girls don't dig a man in a wheelchair. The handicap thing was never-ending. The girls figured that a man being in a wheelchair meant his dick didn't work, it didn't get hard, or he didn't feel a thing, so why bother?

*Get your mind out of the gutter,* he thought.

He made his way home where the front porch had a wheelchair ramp. The living room lights were on, indicating Eshon was home. Kid worked his way up the ramp, placed his key in the lock, and made his way inside.

Eshon was seated on the couch in the living room. The moment Kid was inside she uttered, "They finally found that bitch!"

"Found who?"

"Jessica," she said. "It's all over the news. Her body was found somewhere in New Jersey."

The Kid was calm and silent. He gaped at the TV. The news segment about Jessica was just ending, but Eshon was just starting up. Her hate for Jessica was still palpable, although Jessica was dead.

"Devon may be a scary and crazy muthafucka, but he definitely knows how to put in work. I'm glad she's fuckin' dead. I hated that bitch," she proclaimed with much distaste. "Remind me to bake him a cake for this one."

The Kid remained silent and still. Most likely, she would never know the truth. *He* had located and shot Jessica in the head. He was a cold-hearted and calculated killer. He was more dangerous than Devon would ever be. He was smart, but the wheelchair and unassuming appearance would continue to throw everyone off and make Kid appear more amicable than he really was.

"I know you used to like her, Kid, but I'm glad you didn't get wit' that bitch. She was fuckin' poison and she probably would have ruined your life," Eshon said.

"What's done is done. I'm ready to move on," he said.

"We all are. So what's next for us?"

It was Eshon's favorite question. But what was next for them? The Kid wanted to know too.

"I don't know right now, Eshon. We're living here now, in peace with some money, and I kind of like it here. It's different."

"It's too quiet sometimes."

"I don't mind quiet."

"I miss Harlem," she said.

"I do too, but Harlem is chaotic right now with the feds, the explosion, and people being homeless. Why Brandy wanted to go back to that, I don't know. It was a foolish choice."

"Where else is she gonna go, Kid? She wanted to leave town, but all she know is Harlem. And all I know is Harlem."

"That's why it's always good to expand your horizons. If it's all you know, then it will always be who you are. And the easiest thing in life is to be predictable."

"So what you saying? We predictable?"

"I'm saying, we always going to have to think five, six, and seven moves ahead."

"That's why we have you," Eshon said.

"Me, I'm just a nigga in a wheelchair, Eshon. What can I do?"

"You're my conscience . . . my guardian angel."

"I'm no angel," he replied.

"You're my angel."

"Well, your angel finally lost today in chess."

Eshon was shocked to hear the news. "What? You lost? How? And to who?"

"This girl. She simply outmaneuvered me . . . and beat me at my own game," he said.

"You lost to a girl?"

"She was eighteen."

"You're joking, right?"

"No, I'm not."

"Damn. I'm sorry, Kid," she said.

"What is there to be sorry about? It's only chess, and I'll get my rematch."

"You will."

Just then, Eshon's cell phone rang. She didn't know the number; her cell phone was new and only a handful of people had her number. She looked at Kid and was hesitant to answer the call.

"Who is it?" The Kid asked.

"I don't know. This number never called me before," she responded uneasily.

"Just answer it," he said.

She did, pressing the answer button and said tensely, "Hello?"

"Eshon, it's me, Brandy. We need to talk," she said loudly and quickly, like something was wrong.

"Brandy, why you calling me for a different number?"

"I was scared to call from mine. But listen, the feds came to see me."

"What? Are you serious?" Eshon was shocked by the news.

"You think I would lie about this shit?"

Eshon was listening attentively. The mere mention of FBI and Brandy in the same sentence made her heart flutter with apprehension. But it was about to get worse.

"They're lookin' for you," Brandy said.

Eshon was suddenly flooded with trepidation and fear. "What, lookin' for me...why?"

"They wanna question you about Jessica."

"Fuck!" Eshon cursed.

Jessica was dead, yet she was still a pain in her ass and a risk to Eshon's life.

"They gave me their number for you to call."

"Did you give 'em my number?"

"No, I'm not stupid, Eshon. But I think they might be following me and might have my phone tapped. I think that's why they didn't take me in."

"What did you tell 'em, Brandy? And be very specific."

"I told them that the night we last saw each other was at club Sane. I told them that we went to your cousin's place in Brooklyn—Bed-Stuy, but that's all I told 'em."

Eshon had to sit down.

The Kid was close by, and he knew something was wrong. He was waiting for Eshon to end her call with Brandy. He had a bunch of questions to ask her. Eshon continued to ask questions. Did they know where she lived? And did they have a warrant out for her arrest?

The call ended with Eshon receiving Officer Spielberg's cell phone number and subsequently falling into downright distress. She looked at Kid with an alarmed gaze and said, "The feds are lookin' for me."

"They're what?" The Kid was stunned.

"Somehow we've been marked into their investigation."

"Shit!" he uttered.

"What we gonna do?"

The Kid went into combat mode mentally. The FBI looking for Eshon was a problem. The good news was that Jessica was dead, so what else could link them to Meek or any other crime? The bad news was that Eshon was on the FBI's radar.

"Brandy gave me a name and a number to call," she said.

"What's the name?"

"She said his name was Officer Spielberg. I think he's the one I spoke with about Jessica at the precinct that day."

"He's a city cop? I thought she said it was the feds?"

"I guess he's workin' with the feds."

"Okay, this is what we need to do. You calm down, and you need to call him. It might make you look less suspicious if you reach out to them to talk."

"Are you serious?"

"It's no secret that you and Jessica were once best friends. It was inevitable that the feds were going to find out. People are going to talk."

"And what I'm supposed to say to them?"

"Let me think."

Eshon was extremely nervous. She wasn't ready to tangle with the FBI. She wanted to run away as far as possible—leave town like Brandy once suggested. Maybe her friend was right; New York wasn't a place for them anymore, and it was time for a change.

An hour passed. Kid and Eshon went over the story to tell the officer before they called him. It had to be precise. They wanted to throw the cop off. The Kid wanted Eshon to not repeat verbatim what Brandy had told her—about the fight, and about other things. He wanted her to change her voice to sound purely ghetto and go off on tangents and talk about the many arguments that she had with Jessica.

"Allow the cop to control the conversation. Let him bring you back to corroborate what Brandy said. You can't let y'all stories sound rehearsed," The Kid said.

Eshon nodded. She understood.

She took a deep breath and dialed Spielberg's number. It rang. They both were silent. The Kid looked unflappable for the moment, but he knew it all could go wrong within a heartbeat. Eshon just needed to stay cool and keep to the script.

"This is Officer Spielberg, how can I help you?" Spielberg answered.

Hearing the cop's voice, Eshon's heart almost stopped. For a split moment, she went mute, but then collected herself and did what she was told. "Yeah, this is Eshon Williams. I heard you was lookin' for me?"

"Yes, I'm an officer with the 1st precinct investigating the murder of a Jessica Hernandez. When was the last time you saw her alive?" he asked, surprised.

"Yeah, I heard 'bout that fuckin' bitch gettin' murdered and shit like that. She was always a grimy fuckin' ho," Eshon proclaimed with contempt.

"I heard y'all used to be friends."

"Key word, we 'used' to be friends. And then I couldn't stand that bitch. She tried to fuck wit' my man and I don't play that shit. Why she gotta go fuck wit' mines, huh? Bitch, get your own fuckin' man."

"And when was the last time you had any contact with her?" he interrupted.

Eshon sucked her teeth and replied, "I don't fuckin' remember, like two, maybe three weeks ago. We got into it. I was ready to snatch that bitch bald headed. Like I said, she was a grimy bitch."

"What about club Sane? You were there with her that night, from my understanding?"

Eshon sighed. "I guess so. I mean, that bitch wanted to make up and become friends wit' me. I was cool wit' that bitch, officer. When she moved here from Cali, I befriended that bitch when she had no one. I looked out for that fuckin' bitch and what this bitch do? She tried to stab me in the fuckin' back and talk shit 'bout me in the hood. Can you believe that fuckin' shit? How dare she!"

Quickly, Officer Spielberg saw that he wasn't getting anywhere with this one. She was all over the place, vilifying Jessica's name and spewing hatred to him about Jessica like he was her therapist. But he continued with his questions.

"Can you tell me about this new boyfriend of hers?"

"I heard that bitch got a new man, some clown nigga wit' money. So why was she tryin' to fuck my nigga, huh? She's a selfish fuckin' bitch, and don't get it twisted, it's fucked up that she's dead, you know what I'm sayin', but that bitch was living a foul fuckin' life, real talk, officer."

"So you never met this boyfriend?"

"That bitch never brought him around, like she had something to hide, or thought he was too good to bring him around the fuckin' hood. But anyway, she better be glad she ain't fuckin' introduce him to me—shit—because karma would be a muthafucka and I definitely woulda threw some pussy his way, you fuckin' feel me, officer?" Eshon proclaimed, loud and clear and ghetto fabulous. "An eye for a fuckin' eye! And I know I got the bomb-ass pussy—my shit is fuckin' platinum!"

A deep sigh escaped his mouth. She was a headache over the phone.

"Another question, do you know a Stephanie Brown?" he asked.

Eshon remembered the name she had given to Spielberg that day at the precinct. She reacted with, "She a phony bitch too—some bitch Jessica be chillin' wit' lately, bitch tryin' to be BFF wit' that fake bitch. We don't fuckin' rock like that, officer. But I don't really know that fuckin' bitch."

Questioning Eshon became a frustrating task for Spielberg. She cursed a lot and she was still angry. It seemed like a dead end. There were more questions, but the same ghetto attitude and anger spewed out.

By the time he hung up the phone, he was completely convinced that she wasn't the same girl looking for Jessica at the precinct. There was no love there. And no one knew the name or the location of this mystery man Jessica was seeing. They didn't even know what he looked like. But he was confident that Jessica's cell phone records would give them a clue.

After her talk with the cop, Eshon exhaled loudly.

The Kid was proud of her. "You did good," he said.

"I'm gonna be sick," she uttered.

She shot up out the chair and rushed to the bathroom where she threw up chunks into the toilet. Her stomach couldn't take the stress any longer.

# 27

The EgyptAir flight from Cairo landed at JFK Airport in Queens early in the morning after a thirteen-hour trip. When the plane touched down on the runaway, almost every passenger had jet lag from the long journey across several time zones. Passengers departed the plane and made their way into U.S. Customs to the grueling ritual of passenger and luggage searches, and questioning. Among those trying to make their way through U.S. Customs were Shahib Abu Mudada and his wife, Asma.

They reached Passport Control where their immigration status had to be confirmed, and their passports and visas were checked; both of theirs were valid.

And then came the questions.

"And what is the purpose for your visit to the United States?" a male custom agent asked the couple.

"Pleasure. Our son is getting married tomorrow," Shahib answered.

"And how long will you be staying?" the agent asked.

"A week," he said.

"Do you have anything to declare?"

"No, sir."

He locked eyes with Shahib and watched his movement. Shahib stood in front of the agent dressed in a pair of khaki pants, black sandals, and a white button down shirt. His appearance was strongly Middle Eastern with short-cropped jet-black hair, graying sideburns, and a goatee. He was levelheaded, but deadly—and one-hundred-percent committed to the Al-Qaeda.

It wasn't his first trip to the United States, but it had been a long time since he had last set foot on U.S. soil. He remained serene. His wife was the same, standing by her husband's side with a smile. On the inside, she hated everything about America and despised their government and their ways. She loathed this trip, but it was necessary. She was a beautiful woman dressed a hijab headscarf and an abaya.

Everything was high-tech security; fingerprints were scanned and their pictures taken. The agent saw nothing wrong and stamped their customs forms. They were free to move along and enter the United States.

"See? So simple," Shahib said to his wife.

They walked through the terminal coolly, pulling along their rolling luggage. Outside the terminal, there was a fleet of cars, buses, and taxis waiting to pick up the arriving passengers. Shahib and his wife stepped out into the heat and were immediately approached by Amir. Amir greeted the couple with respect and the saying, "*As-salamu-alykum*," which meant *Peace be upon you*.

"*Waalaykuu salaam*," Shahib replied—*And upon you, peace*.

The couple was escorted to a classy dark Mercedes Benz. Some onlookers believed that Shahib and Asma were royalty, diplomats, or oil tycoons. They got comfortable in the backseat. Amir climbed into the driver's seat.

"Take me to my son immediately," Shahib instructed.

Amir nodded and drove off.

The bombings had become international news with the world up in arms, and Shahib was displeased. The news of their son shot and two million dollars gone—it was distressing.

Amir jumped onto the Van Wyck Expressway and drove north, toward the Whitestone Bridge. Shahib sat in silence next to his wife and they both looked out the window, staring at the heavy traffic, the people, and the urban surroundings, and already had absolute distaste for the city. Asma took hold of her husband's hand. She needed his touch and his strength. The news of her son shot and in trouble was challenging for her to hear. Nothing was going to stop her from reaching him, even if she had to swim the entire Atlantic Ocean herself. A mother's love and protection was stronger than any material on earth.

Amir drove across the Whitestone Bridge where the traffic had improved and continued north toward Westchester. Soon, they would reunite with their son, and they couldn't wait. Asma wanted to hug and love her son, but Shahib wanted an explanation.

\*\*\*

Maserati Meek woke up to a morning blow job from Cindy. As he lay on his back, she disappeared underneath the sheets, started stroking his dick and sucking the top of his head, and eventually wrapped her full lips around his dick and bobbed her head up and down. He howled like a wolf to a moon, the effects of her sexuality domineering over his manhood.

He could feel her about to make him come. She used her hands to explore his body and she was plunging him into complete bliss. When she was done, Meek swore he could see stars in the morning. The two of them rested nestled against each other. His gunshot wound was healing fine. He could feel his body returning to normal. The sexual distraction was needed.

"You wanna fuck me again?" Cindy asked.

"I need rest."

"I need some dick again," she said.

He chuckled. "You are like the Energizer Bunny, eh? You keep going and going . . ."

"Only with something that I really like."

She could be aggressive, but she was falling in love with him. The look in her eyes was the same look Jessica had when they would lie together naked after wicked lovemaking. Meek held Cindy in his arms. Every inch of her was softer than cotton candy at a carnival. He could eat her alive, she was so sweet. They talked and they were both able to laugh. With her head placed against his chest she could hear his heart beating. It was their sensual moment. They were in good spirits.

But then their moment was soon interrupted when the bedroom door swung open abruptly and Shahib charged into the room, followed by Asma. What they saw bothered them greatly. Maserati Meek was taken aback by their sudden presence. He rose up slightly, not knowing what to truly expect from his father.

"Father!" was the only word he could utter, shocked by their sudden presence.

"What is this, Akar? You lie with whores now?" Shahib shouted. He glared down at Cindy naked against his son. "You're American now? You take American women to your bed? Non-Muslim whores who corrupt your mind!"

Cindy was completely stunned by his comment. How dare he? "Excuse me!" Cindy exclaimed.

Asma stood erect with outrage too in the bedroom. Her eyes glared with disappointment and disgrace at her son. Akar with a non-Muslim woman? It too much for her to tolerate. She marched toward the bed and forcefully grabbed Cindy's arm, trying to pull the woman away from her son.

But Cindy wasn't about to be bullied by his parents. She resisted. She shouted, "Bitch, what is your fuckin' problem?"

Asma slapped her face and exclaimed, "Leave here!"

The attack came as a shock to Cindy. She clutched the side of her face and glared at Asma. Asma was ready to skin her alive. Although she

180

obeyed her husband faithfully, and sometimes was quiet, she was hardly timid or meek. She and her husband tolerated what their son was into in America because the money helped fund Al-Qaeda.

Meek's parents, just like Meek and his soldiers were hypocrites—just as any other ordinary person who serves two gods. On the one hand they prayed several times a day, read the Kuron, funded Al-Qaeda, and pledged allegiance to Allah. But there was a flipside to these radicals who played God by doing "Allah's" bidding by blowing up innocent people. They turned a blind eye to their son's drug dealing and allowed him to immerse himself into American culture when it suited him or them and then cried injustice.

Cindy stood naked in front of Asma, not caring who was in the bedroom. She shouted, "You crazy fuckin bitch, don't you ever touch me again!"

The second slap came just as fast as the first one. It was so violent that it made Cindy's head spin and her face bleed. She had been cut by Asma's diamond ring.

Cindy was about to react, but she nearly bit off her tongue trying to remain calm. She found herself in a no-win situation. She was outnumbered, and worst of all, Meek wasn't coming to her rescue. He simply lay there nonchalantly. And there was something in Shahib Abu Mudada's eyes that let her know that if she said another word or retaliated against his wife, then she wouldn't leave the room alive. Her heart started to beat faster with trepidation.

"You are nothing to us, so leave this room now before you regret this union with my son," Shahib warned her.

Cindy didn't say a word although her eyes were filled with rage. She simply collected her things and left the room naked. Shahib and Asma didn't even give her a second look. They considered their son's young whore nothing but a bug on their shoe.

"Amir, escort her out. We need to have a word with our son," said Shahib.

Amir nodded. He walked behind Cindy to ensure her departure from the home.

Shahib closed the bedroom door. Maserati Meek—Akar—removed himself from the bed with the bed sheet covering his private parts to respect his mother.

"Father—"

*Slap!*

The blow hit Meek so hard, it almost made him cross-eyed. He felt like Cindy. It was his turn to face his parents' wrath.

"You are a fool! You create unwanted attention toward yourself when the time is not right. What is wrong with you? What is this I hear of millions of dollars lost, you are shot, and these bombings of a ghetto and a nightclub? You use our people for your own personal vendetta."

"You don't understand, Father. I'm at war."

"War? With whom?"

"These kafirs," he said.

"Kafirs. Are these the same kafirs you are in business with?"

"No!"

"Then I want to know who they are. Sit and we talk."

Shahib's look upon his son was cold and fierce. He was the ultimate authority, and the remaining bombers pledged their allegiance to him and their cause.

Shahib and Meek talked. Asma stood off to the side and was silent. It was time for the men to talk business. She knew her role—subordinate to her husband. Long ago she was forced into an arranged marriage with Shahib, but over the years she grew to love him. Asma felt fortunate to have her husband in her life. He treated her kindly and gave her a lifestyle of money and influence.

Maserati Meek filled his parents in on the escalating war with Panamanian Pete. The bloodshed and the bombings were halting his currency flow. The war was bad for business. The money Maserati Meek made from the streets was helping to fund Al-Qaeda, and now the shooting, the bombings, and the loss of millions of dollars was a major setback for them.

"No more suicide bombers," Shahib ordered his son.

Meek nodded.

"We fix this now," said Shahib with conviction.

Akar was the prince, but his father was the king. And right now the king was frustrated with his prince. The CIA, FBI, DHS, and the ATF were intensely investigating and detaining any obviously Muslim people in the States on work visas—and it was crippling their cause and their money. Too much heat had been generated from Meek's reckless actions. Anyone on a watch list was now under heavy surveillance by the FBI. Shahib felt lucky that he and his wife had made it through customs in one piece. But he made sure to dot his I's and cross his T's.

"From now on, we will do things up close and personal—either knife or gun to rid ourselves of our enemies and expunge our strife. But no more suicide bombings, Akar, do you understand me?"

"Yes, Father."

# 28

Devon set up the meet between Panamanian Pete and The Kid. It was a risky move, but The Kid felt that it was a necessary move. Papa John and Devon were against it, but The Kid assured them that he knew what he was doing. He had a plan, and Pete was part of it.

"Sometimes you have to expose your king in order to get what you want," The Kid had said.

"This ain't fuckin' chess," Devon had griped. "This real life."

"Life is a game of chess, Devon. We all are just trying to stay on the board and make it to the other side."

The van stopped in front of the bodega on Nostrand Avenue in Bed-Stuy. The area was swamped with folks on a warm summer evening. Devon climbed out of the driver's seat and Papa John climbed out of the passenger seat. They then opened the door and removed the wheelchair ramp for The Kid. They helped him out of the van and onto the sidewalk.

"I'm still not too sure 'bout this," Devon said.

"Just trust me," said The Kid.

Papa John wheeled Kid toward the bodega that was huddled in the middle of the block among other storefronts. They went into the cramped and dirty bodega and were met by two of Pete's men. Aside from the store clerk, who minded his business, the store was empty for the moment.

The armed men met The Kid and his crew with foul looks, but it didn't intimidate The Kid. He was determined to see Panamanian Pete. He came with gifts, clutching a small satchel containing fifty thousand dollars. The fifty grand was huge for them, because their money was dwindling rapidly and almost becoming stagnant. Their drug connect had dried up, and Devon and Papa John hadn't done a lick since Kip's death. The Kid saw one way to garner a huge source of income, but it was going to take small money for them to make a huge sum of money.

All three men were searched against their will. Devon was reluctant to remove his guns from his person, but they weren't going to meet with the boss unless they were unarmed.

"This is fuckin' crazy," Devon voiced loudly.

Right there he was ready to kill the two men, itching to dominate the situation. He was like a five-hundred-pound gorilla ready to pound his fists against his chest and charge to create destruction. But it would have been suicide. Brooklyn was Panamanian Pete's hub—his hometown—and they were way too far behind enemy lines to act a fool.

"Devon, just chill," The Kid said.

Devon acquiesced to the decision for peace and to talking with Pete. Papa John was following the flow. He wanted to make it out of Brooklyn alive. He was thinking about Dina tonight.

The men were stripped of their weapons and allowed to continue to the back of the store. They were guided through a door, down a short hallway and into a room cluttered with commodities and boxes. Panamanian Pete sat behind an old desk smoking a cigar. Two men, definitely armed and dangerous, flanked him. The room they were in was windowless and looked more like a storage room than an office.

The door closed behind the last man. The Kid was face-to-face with Panamanian Pete himself. He was one of the biggest fish in the lake, and if he wanted to, he could swallow Kid and his crew whole. Plus, Kip was responsible for killing his brother and taking his $800,000. But Kid still felt that it wasn't a bad idea for them to meet and talk.

Pete smoked his cigar and looked fiercely at the handicapped nigga in a wheelchair holding a satchel. He'd had no idea Kid couldn't walk.

"What the fuck can a crippled nigga in a wheelchair do for me?" Pete barked out.

"I just came to talk," said Kid.

Pete laughed. "Talk with you? I know Devon, and I barely know this nigga here." He pointed to Papa John. "But I don't know you, nigga."

"You knew my brother, right? Kip?"

"I heard stories about that nigga."

"Well, he was my brother," The Kid said.

"And?"

"First off, I'd like to give my condolences on your loss too. I'm sorry about your brother," The Kid said.

"If you think we got something in common because we both lost our kin, then you're mistaken, you crippled little nigga. I only took this meeting with you because of Devon."

Pete looked at Devon and said, "A man with your experience should come and work for my organization one day. We could use a killer like you, Devon. You'd be welcomed here."

Devon simply smirked. If only Pete knew the truth about his brother's murder, how open would his arms be toward Devon?

"I'm good where I'm at," Devon replied coolly.

"If you ever change your mind—"

"I won't," Devon quickly interrupted him.

Panamanian Pete puffed on his cigar. He fixed his eyes on Kid. "If you came here to waste my time, I guarantee y'all won't leave here alive."

"We didn't," The Kid replied with confidence in his voice.

"You have one minute to catch my attention."

The Kid knew his first move, and it wasn't with words. He handed over the satchel to one of Pete's goons. The man took it and placed it on Pete's desk. Pete took the bag and opened it. He saw the money but remained offhand about it.

"There's fifty thousand dollars inside," The Kid said.

"Fifty grand . . . for what reason?" asked Pete.

"Simply for information," The Kid said.

"Information on what or who?"

"We have a common enemy, Mr. Pete, and we both want the same thing: Maserati Meek, dead. He's still alive after your attempt to kill him."

Panamanian Pete had heard the same thing. It was difficult news to hear. The man had nine lives.

The Kid continued with, "You were able to get close to him. I just want information on Meek, Mr. Pete. I want him dead, and I'm willing to do it myself. Me and my crew, we'll take all the risk and we'll hunt him down. I promise you it will get done. All I need from you is the same source that linked you to Meek's business. I'm ready to take Maserati Meek for everything he has, and I'll cut you in with the profit. You have my word, Mr. Pete."

Pete was quiet but was listening. The Kid had his ear. He took another puff from his cigar and looked at Kid poker-faced. No one had any idea what he was thinking. Had he gone for the proposition, or did he feel that the meeting was a waste of his time?

"Fifty thousand just for information," said Pete coolly.

"That's all I'm asking for, and we'll do all the legwork."

"You know what? You got balls, kid, especially for someone that can't walk, and I respect that. We have a deal. I'll hand over my sources, and I'll expect you to get things done. Do you understand me?"

"I do," replied Kid.

"If you fail to do so, or if you fuck me over, I'll kill you and your entire family. Whatever you love, expect it to die painfully slow," Pete warned in a stern voice.

The Kid nodded.

Everyone could breathe again. The deal had been set into motion. Now it was time for action—for The Kid to deliver what he promised on. The Kid spun himself around, and they all were ready to exit the cluttered room. But before they could leave, Panamanian Pete spoke to them with an afterthought, saying, "You got one month to make it happen."

The Kid simply nodded. All he needed was the intel, and he was sure he could make Maserati Meek's demise happen. He was yearning to do what Panamanian Pete failed to do. But this time, he saw his own payday too. It was one he hopefully could live a good life off of.

***

It was after midnight when Papa John parked on the suburban block and killed the ignition to the SUV. He sat a few cars away, watching his father's place. Like always, the area was quiet. No passing cars, no people on foot, and almost every house was dark and still. Residents went to bed early in this part of town. Papa John lit a Newport and chilled. He spotted his father's Benz parked in the driveway. He texted Dina's phone. She replied: FIFTEEN MINUTES AND YOUR FATHER WILL BE GONE. Papa John sat back and waited, smoking his cigarette. Fifteen minutes seemed like forever when he was horny like hell, but he had no choice.

It had been a trying day for him. Meeting with Panamanian Pete was nerve-wracking. He felt that The Kid had put them in a situation that was a no-win. How were they going to find Maserati Meek? The man had money and power, and he was in hiding. Where would they start? For all they knew, Meek could have fled the country and gone back to Egypt— and if so, there was no way to get at him then. And could they trust Pete? Papa John strongly felt that Panamanian Pete was just as dangerous to them as Maserati Meek. Was Pete truly the lesser evil?

Papa John pulled on his cigarette, finished it down to the butt, and then flicked it out the window. Ten minutes had gone by, and there was no sign of life yet. His father was still home. He was tempted to call Dina to see what the holdup was. He gave himself five more minutes.

Three minutes later, finally, his father made his way out the home and into his car. He started the vehicle and the Benz went backing out the driveway and drove away.

"It's about fuckin' time," he uttered.

He could feel that pussy already pleasing him. He was aching to wrap his arms around Dina and go to work on her. To be on the safe side, he waited an extra five minutes, and then he called Dina and asked if it was cool to come inside.

"Yes," she replied.

Papa John climbed out the vehicle and walked toward the house. He implemented the same routine—keep his head down, move coolly in the dark, and go to the back of the house, enter through the back door. Everything went smoothly. Dina was standing in the doorway, butt-naked this time. Papa John's eyes lit up with excitement. He hugged her passionately and then thrust his tongue into her mouth. They kissed.

"Damn, I missed you," he said.

"Ooooh, I missed you too," she said.

He entered the house, their bodies and lips still latched to each other. She undid his jeans and reached into his pants to feel his glory. Papa John could feel his arousal escalating. Her hand against his erect manhood was tantalizing. Dina was hot and heavy too. She could feel her pussy running wet for him.

He kissed the side of her neck and grabbed her healthy tit. Dina exhaled with repentance. She promised herself not to ever see him again, but she couldn't resist the temptation. When he contacted her, she replied in anticipation. It was so hard to stay away from him. She was either pregnant by him or his father. So far, the pregnancy hadn't come up. It wasn't an issue yet, but she needed to address it.

Once again she pulled herself away from their steamy episode. She looked at him and said, "Are you going to ask?"

"About what?"

"Seriously, Papa John? Remember? I'm pregnant."

"I know. Did you tell him yet?"

"No. I can't tell him until I know what I'm gonna do with it."

"And what are you gonna do? You gonna have this baby or not?"

She sighed. "I'm scared."

"Get an abortion then," he suggested.

"It's so easy for you to say that. You're not carrying it, and you're not engaged to your father," she said.

"But we both wanted the same thing."

"Things are getting complicated."

"It don't have to be. Two choices, you can get an abortion or you can end this affair and we can go our separate ways," he declared.

Papa John was bluffing; he wasn't ready to end the affair with Dina. She felt like the best thing that ever happened to him, although she was engaged to his father. No more Dina would be like falling from heaven—an angel losing its wings.

He stared intensely at Dina, and said something to her that he couldn't believe himself. "I think I love you."

"What?" she was shocked by what he said.

"I wanna be with you."

"How would we make it work?"

"Look, I know this shit here is tricky between us, but we can find some way to work it out."

"Do you want me to get an abortion?" she asked him.

"I don't know. This baby could be my pops' too."

"How did we get here?" she asked rhetorically.

"We got here because you got some good pussy," he was able to joke. She laughed. "So I've been told."

"Nah, but fo' real, you is special, Dina. I could see why and how my pops fell in love wit' you and put a ring on your finger."

"You is a trip, Papa John."

"You make me a trip. Hey, let's finish what we started by the door and we can talk about this later," he suggested.

She smiled and put her hands into his unbuttoned pants and wrapped her fingers around his thick dick.

"Yeah, just like that," he moaned.

"Like that, huh?"

"Yeah, like that," he replied breathlessly.

Every part of him was lit up with stimulation. He closed his eyes and appreciated how she touched him. The hand job was magnifying his erection. She kissed his lips, and then their tongues danced. Each part of Papa John ached for her. His jeans dropped lower, and her stroking continued until he felt on the edge of exploding.

They became lost in each other—paradise was right within their reach. Until they heard the quake of his voice boom out.

"What the fuck is this?" Darryl yelled.

Dina and Papa John quickly pivoted in fear and in awe. There was Papa John's father burning with rage. His eyes were red like the pits of hell. He charged toward Papa John like a bull, swung fiercely, and struck him with a hard punch to his face. Papa John staggered backwards, but he didn't fall. Darryl attacked him again with another punch to his face, and then his fist thrust into Papa John's stomach. Papa John folded like a chair and fell to the ground. Darryl continued with his onslaught.

"You think I didn't fuckin know?!" Darryl screamed. "You think I'm a fuckin' fool?! My own son and my fiancée having sex in my house!"

Father fought son, but the son shot up with a bolt of energy and desperately tried to defend himself. Papa John was able to release a few punches of his own. However, the wrath of his father was strong, and Darryl picked up his son like a Titan and tossed him across the room like a rag doll. Their bodies clashed and tussled inside the living room, knocking over furniture and making glass shatter and pictures fall from the walls they hung from. There was no way Papa John could get the best of his father. Darryl was a trained officer—a warrior licensed to carry firearms.

Dina screamed from the attack. She stood there shocked and helpless. This wasn't happening. It wasn't supposed to end like this, but it was ending, whether she liked it or not. Right in front of her eyes, her worst nightmare came true. She rushed to break up the fight, but it was like trying to wrestle apart two snarling wolves with their sharp teeth exposed. Someone was going to get bit.

"Please, stop it!" she shouted. "Get off him!"

Darryl was on top of his son, punching away zealously. Dina tried to wrestle her fiancé off her lover. She frantically tried to stop Darryl from beating his own son to death. She grasped at him, shouting loudly. Papa John was on the floor bloodied and bruised. She saw that he couldn't take any more punishment.

"Get off him, Darryl! You're gonna kill him!"

"Fuck him!"

Darryl pushed Dina off him forcefully and sent her flying across the room and crashing against the china cabinet. Shards of glass fell down on her. She collapsed.

"She's pregnant!" Papa John shouted.

Darryl tuned everything out. He was completely consumed by rage. Papa John struggled with him on the ground and saw only one option. He reached for that option in panic. He unlatched his father's holster and hastily freed the gun, and it went off—*bang!*

In an instant, Darryl felt the bullet from his gun tear through his abdomen with his shirt turning crimson. He finally stopped attacking his son and pressed his hand against the fresh gunshot wound. He couldn't believe it. He looked at his son wide-eyed and uttered the words, "You shot me."

Dina screamed. "What have you done?"

"I didn't have a choice," Papa John said. "I didn't have a choice!"

Darryl suddenly became weak. He stumbled and buckled on his side. He was still alive. Papa John was able to lift himself to his feet. He still held onto the smoking gun. He too was in awe at what he'd done. Not only had he shot a cop—he had shot his own father.

"Shit!" Papa John uttered.

It had just . . . happened.

"Ohmygod!" Dina shouted. She ran to her fiancé's aid. She fell to her knees and scooped Darryl into her arms. Her tears started to fall from her eyes. Instantly, she put the blame on herself.

"I'm sorry! Baby, I'm so sorry!" she hollered.

"Call 911," he shouted.

Dina turned to Papa John with eyes filled with tears and screamed madly, "Get out! Get the fuck out!"

Papa John saw one way out—to run away. She didn't want him there. She didn't want his help. He eyed his father that was crippled to the floor from his injury and there was empathy in his expression. He looked at Dina holding onto her fiancé feverishly and crying hysterically, fearing she might lose him.

He took off running from the house with Darryl's gun still in his hands. He arrowed into the SUV like bull's-eye, started the vehicle, and sped away, not knowing if his father would live or die. But he knew one thing for sure—his affair with Dina had ended. There was no way he would be able to see her again. He hadn't planned for any of this to happen—to fall in love with Dina or to hurt his pops. It just all came out of nowhere, like a shot to the head.

Papa John drove far away from Whitestone, Queens. He cried. He felt fear and worry. Would Dina rat him out to the police? He didn't know what to expect. He didn't know—if his pops did live, would he come gunning for his own son?

Right now, the only thing on his mind was his own well-being. He drove north, toward New Rochelle. He continued to wipe the tears away, feeling like they would never end.

# 29

Rodney, one of Panamanian Pete's trusted soldiers, put the pipe to his lips and inhaled a good portion of the crack cocaine. The high hit him as soon as the smoke filled his lungs. He leaned back, feeling his whole body buzzing in pure sensual stimulation. He needed another hit. He kissed the pipe again, and this hit felt even better than the last.

He sat shirtless on his bed in his one-bedroom Brooklyn apartment. Beside him were a few loaded guns and ten thousand dollars in cash. He needed the money. But sudden guilt riddled Rodney. He had not only sold his soul a long time ago, but he'd betrayed the hand that was feeding him. He gave them up for his addiction. They somehow knew to come to him, and he wasn't difficult to persuade.

The drugs had changed him. No one knew about his crack addiction except for his partner in crime, G-Dep. G-Dep knew about his demons, but Rodney trusted the man with his sickness.

He took another hit, and his eyes narrowed. Soon, his high started to fade. It was one bad thing about crack—the pleasure didn't last long. After blowing out the smoke, he floated for about a minute on cloud nine and then came crashing back down to his reality.

For the moment, he was a functioning addict. He had been a killer for Panamanian Pete for many years. He did the man's dirty work—found himself waist deep in murders, addiction, and disease—being HIV-positive was his other big secret. His life had been hell on earth since the day he was born. He had been abandoned by his mother, beaten by his father, raped by his uncles, and was a child scorned since he could walk.

He finished off an eight ball of crack in a few short hours and was ready for more. Rodney preferred to smoke himself to death. The guilt inside him was strong. He couldn't live with what he had done clear-headedly. He had to escape somehow, some way, and running face-first into his addiction was the only way for him.

He gave them up—just like that. They knew when and how to come at him. After years of loyalty, how was it so easy?

***

G-Dep kissed his side-bitch goodbye passionately in the apartment doorway. It had been another night of rough and crazy sex between them. He groped her tits for fun, hugged her thick and naked body, and made his exit from her Bronx apartment. He rambled down the stairway with a .9mm tucked into his waistband, concealed by his T-shirt and a jacket that he zipped up.

Pleasure was over, and now it was time for business. He had to meet with Rodney, and together they would meet with Panamanian Pete at The Bottom's Up for another job he had for them. By the sound of Pete's voice on the phone, this job seemed really important.

G-Dep stepped onto the sidewalk and stopped for a moment to light a cigarette. He inhaled the smoke and moved toward the burgundy Beamer parked across the two-way street. Traffic moved back and forth, and it being a summer night, the Bronx looked like a minor block party. Residents lingered outside in front of their buildings, in the parks, and on their steps, and leaned against parked cars drinking liquor and beer. The young females, dressed for the warm weather, were gossiping and flirting with the fellows. It was a typical Bronx night. G-Dep walked past it all casually, and though it was Blood gang territory, they knew not to fuck with him. His status ran deeper than the concrete. His reputation preceded him.

He removed his car keys from his jacket and pressed the alarm to deactivate it. He slid into the driver's seat and started the car. He removed the .9mm from his waist for comfort while driving and hid it underneath his seat. He glanced in his mirrors and put the vehicle into drive. The windows were down because it was another warm night in the hood. With his seat leaned back, he attempted to pull out of the parking spot. Then suddenly they came out of nowhere—three shooters with their arms outstretched toward the Beamer with pistols at the end. They took aim for G-Dep and opened fire.

*Pop! Pop! Pop . . . Pop!*

*Boom! Boom! Boom!*

G-Dep found himself under fire; bullets slammed into him. He jerked from the shots but managed to hammer his foot against the gas pedal and desperately attempted to flee the shooters. The car sped off wildly into the street and raced down the block, but G-Dep suddenly passed out from his wounds and his Beamer violently slammed into three parked cars and flipped over. The impact was loud, and the gunfire had sent people flying in fear in every direction.

The shooters ran toward the accident where G-Dep was pinned inside the car and unconscious. They fired more bullets into his body, making sure he was dead. It was overkill.

A minivan pulled up, and the shooters hurried into it. The van took off, leaving behind a gruesome murder. When the smoke cleared, G-Dep was dead, riddled with bullets, his body twisted and bloody in the wreckage.

\*\*\*

Panamanian Pete smoked his cigar and tilted himself back in the leather chair. The closed office door slightly muffled the music from the strip club. He liberated the cigar smoke from his mouth and closed his eyes. His legs were spread and he could feel the wetness of her mouth engulfing him.

Passion was positioned between his legs, hunched forward, his dick in her mouth. He looked down at the mass of black hair planted in his lap and played in it. He moaned. Her suction and salivating mouth continued to carry him nearer to an orgasm. She cupped his balls and licked his dick so good, that Pete felt he would deflate from pleasure.

"Damn, Passion, you know how to work a nigga good—oh shit, keep doing that," Pete said.

Her head rapidly bobbed up and down in his lap, his thick dick cramped in her mouth. She tried to suck his dick dry. She moaned and jerked him off, her saliva becoming a lubricant.

"Right there! Fuck yeah, you about to make me come!" he announced excitedly.

While enjoying her oral pleasure, Pete's cell phone rang against his desk. He was too excited from his near-orgasm to care who was calling him at the moment. The only thing that mattered right now was busting a nut.

Passion continued to work her sugary magic on him. She was ready to feel his release into her mouth. She sucked the height of his lust, taking him to the point of no return, with his flood rushing to escape. After a few more hard licks and soft sucks, Pete freed his semen into her mouth and like the freak she was, she swallowed every last bit of it. She wiped her mouth and lifted herself from her knees. Panamanian Pete sat spent for a moment, exhaling with satisfaction. He picked himself up from the chair and fixed his clothes.

Passion smiled. He didn't smile back. It was back to business. He had a club to run, drugs to move, people to kill, and money to make.

"You can let yourself out now," he said to her.

She knew the deal. She was only there for his sexual needs. After he came, she became another face, another employee of his. Passion collected herself and left the room. It was back to work.

Pete finally picked up his cell phone and checked to see what call he'd missed. The number was new to him. He shrugged it off.

"Where are these idiots?" he asked, referring to Rodney and G-Dep.

He didn't know yet. G-Dep's death had happened only an hour ago. He dialed Rodney's phone first, but there was no answer. Next, he called G-Dep with the same results. Not getting in contact with his most ruthless killers frustrated Panamanian Pete. A drink was needed. He walked out his office and signaled one of his female bartenders, and she rushed over.

"Bring a bottle of Cîroc to my office," he said.

She nodded. The boss came first.

Pete scanned his club and everything was normal and live. Two strippers were on the stage dancing butt-naked to Rihanna's "Pour it Up!" Money was being tossed their way, the bar was busy, the music was loud, and the females worked the customers with lap dances. G-strings were decorated with dollar bills folded lengthwise tucked in around the sides, and his security was tight and watching it all.

Pete turned and went back into his office. He lit another cigar and once again tried to dial his two killers again. Nothing. He got their voicemail.

A knock on his door came—it was the bartender. She entered his office with a bottle of Cîroc and a champagne glass and placed it on his desk. He thanked her and she walked out. Pete poured himself a glass and gulped the clear liquor. He sat back and seethed with anger at not being able to reach Rodney or G-Dep.

A slight disturbance in the club caught Pete's attention. Suddenly, the music stopped and it sounded like something was going on. One of his employees rushed into his office and said, "Mr. Pete, the police are here."

"What? They're in my club for what?"

"They just asked for you," said the employee.

Panamanian Pete removed himself from his chair. He left his cigar smoking in the ashtray. He approached the door, but three detectives flashing gold badges barged into the office abruptly. Two of Pete's armed goons were right behind them. They were unafraid of the authority.

"What the fuck is this?" Pete growled at them.

"We have a warrant for your arrest," one of the detectives said.

"Warrant? For what?"

"For murder."

"Murder? What the fuck is this?"

The detectives showed him the warrant. He looked over it. It was legit, but he was still reluctant. He stood teed off with his fists clenched.

One of the detectives turned his attention to the two goons and warned them to disarm themselves. He already had his hand on his holstered gun.

"Do it, or you two get handcuffed too," he warned the thugs.

Reluctantly, they removed the Glocks they carried and placed them on Pete's desk. Next, the handcuffs came out.

Pete scowled heavily. "Tonight, y'all do this?"

"You do the crime, you do the time."

"I won't do time. Murder—I'm no killer, and my lawyers will have a field day on y'all asses. You hear me? I run this town! So enjoy this fuckin' moment, detectives, because I'll be out soon," he exclaimed.

They put the handcuffs on Panamanian Pete. His unarmed goons could only watch. Though he was incapacitated, he still stood tall and strong in his four-thousand-dollar suit with his hard eyes unwavering.

"Let's just get this shit over with so I can get back home," Pete said.

"It'll be over, all right," said one of the detectives.

Panamanian Pete locked eyes with the man and stared into his soul. What he suddenly saw terrified him. He'd made a mistake in believing them. He shouted to his goons, "They're not cops, they're hit men!"

The detectives quickly brandished their guns and opened fire on Panamanian Pete and his two thugs. The first shot struck Panamanian Pete between the eyes at point-blank range. His head twisted back violently and his blood splattered everywhere. The second shot struck him in the face, and the third crushed his neck. His body crumbled to the floor with his flesh warped from the barrage of bullets. His two goons received the same fate. Bullets ripped into their frames, and they dropped faster than falling rocks. Their bodies sprawled in death against the office floor. The killers stood over all three bodies and pumped several more rounds into their heads, creating a much more gruesome scene.

The loud gunfire that echoed from the office sent patrons inside the club running for the exit. Strippers rushed to the dressing room, and everyone else took needed cover and felt panic. No one had any idea what was going on. Who was shooting, the cops or their boss?

Chaos continued to ensue. The club had been disrupted with terror, and when the office door opened and the three detectives exited with their smoking guns out, blood on their clothing, and their faces hardened with malice, people already knew the result—Panamanian Pete was dead, and most likely his two men.

"They ain't cops!" someone shouted.

But who would dare to stop them? They had just killed one of the powerful men in the city—a drug lord. If a brave soul interfered, then what would be their fate? No, they allowed the killers to walk away unharmed with no hindrance. Their movement was cold and undaunted, as they eyed the cowering patrons as they left and said nothing.

Passion was the first to remove herself from her hiding space. She ran to the office and what she saw made her scream her head off. She saw Panamanian Pete's mangled body in the carnage. She ran to aid him, but it was useless. His blood covered her hands as his body lay limp in her arms.

## 30

The Kid knew how to do the legwork. Thanks to Panamanian Pete and the sources he paid for, he received enough intel on Maserati Meek to know when the man would take a piss. It was tedious work, but it needed to be done. Three weeks went by with Kid thoroughly doing his investigation via the streets, paperwork, and the internet. From the sources, Kid was able to look into Meek's real estate and saw that Meek had property all over the city under different names. He had businesses too, and a handful of shell companies helped launder his money overseas.

In the shadows, The Kid followed the breadcrumbs and finally came to the light. That light led him to a nice home in Westchester. The Kid sat parked across the street in a Ford Taurus, armed and dressed in black. He spied on the home with binoculars and noticed several Middle Eastern men came and went, but there were two that definitely caught his attention: a man and a woman. They were older, well dressed, and appeared to have authority over the Egyptians and looked to be important to Meek.

"His parents," The Kid deduced.

He smiled. It would have been easy to kill them all right there, but Kid had a master plan—and that master plan included getting paid. He wanted a few million, and now he saw how he was going to get his money. He drove off and planned to make his move soon on Meek.

Things had become complicated with his crew. Papa John had shot his father. Though he hadn't died, he was still a cop, and a cop being shot in New York meant trouble for the suspect and anyone connected to him. However, Papa John was needed. So The Kid told him to go north for a moment, to Buffalo, where Kid had a friend to hide him. The Kid assured Papa John that if his plan was executed well, they would all become rich and live well elsewhere.

Devon took to the streets peddling drugs and robbing dealers, although The Kid warned him to chill and keep a low profile. But Devon was a greased machine that needed to keep operating. There was no such thing as a time-out from the game for him, or keeping a low profile.

The news about Panamanian Pete's murder reached Kid via Devon while he sat playing video games in the living room. It was shocking to hear, but The Kid wasn't going to lose any sleep over it. It was the life. You play the game, you live, and you die. The Kid was grateful that he reached Pete just in time to get what he needed from him. One drug kingpin was dead and there was one left, in hiding. Once Meek was gone, the market in New York was going to be left wide open.

The Kid and Devon stalked the parents, learning their movements. When the time was right, they were going to strike faster than lightning itself. They were staying at the swanky Marriot in New York City and traveling to Westchester to see their son daily. Armed goons protected them. Getting to them would be difficult, but it wouldn't be impossible.

"So how we gonna do this?" Devon asked.

"First, with Papa John's help," answered Kid.

"That fool done shot a cop. You think he gonna come out of hiding?"

"He will. With the payday I'm looking at, he'll have enough money to go wherever he wants," The Kid said.

Two days later, Papa John arrived from Buffalo. They all converged at Kid's New Rochelle residence.

***

They started following them from the Marriot uptown. Shahib and his wife exited the hotel lobby and climbed into a black Mercedes. Two suited men, armed with obscured guns, escorted them. Through the thick traffic, Papa John followed them closely but subtly.

"Don't lose them," The Kid said.

"I won't," Papa John assured him.

From Manhattan, they merged onto I-87 North. The Benz traveled north for several miles with the minivan following three to four cars behind them.

"You think they know they're being followed?" Papa John asked.

"Nah, we good," The Kid said.

Devon kept his gun close and his eyes fixed on his payday. He was ready to do what he did best with his gun. "I'm ready to get this money, fo' real. I'm ready to get paid."

"We all are," Kid said.

They would soon approach Westchester County, and The Kid knew that they needed to make their move now or never. They had to execute a guerilla-style kidnapping—quick and rough, no holds barred. If there was one mistake, then they were all dead.

The couple was seated in the backseat, while the two guards sat up front. Papa John steered the van from being three cars behind them to two. Then they were right behind the Benz. They were off the highway and on a less populated street.

"Let me know when," Papa John said.

The Kid timed the moment. He looked around the area and spotted no surveillance cameras, no people, no cops. When they drove to the next block, he exclaimed, "Do it now!"

Papa John pressed heavily on the gas pedal, sending the van speeding toward the Mercedes Benz, and he purposely rammed the van into the back. The car jerked forward and jumped the curb, causing the Benz to stop. Each man in the van felt the intensity of the situation.

The front doors of the Benz opened. The two guards were climbing out. One was already removing his gun from his suit jacket. The Kid and Devon were ready. They were masked up with Glocks in their hands. The Kid would be without his wheelchair. They burst from the van and quickly opened fire on the two men—gunning them down where they stood.

The Kid immediately went for the prize, Shahib Abu Mudada and his wife, Asma. He snatched open the door and thrust the gun into Asma's face, shouting, "Get the fuck out the car before I shoot this bitch!"

They needed to hurry. It was broad daylight, and though the suburban area was sparse with people and traffic, there was no telling who was watching them and calling 911.

Shahib frowned angrily and locked eyes with the masked gunman who had a gun to his wife's head. The look in the man's eyes said to Shahib that he meant business. But Shahib didn't want to succumb to their demands. He hesitated.

The Kid didn't have time for games. He shot a bullet into the headrest. It was loud. It was intense. Asma jumped from it.

"Bitch, I said get the get the fuck out the car!" The Kid shouted. He roughly grabbed Asma by her arm and yanked her from the car with brute force. She fell to the ground on her side. Shahib flared with anger. He bolted from the backseat to defend his wife, but Devon quickly slammed the butt of the pistol against his head, and he dropped to his knees.

"What the fuck he told you, nigga? Get out the fuckin' car! You think we playin'?!" Devon shouted.

Meek's parents were thrown into the back of the van and it sped off, leaving the two guards dead on the road. The van traveled west across the George Washington Bridge and into New Jersey. Then it went south and arrived in Newark. For the duration of the ride, the couple were assaulted and tied up by their wrists. They were then removed from the van and forcibly shepherded into the basement of an abandoned building on South 11th Street right next to a huge junkie lot.

"Get your fucking hands off me! You will die! You hear me?" Shahib screamed out. "I will castrate you in the name of Allah! Take your hands off me and my wife!"

Devon punched him in the face and threw him to the cold, dirty floor of the basement. Shahib's face was bruised from the attacks, and though confined, fire still burned in his soul. He struggled with his captors. He refused to be defeated.

"Shut the fuck up, nigga! You ain't in no position to give orders here. This ain't Egypt, bitch! You in America, muthafucka!" Devon shouted.

Shahib glared up at Devon and his other captors. There was no way he would relent to men he felt were beneath him. He clenched his fists and attempted to stand up, but Devon kicked him back down.

"Stay the fuck down, nigga, or next time you stay down for good!" Devon said gruffly, as he pointed his gun at Shahib's face. His finger was on the trigger, and he was itching to take the man's face apart with a bullet.

The Kid gripped Asma by her arm strongly. She scowled at him. She was reluctant to yield to these men. "Take your hands off me!"

The Kid smirked at her, caught off guard by her insulting him when she was in no position to do so.

"Bitch, you and your husband got some mouth on y'all," said Kid.

"I hate Americans!" she shouted in her thick Middle Eastern accent. She then spit in Kid's face. Her phlegm trickled down his cheek.

The Kid made a fist and punched her square in the face. She went flying backwards and landed on her back.

Seeing this enraged Shahib. He leaped from the ground to aid his wife, but once again, Devon was there to put him down like a dog. Devon struck him again with the butt of the gun. It cracked against his face and

Shahib dropped to the ground. The side of his face throbbed in pain.

"I told you, nigga, stay the fuck down," Devon growled. He turned to Kid and said, "Let me just kill these muthafuckas right now."

"Not right now," Kid responded coolly. "We need them to send a message to Meek."

Devon frowned and glared at Shahib. The core of his heart despised everything these sand niggas stood for. He hated the way they looked. He hated the way they talked. They were terrorists. They had attacked his home. Shahib's son had killed Kip. It took everything inside of Devon not to explode and tear apart the two captives.

"What kind of message you tryin' to send?" Papa John asked.

"One that will definitely get Meek's attention," The Kid replied.

The Kid looked at Shahib and his wife, stone-faced. He started turning the wheels to his plan. He brandished a knife and said, "We send the sand nigga a finger."

Devon smiled, loving the idea. "Let's send the nigga a whole hand."

"Just a finger," The Kid replied.

"That ain't shit. You a cut off a nigga's hand and that will definitely open a nigga eyes to show we serious."

"They already know we're serious," replied Kid.

"I'll do it then," Devon quickly volunteered.

Shahib and Asma hugged the concrete floor. They were silent. Asma threw a worried gaze over to her husband. She wanted to remain strong, but fear was consuming her. Her husband was helpless to defend her, and they were in a no-win predicament. Asma wanted to believe there was hope, but the look in their captors' eyes said the worst was yet to come. She watched in terror as Devon moved toward her with the large butcher's knife in his hand. His eyes were oddly fixed on her, a grin on his face.

"Don't touch her!" Shahib yelled.

"Or what? What you gonna do, you sand nigga bitch!" Devon retorted.

Devon was ready to cut off the wife's finger, but The Kid intervened, saying, "No, not her. Do him."

"What? You sure?"

"Yeah, do the husband. In their culture he has more worth. Do him."

"A'ight." Devon shifted in the direction of the husband.

Papa John held Shahib down and outstretched his arm. Shahib tried to oppose, but Papa John was stronger. He nearly broke Shahib's arm pinning him down.

The Kid put his gun to Shahib's head. "Your finger or your brains... pick one, nigga."

Shahib grimaced and relented. His right hand stretched out and his fingers spread. Devon crouched with the knife in his hand and chose the index finger to sever.

"Please, do not do this to my husband," Asma cried out. "Allah will punish you . . . just let him go."

"Asma, it will be okay. Turn away," Shahib said.

She refused to turn away from his pain. Her eyes leaked tears. She stuck her eyes on her husband, looking on in anguish as Devon readied himself to cut off the finger.

"Bitch, your turn will come too," Devon expressed to her before he did his cutting.

He placed the sharp knife against Shahib index finger. Shahib didn't budge. He didn't close his eyes either. He was ready for the physical attack to his body.

Devon smirked and thrust the blade against the finger, simply severing it in half. Blood spilled against the concrete. Shahib didn't cringe, nor, did he holler from pain. He barely made a sound. It was like he was a machine.

Devon picked up the finger and looked at it like it was trophy. "I still think we should take the entire hand."

Asma cringed and hollered. The tears drained from her eyes and she screamed out, "You monsters!"

Hearing her call them monsters, Devon stood up and marched her way. "You call *us* monsters, when your people bomb buildings and kill hundreds of innocent people!"

Asma scowled as Devon towered over her ominously. She breathed with contempt inside her body—her chest heaving in and out with absolute rage for all of them.

Devon continued with, "You want me to show you a fuckin' monster? I'll show you the monster inside of me." He kicked Asma in her stomach, and she hollered and folded from the blow.

Shahib shouted, "Don't you touch her!"

"Or what, muthafucka? Huh? What the fuck you gonna do?" Devon mocked.

Shahib lay powerless, his hand disfigured, and his rage to attack curbed by sheer disadvantage. He looked fiercely at Devon crowding his wife. Devon looked back, and his eyes displayed something tremendously menacing that made Shahib tremble with worry. The look was obvious.

"Yeah, I see the way this bitch been lookin' at me," Devon said chillingly. "Like I ain't shit!"

"Leave her!" Shahib cried out.

Devon kicked his wife in the stomach again, and she coughed and winced from the blow. Devon repeatedly struck her and said, "You wanna see a monster, bitch? I'll show you one."

She desperately tried to fight back, but he was too strong—and too possessed. He punched her in the face, bloodying her lip, and then wrapped his hands around her slim neck and squeezed.

"No! No!" she hollered, straining to breathe.

The Kid and Papa John stood in silence and watched Devon attack the wife. There would be no stopping him. He wrestled with her and tore her hijab, and her face became more visible. She tried to kick and scratch frantically to prevent herself from getting murdered. Devon was impervious to her aggression. His hands were still around her neck, but they changed to become wrapped around her pretty face, gripping tightly. Smothering her nose and mouth with his dirty palm, he quickly bashed her head backwards onto the concrete. The blow put her in a minor daze, and Devon continued on with his onslaught. He banged the back of her head against the concrete again, and blood ran from the back of her head and onto the ground.

"You done?" Papa John asked nonchalantly.

Asma laid there crushed and in tears. She couldn't stop him. She closed her eyes and felt the urge to die.

It was back to business. Shahib's finger was wrapped in cloth. It would immediately be sent to Maserati Meek.

# 31

The sudden absence of his parents consumed Maserati Meek with worry. Neither his father nor his mother were answering their phones, and there was no word from his guards. Hours had passed since they'd left the hotel. They'd simply vanished.

Meek paced the bedroom and steadily looked out the window, hoping to see a car pull up. He called again; their phones went straight to voicemail. He looked out the bedroom window again. Everything was still and quiet—maybe a little too quiet. His enemies were dead. Thanks to Rodney, his men were able to finally take care of Panamanian Pete. But once again, panic set in. The feds had gotten to them—arrested his parents and held them in custody, he assumed. They had been snatched off the streets and questioned. He believed that if they had gotten to his father, then they were on to him, too. And it would only be a matter of time before the FBI came raining down on his Westchester whereabouts.

"Amir," he called out.

Amir entered the room, ready to hear instructions.

"We must go! Get everyone ready," Meek said.

"Is there something wrong?"

"Everything is wrong. The FBI, they might come for us. We must leave again."

Amir nodded. He left to do what he was told. As they had done in Brooklyn, everything they left behind would be destroyed. Maserati Meek started to pack bags and ready his men for a sudden departure. This time he planned on fleeing the metro area. He had properties everywhere.

The package came to the doorstep. It was a small box. One of Meek's bombers picked it up. There was no return address, but it was addressed to Maserati Meek. His name was written in black marker across the box. It was brought inside the house and placed on the mahogany table in the living room. Maserati Meek entered the living room and stared at the package.

"Where did it come from?"

"It's just came out of nowhere," said his man.

Meek warily approached the box. He nodded for one of his men to open it. A man named Gulnaz took the box into his hand and slowly lifted back the flaps. Inside was Shahib Abu Mudada's finger with his signature ring. A note and a burner phone accompanied the gruesome gift.

"It's his finger," uttered Gulnaz.

"Whose finger?" Meek asked.

"Your father's."

Maserati Meek was completely speechless. He read the note: *We have them both. More to cut off. We'll call you with the details. Don't leave town. -Ghost.*

Meek screamed in agony. Right away, he attacked his men, slapping Amir in the face and punching the second man closest to him in his face. "Where were you all? This is your fault! They have my mother and father!"

"We'll find them, Akar," Amir said.

All the men fell to their knees and began praying to Allah to save Shahib Abu Mudada and his wife.

\*\*\*

The phone call from a blocked number came soon. Maserati Meek answered, and on the other end was a disguised voice.

"We want three million dollars, or else you'll find your parents' bodies scattered all around the Tri-State area."

"Who is this, eh? How do I know my parents are still alive?"

"They're still alive," the caller replied.

"I want proof," Meek said.

"I'll give you proof. How about another finger? Or maybe the entire hand this time? Or I'll send you your mother's tits in a box," Ghost threatened.

"I swear to you, whoever you are, if you place another hand on my father or my mother, I will find you and I will kill you. Do you know who I am?" Maserati Meek yelled through a tightened jaw.

The phone went dead. Meek feared the worst, and panic set in. He had lost his temper. He had no way in calling the number back. He gripped the cell phone so tightly it was ready to break in half. Then, it rang again. It had to be Ghost calling back.

Meek answered the phone right away and instantly heard his father's screaming in the background. It was an agonizing shriek that made Maserati Meek boil with rage. He felt helpless. There wasn't anything he could do at the moment. He had no idea where his parents were, or who was holding them captive.

"Shall we start again?" Ghost said smugly.

The screaming in the background stopped.

Ghost continued with, "First, we know everything about you; it's the reason I'm asking for three million dollars. I know you can afford it. You have two days. I'll call you an hour before you make the drop to give you the location. And if you try anything, you already know the gravity of the situation. Your mother is a very beautiful woman, and she might end up pregnant with your little brother or sister."

The call ended. Meek started to shed tears. He envisioned his mother being raped by these animals, and it was a heart-wrenching thought. So many wild images ran through his mind. He huffed. He dropped to his knees and started to pray to Allah for his parents' safe return to him. He believed that all of his enemies were dead, so who would dare come after him? This caller, he was firm and unwavering, and he cared nothing about his threats. The voice was cloaked by a machine, so there was no telling who it was.

He would pay the three million dollars because his parents were needed alive, especially his father. Shahib Abu Mudada was a major player in their cause. He was needed. To lose his father would bring about a huge setback to Al-Queda.

Maserati Meek would be willing to spend another five million to hunt this man named Ghost down to the ends of the earth. The money meant nothing to him. Once he had his revenge on the people who had taken his parents, he would go back to making millions in the drug game.

Ghost. This man named Ghost would be his main priority. He and his men abandoned the Westchester residence, destroying everything inside and setting the place ablaze. It was habitual for them. If the feds did come to the address, they didn't want anything traced back to them—no fingerprints, no DNA, nothing! And the place had been contaminated. This man named Ghost had been able to track him there, and it spooked Maserati Meek.

Meek climbed into the backseat of a black Escalade and it drove off, nearing the city. He would put together the three million dollars for Ghost. It had been three hours since the phone call. He had two days to plot his revenge on this man. The things Meek wanted to do to the people who had kidnapped his parents and violated his mother—it would be extreme pain and agony. He would have no mercy for any of them.

His suicide bombers were ready to counter with extreme violence in the name of Allah, and for Shahib Abu Mudada. They were ready to blow up half the city if necessary—no one and nowhere was safe.

Not only did Maserati Meek reach out to his Egyptian brothers, he also rounded up his old drug crew and acquired some new shooters on deck. They all came with a hefty price. He spared no expenses. Nearly thirty armed and dangerous men were at the ready to implement severe and deadly violence on the people who had kidnapped his parents.

# 32

The Kid had no doubt that Maserati Meek would pay the ransom for his parents soon. He could hear the desperation in Meek's voice, and it was a pleasure to hear him squirm and quiver, knowing that he was in no position to negotiate. It was the sweetest revenge.

Three million dollars was a lot of money, and once The Kid had it in his possession, he didn't see himself staying in New York for too long. There were memories, good and bad, but he felt that it was time to go. He wanted to travel far away—no place in his mind yet, but he wanted to live somewhere where he didn't have to pretend to be handicapped anymore. He wanted to walk freely and live his life peacefully with his money. He didn't want to live a lie anymore.

He made his way back to his New Rochelle residence alone. He'd sent Eshon to stay with a friend for the night, and he welcomed the brief solitude. He pulled into the driveway to seclude himself from any nosy neighbors and made his way inside the house through the back door, pushing his own wheelchair.

Inside the house, he walked freely, packing everything he needed to take with him, including a small arsenal. He paused on a picture of himself and Kip in the park on a sunny summer day. It was taken when they were young, maybe adolescents. He and Kip had the biggest smiles on their faces. Kip had always had his back, and now Kid felt he needed to have his brother's back, though he was dead. He was determined to make

Maserati Meek pay for killing his brother. Kip was the only family he had, and in the blink of an eye, it was taken away from him.

Kid went into the bathroom and took a shower. He wiped the fog from the mirror and took a long look at himself. He saw a natural-born killer, and he saw a man who was alone. He saw a man who had been angry for many years, hiding his anger from being in a wheelchair for so long, and then he released it by doing gruesome murders.

They never saw him coming. He was that good at killing people. For a long time, he worked alone. He tightened his fingers into a fist and banged it against the sink countertop. An impulsive rage struck him. He thought about Jessica. He thought about love. He had never had what Kip and Eshon had. He wanted to feel that same love. But the girls always looked at him as a cripple when he hadn't been one for quite a few years. Pretending to be one had had its effect on him. At that very moment, with Kip dead and gone, he realized that all his anger, rage, inadequate feelings were his own fault. He created his own prison to keep his brother close and now resented the time he spent in it.

Chess and video games were his outlet, but The Kid craved something more. His body needed the affection, and he thought about the time he caught a glimpse of Eshon's naked frame in the bathroom. She didn't shy away so suddenly, but she made it clear to him that he would only be a friend to her. They had grown very close, but only as friends. And would it be right, anyway, to have an interest in his brother's girl?

Then The Kid thought about her—Jackie. She was beautiful and smart, and she felt special. The Kid was able to smile when he thought about her attitude and her beauty. Seared into his memory were her high cheekbones and her long lashes, and her long black hair and her ebony skin. She was dressed like a peasant, but she had the beauty of royalty.

He wanted to see her again. Once he got the payment from Meek, he didn't know where the wind might take him.

Kid had the impulse to walk to the YMCA and astonish everyone there, but it would be foolish. He had to continue his ruse. He got dressed and pressed his behind down into the wheelchair once again, rolled himself out of the house via the wheelchair ramp, and headed toward the Y. He had no idea if Jackie would be there or not, but he would look for her.

Two hours went by, and The Kid found himself engrossed in several games of chess. He'd won eight games so far, and the competition was growing tiresome. Every so often he would glance around to see if Jackie was in the building, but there was no sight of her. He started to give up, feeling it was a one-time thing. He wouldn't see her again.

Another hour went by; he'd won his umpteenth game. He made a little money on the side—nothing much, but it was fun. After his last match, he was ready to leave. He was about to push himself away from the table when he all of a sudden heard her say, "You came back for another ass-whooping?"

He turned to see Jackie looking at him, unsmiling.

"I came for my rematch and to see you again. I've been thinking about you," he said.

"I don't know why. I'm nobody special."

"You beat me."

"I saw you coming," she replied coolly.

Her appearance was the same: blue jeans, a T-shirt, old sneakers, and her long hair pulled back into a ponytail. She sat opposite Kid at the table.

"Black or white?" she asked him.

"I like black," he said.

"White it is for you then," she said.

He laughed. "You are something else."

"Anyway, are you going to make it an interesting game this time?"

"You care to place a little wager?"

"I don't bet. Besides, I have no money on me."

"Let's not play for money. Let's play for information and time," he suggested.

"What?"

"If I win, you tell me everything I want to know about you. And I get a kiss from you . . . maybe a date, too."

She looked at him straight-faced. "And what do I get when I win?"

"I'll take you out, somewhere special. Your choice."

"It sounds a little unbalanced and unfair for me. How do you know that I want to go out with you?"

"Well, you can pick."

"If I win, then I want you to leave me alone," she said clearly.

"Wow, really?"

She nodded, looking him directly in the eyes. "If you're confident about your game, then you'll take the bet."

The Kid sighed. He then huffed and said, "We have a bet."

"I hope you're a man of your word when you lose," she said.

"I am." He didn't plan on losing this game. "Ladies first," he suggested.

She moved her pawn. He moved his. Two more pawns were moved, followed by her knight, his bishop, and her queen. The two became exceptionally focused on the game. Their eyes were completely lowered to the pieces on the chessboard and magnetized by every single move made. The Kid became more aggressive with his movement. He looked six moves ahead, trying to find Jackie's weakness. But she was highly skilled.

Twenty minutes went by and the game was close. It became so close that it concluded in a draw. Jackie had no legal move, and her piece wasn't in check.

"Damn, that never happened before," The Kid said.

"There's a first time for anything."

"So, who wins the bet?" he asked playfully.

"No one . . . unless you want to go at it again?"

He smiled at her, saying, "I want to get to know you better, and I want my date. So let's play."

Their pieces were rounded up again, and a new game started. She went first again. A small group gathered around to watch and learn the game from the two best.

The Kid had tunnel vision and moved his pieces on the board like he was a machine. His technique was uncanny. Early on, he did a castling move with his king. It threw Jackie off guard somewhat, but she found her footing and attacked. Piece after piece was moved on the board and some taken by the other side. The pieces on the board started to dwindle. Jackie became a predator with her queen and bishop, but The Kid was fierce with his rooks and his knight.

Unfortunately, in the end, their game concluded in a draw again. They both were left scratching their heads.

"Again?" he asked.

"Maybe next time," she said, getting up from the chair.

He didn't want to let her go so easily. He followed behind her outside.

"Hey, can we at least talk?" he said.

"About what?"

"What do you like to do at least?"

"Play chess," she replied.

"You know, you are one hard nut to crack."

"Who said I wanted to be cracked open, so you can look inside?"

"Why do you play so hard to get? Is it because I'm in a wheelchair? Look, I really like you. I know I didn't win, and you didn't win either, but I'd love to take you out on a date. Just give a handicapped nigga a chance."

She stopped and turned to face him. "You're relentless aren't you?"

"Being in this chair, I have to be."

She finally smiled. "My parents are strict, so I can't be seen with you."

"I'll become the invisible man," he joked.

"I'll take your information and maybe I'll contact you, maybe I won't."

"You don't have a cell phone number?"

"My folks are poor," she admitted.

"A'ight, we can work it out. I might be leaving town soon," he said.

"Really? Why?"

"Just for personal reasons."

"If you're leaving town, why try and get with me?"

"If I do, I'll come back for you and we can make something happen. I promise," he said with conviction in his tone. "I really want to see you. I think you're special even though this is just my second time meeting you."

Jackie started to look skeptical, but she still took down his information.

"Where you going?" she asked him.

"I don't know. Maybe I might stay and hang out with you."

"You need to make up your mind soon. I don't like to play games."

"Believe me; I'm not playing games with you. I'm so serious. And don't think because I'm in this wheelchair that you need to feel sorry for me. Believe me; I might surprise you with many things."

"Look, I have to go. It's getting late, and I don't want my parents to worry. I'll call, or maybe I won't."

She strutted off, and The Kid sat there and watched her fade away from his view once more. Damn, he wanted her in his life for some reason. Was it her skill at playing chess? Her beauty? Her elusiveness? Maybe it was all of those combined into one petite and cute young girl. Whatever it was, he couldn't stop thinking about her.

Finally, he wheeled himself in the opposite direction. He wondered if he liked her enough to one day reveal the truth about himself—that he was able to walk, and his other, darker secrets. Only time would tell.

\*\*\*

Jackie strutted toward the modest looking home on the tree-lined New Rochelle street. She quickly climbed the stairs, placed her key inside the lock, and entered the home. The crackling of police radios, surveillance equipment strewn in the living room, and the men moving around the home with holstered Glocks and "FBI" stenciled across their attire was a clear indication of her identity.

"Why do you keep toying with him, Agent Moore?" one of the agents asked.

"Because, I don't want to spook him. He's smart," she said.

"He's a fuckin' cripple."

"Yes, but I believe there's more to him than meets the eye."

"It's your case and your career if you're wrong."

"I'm not wrong. He's linked somehow. I just have to find a way inside."

The façade of a young teenager quickly evaporated, and her professionalism as an undercover FBI agent resurfaced. Her eyes became sharper and her speech a lot more adult. Agent Daphne Moore was twenty-nine years old with a young-looking, Barbie-doll face that made her stand out. But she had an old and serious soul to her. She was motivated and ambitious. She had graduated from John Jay College of Criminal Justice at the top of her class and soon joined the NYPD task force. After four years as a top cop, she became a federal agent.

The Kid had made her radar via his brother Kip Kane. Kip's meeting with Maserati Meek sparked interest from the feds. Who was Kip, and what made him important to the Egyptian drug lord? Meek was a dangerous man who had slowly but surely become a blip on the FBI's radar. The feds acquired a few pictures of Kip, but so far, they had nothing on him.

Agent Moore found it odd that a slew of men associated with Kip Kane were being viciously murdered. There was Uncle Junior and his crew viciously gunned down in Brooklyn—not too long after their confrontation with his little brother Kid. A man named Jay P, who was connected to Maserati Meek, had been slaughtered with his girlfriend in their bedroom, and there were others being hunted down like animals and murdered cruelly by someone. Agent Moore knew Kip to be a murderer, a hired killer for Meek—but these murders were different, she felt. Her gut instinct told her that these killings were personal for some reason, and they weren't executed by Kip. Her instincts never lied. She convinced her superiors to open a case on what was left of Kip's crew, including his younger brother—but so far, there wasn't much. But she was determined to find something on everyone and make her case by any means necessary.

She had his cell phone number, an address, and information that he might be leaving town. For what reasons, she still didn't know.

# 33

The FBI surveillance team began to quietly disperse the modest New Rochelle home once Agent Moore debriefed everyone. Something Kid said about leaving town was bugging her. Where was he going and why? Of course she wanted to ask specific questions about his upcoming departure, but she didn't want to seem too interested when her cover was to be elusive and blasé. Where would this take her investigation? And were Devon Francis and "Papa" John Jakes leaving too?

What if Kid wasn't connected? He could just be a man in a wheelchair who happened to have a dead brother that was in bed with a crazy Egyptian drug lord. She had so many questions that she wanted answered, quickly. Maybe playing coy wasn't the best route when someone was blowing up New York. Innocent lives were taken, and she was no closer to solving the case. She had a lot riding on this case and was determined to prove her worth. Law enforcement is a man's world—a competitive arena—and Daphne was never going to fuck her way to the top. She knew other agencies were vying to solve this case, and her supervisor assigned it to her.

"You coming, Agent Moore?" one agent asked.

"Not yet. I want to go over a few things."

"You work too hard. There's always tomorrow."

Agent Lanier was the last to exit the home, leaving Agent Moore to her work. She had already grabbed a beer from the fridge and was nibbling on a slice of leftover pizza they had ordered hours earlier.

Daphne stared at the pyramid wall of suspects. Akar Mudada, AKA Maserati Meek, was at the top, and Kip Kane was there with a large X across his face along with several other dead goons. On another line was Devon and Papa John, who was also wanted for the attempted murder of his father, a NYPD detective. Last on the list was Kid Kane, chess champion. Why did she have a strong feeling that he should be moved up the ladder? Well, that's what her gut told her. But her heart, it said that he should be excluded altogether.

Daphne decided that she had done enough for the day. In order to move forward in this investigation she had to definitively include or exclude Kid Kane. To do that, she had to see him again and quickly, as he was leaving town.

***

The Kid sat perched in his wheelchair across the street from Jackie's home. He had followed her, keeping a safe distance back. Kid didn't think he would follow her. In fact, he had begun wheeling himself home but felt a strong urge not to. He felt connected to Jackie, and for some reason he couldn't get her out of this mind. He was familiar with wanting what he couldn't have. How could he ever forget Jessica? But Jackie was different. She was smart, sassy, and a challenge. Most importantly, she was an excellent chess player. He'd only just met her, and already Kid wanted to marry her. He just couldn't get her out of his head.

The whole time Jackie walked briskly home she was talking on a cell phone that she said she didn't own and never turned around. As Kid wheeled himself behind her, he felt a like a stalker. But following her was satisfying. He would get to know one more thing about her that he hadn't, that she wouldn't dare disclose.

As Kid's strong arms pushed him toward his destination he thought about rescuing her from strict parents and whisking her off into the sunset. They'd get married and before long he would experience a "medical miracle" and walk again. She would love him and have his babies, and he would always protect her. The Kid pictured them both playing professional chess tournaments and living a life of leisure. Eshon was in his daydream too. She would find a new love and come around to be an aunt to Kid and Jackie's children.

Initially Kid had the intention of knocking on her door, meeting her parents, and asking her once again on a date. Now, seeing the cell phone, Kid felt that she was hiding something, and he was determined to find out what that something might be.

As Jackie crossed the wide street and entered a small, modest house with a picket fence, the unmistakable array of unmarked black Fords with official license plates caught his attention. Was this a law enforcement neighborhood?

Kid didn't have any plans on loitering, but he couldn't pull himself away. With a blank stare he looked at the home. His hunch was realized when less than thirty minutes later the boys in blue with alphabets scribbled across their windbreakers emerged. Everyone looked fatigued—rubbing their eyes, yawning, and staggering to their vehicles. Ever since the explosions most agents were pulling doubles and triples.

The Kid was confused. Why were a half-dozen FBI agents coming out of Jackie's home? She was an eighteen-year-old girl that he had just met. Could one of them be her father and that's why she was always rushing home? The question was answered when his beautiful crush came out of the home in full government regalia. Jackie was putting on her windbreaker and he could clearly see a holstered gun. Kid was flabbergasted. He had been played, just like Jessica had played him.

***

Kid could not sleep that night. How did he keep finding himself in these situations with women? They were so cunning. He wished Eshon was there so he could tell her what had happened. Obviously, Jackie was connected to the federal investigators that had knocked on Brandy's door and also the local cop, Officer Spielberg.

Kid couldn't figure out how they had gotten on to them. What had they done wrong? Truthfully, the only person to blame would be him because he was the one moving the pieces on the chessboard.

He knew what he had to do, but somehow couldn't come to terms with it. How could he kill Jackie? The intelligent, chess playing, snarky, devious, duplicitous, FBI agent Jackie?

# 34

The next morning Eshon was back and had breakfast made. Usually Kid ate a healthy portion of pork bacon, eggs, and grits, but he had no appetite today. He felt sick to his stomach.

He wrestled with whether the short time he and Jackie had spent together was real. How much of Jackie was really her and how much was just her cover? It can't all be fake, he thought. You can't pretend to love chess—not at the level she played. How could the FBI handpick someone that would be perfect for him?

He hated to admit it, but he had been outsmarted. Kid thought about snatching up his crew and leaving town, but with what money? He had a plan and he had already pressed play, so could he hit pause? The reasonable side of him said that if they had something tangible then Jackie wouldn't be meeting him at the Y. And she hadn't even begun digging into his personal life with questions, which was indicative that they were at the beginning stages. He still had time to finish his Maserati Meek business and avenge his brother's murder.

\*\*\*

To any other man it would have come as a great shock that Jackie showed up at the Y, but Kid knew she would come back so quickly because he had told her he was leaving town. A good agent would need questions answered. As soon as she walked in, Kid's heart skipped a beat. He couldn't help but be drawn to her.

"Ready to lose again, loser?" she asked him.

He grinned, and it was genuine. "Not today."

"That's what they all say. Good luck."

"I don't need luck when I got skills."

"Skills, huh?"

"In many things," Kid flirted. "But you wouldn't know that because you won't give me a chance."

"I'll tell you what, if you win today then I might let you take me out." Jackie had done a 180. She could no longer play hard to get.

"Might? I'll take it. Start thinking about where you want to go, because I'm winning."

The chess match was awkward at best, bizarre at worst. Both Jackie and Kid were trying to lose. Jackie wanted alone time with him. She knew he was sweet on her and wanted his guard down. Meanwhile, Kid didn't trust himself around her. He didn't know if he wanted to kiss her or kill her. It turned out that Jackie was the better loser.

She stood up from the table. "I hope you have more than five dollars in your pockets because I'm hungry."

"Don't worry about my finances, gorgeous. Where we're going you'll be well fed." Kid grinned cockily. "Your chariot awaits. Hop on!" He gestured to his chair like Vanna White.

Jackie was confused. Did he want her to sit on his lap? Kid extended his hand and she took it. He pulled Jackie close and she sat squarely on his lap.

"Hold on tight," he whispered. "It might get a little rough." Their eyes met and Jackie had to look away first. Why was she feeling all warm and tingly with this guy? It was unprofessional and she knew she needed to maintain her boundaries.

As Kid rolled his wheelchair down tree lined blocks and uneven pavements, Jackie marveled at his strength. It was one thing to get around on his own, a whole other level to do it with additional weight. All sorts of thoughts swirled around her head, like how did he look naked? Did his dick function? And if they fucked would he want her to sit on his face? She blushed.

"What are you thinking about?"

"Excuse me?" she said, embarrassed as if he had read her mind.

"You . . . you were in deep thought and then your face lit up like something good crossed your mind. What was it? Share it with me."

Jackie bit her lip. "I was reliving all the times I outmaneuvered you in chess."

"You lie like a rug."

"I swear!" she said and giggled.

"I don't believe you. I think you were thinking about me—us— making sweet love."

Jackie's face turned beet red. She placed both hands over her face and shook her head vigorously. "That's not true!"

Kid stopped his wheelchair and removed her hands from her face. "It's what I think about . . ."

Jackie leaned in and she kissed his soft lips. He slid his tongue into her mouth and they deeply connected. He wanted her, and she could feel how much as she sat on his lap. Kid pulled back first; he had to control his emotions. She was the enemy.

The next couple blocks they were silent. Kid noticed at least two unmarked cars continuously passing them, which irked him.

"We're here," he announced proudly.

"Chipotle?"

"My favorite spot. And don't worry, you can order from the left side of the menu."

Jackie hopped off and helped wheel Kid into the restaurant. They ordered and sat down to eat. Occasionally Kid would see her make eye contact with an unidentified white male.

"Tell me about yourself," she finally asked.

"Me? Not much to tell."

"Well, you can either tell me something or we'll eat in silence. Not much of a date, right?"

He smiled.

"Did I say something funny?"

"You said *date* as if you were looking forward to it."

"Maybe I was, but right now I'm bored."

"Ouch. Ok, well, don't forget that you asked."

Jackie adjusted her posture to signal that he had her full attention. Kid told her everything he was sure she knew about him, leaving out any details that could land him in jail. He went into detail about being adopted, his bike accident with Kip, therapy, his brother getting murdered, and then his Nana passing away shortly thereafter.

"I thought that I wouldn't have anyone after Kip and Nana died, but his friends stepped in and helped me get through the loss." Kid readjusted his wire-rimmed glasses.

"That must have been tough. So, who murdered him?"

Kid played along. "Can you keep a secret?"

"A secret? Who would I tell? My parents? Please. I hate them."

Kid looked around as if he was afraid of someone overhearing. He could tell he had on her the edge of her chair. "My brother was overprotective of me since the accident, so he never confided in me what he did for a living, but I knew it wasn't legit. While I was hustling, he was too."

"You hustle drugs?" she asked, wide-eyed and innocent.

He chuckled and looked down at his legs. "I'm flattered, but no. Chess. I made money playing for money. One day my brother confided in me that a very dangerous person wanted him to do something major—like real big—something that could hurt a lot of people. When he refused, that person threatened my life. I was terrified . . ." Kid put his head down.

"Go on," she coaxed.

"I'm a little embarrassed to tell you this."

Jackie touched his hands. "You can tell me anything."

Kid exhaled. "I was really scared to be alone or go outside. Kip didn't want me to get hurt, but he just couldn't do what the madman wanted him to do."

"And what was that?"

Kid shook his head. "You won't believe me if I told you, so let's just let it go."

Jackie didn't have time to wait for him to fully trust her or warm up to her. She needed to know now. "You just don't get me, do you? I don't let anyone in. I have no one . . . nothing but chess, and . . . now you. I feel connected to you in a way that I've never felt with anyone. Ever. So please, don't shut me out when I'm ready to let you in."

"Have you ever heard of homegrown terrorism?"

She nodded.

"Well, this guy wanted my brother to find willing participants from low income neighborhoods like where we lived to strap a bomb to themselves and blow up buildings and landmarks or something around New York. Each sacrificial lamb's family would receive a large sum of money, but my brother refused."

"Did your brother convert? Why was he chosen?"

"Kip?" The Kid smirked. "He wasn't converting or pleading allegiance to Jihad, Allah, ISIS or any other faction. He was targeted because he would be least suspected, he had the heart of a lion, and he had a vulnerable brother in a wheelchair to threaten."

Jackie thought for a moment. Was this really adding up?

Kid continued. "Before he was killed, Kip tried reasoning with this guy, but he couldn't. I had gotten into a scuffle at the park over a chess game, and to show Kip that he was a team player, the guy went and murdered everyone involved. That spooked Kip, and he made arrangements for us to move down south."

"If it was the way you say, why didn't your brother go to the police?"

"Oh, he was. The moment he found out about Uncle Junior and his relatives getting murdered he planned on going to the police until the detectives picked him up for a crime that he didn't commit. Kip felt surely if he told them what this madman wanted him to do that they would laugh in his face and pin the murders on him." Kid shook his head as if he were reliving his brother's plight. "We were leaving, and this man knew it. He gunned my brother down in cold blood and left me in this big, cruel world without him."

"Who is this monster?" she finally asked.

"He has some ghetto name like a rapper. A fast car . . . what is it?" Kid snapped his fingers for recollection. "Lamborghini, ummm . . ."

Jackie was on the edge of her seat. "Maserati?"

"That's it! Maserati Meek." Kid fumbled with his glasses again. "He's no rapper, Jackie. He's the real deal. He's Egyptian, quirky, and a sadist. And between you and me, he's responsible for the two recent bombings."

"How can you be sure?"

"The girl that was found murdered on the news in connection with the bombings—Jessica Hernandez? That was his girlfriend, and that was her party. She was trying to get away from him too. I guess he was trying to kill anyone who knew of his plan to blow up New York. Miraculously, we all survived and got out, but Jessica must have gone back to him and he killed her. He's crazy, Jackie. That's why I'm leaving. I don't want to leave you, but if I stay I could put you in harm's way. I'm hoping that the federal government will catch him soon, and then I will come back for you."

"For me?"

"Yes. I can't have my future wife living without her man for long."

Her face glowed with a smile, which turned into a huge grin. "Who said I even like you?"

"That kiss said."

She playfully tossed a straw paper at him. "How will you be safe, Kid? I'm worried now. Why didn't you go to the feds for help?"

"Like my brother, who tried to go to NYPD and ended up dead?"

"We're not NYPD."

Kid's eyes widened.

Jackie's heart pounded. "What?"

"You said 'we're'."

"I said, 'they're' not, silly."

Kid and Jackie talked for hours until the restaurant closed. Her watchdogs had changed shifts and she remained. It was like they didn't exist. The conversation had long ago shifted from Meek, bombings, and murder. They discussed their likes, dreams, favorite foods, politics, religion, how many children each one wanted, and then Jackie got personal. She wanted to know if Kid got aroused and could perform. She wasn't wearing a wire so she could speak freely.

"Come back home with me and find out."

"I might sneak out tonight. Just keep your window unlocked."

"There you go again with the might."

"Well, being definitive is boring. I like teetering the fine line of uncertainty."

# 35

Several NYPD officers, including Emergency Service Units, converged onto the Bushwick property with their guns drawn, ready for anything that came their way. Their daunting toys were out to play—including the battling ram clutched by one officer—and they were there to execute a no-knock warrant on Papa John's last known address. His baby mama Tina stayed there with her kids.

The sudden police activity outside the front door alerted the neighbors, and they stood there in awe to watch the show. The front door came crashing open, and hordes of cops rushed into the building with their guns pointing everywhere.

Tina and the kids were startled by the sudden disruption. It was early in the morning and she was getting them ready for school. The heavy police presence inside her home halted her plans, and she found herself under siege. They started to ask questions, but she had no idea where her baby father was at. She hadn't seen him in weeks. They were aggressive with threats to her, but she was clueless as to his whereabouts.

"He shot his own father," they exclaimed.

Tina didn't want to believe it. But they were inside her home for a reason, scaring her children, including Papa John's autistic son.

They made no arrest and left her home a mess. The minute they were out of her sight, Tina hurried to a neighbor friend and used her phone to warn Papa John.

***

Papa John had to go deeper into hiding, fearing arrest and incarceration. The Kid assured him that everything would be okay. He had a plan for them all. He had the perfect method to collect three million from Meek without endangering his crew.

Time was winding down for Maserati Meek. The Kid was ready to make the call and give him the location to meet. His parents were still tied up and being held prisoner in New Jersey. Shahib Abu Mudada and his wife continued to be beaten and tortured by Devon. When Papa John and Kid walked into the basement, the couple almost looked unrecognizable. Asma's face was completely swollen and bleeding. She was chained to a concrete pillar. She had been completely broken. Her husband was also in very bad shape. For fun, when he was alone with Shahib, Devon had severed his right hand, despite what The Kid had instructed him.

"What the fuck you do to them?" The Kid barked.

"What? They still alive, ain't they?"

The Kid stared at Shahib and his wife and shook his head in disgust. They were barely alive. He needed to take a picture of the couple and send it to Meek for proof of life. He took a picture of Shahib's face and made a quick video recording. It was immediately sent to the burner they'd sent to Maserati Meek.

"We need to go. It's almost payday," The Kid announced.

Devon and Papa John smiled. They exited the abandoned building, climbed into a van, and drove toward the Bronx.

***

The next morning Agent Moore held a conference with her fellow agents and her superiors. She debriefed the whole room on the intel she had gotten from Kid Kane. Most of what he had to say they knew, but the candid talk had filled in the blanks.

"Are you sure he's not involved in any way?" Special Agent Hanks, her supervisor had asked.

"He's not. This guy isn't involved, and he's told me everything he knows. He's terrified. Once we build a case against Akar Mudada we could call him to help corroborate a few loose ends. He's connected Jessica Hernandez and Mudada, AKA Maserati Meek. Seems a local officer has been looking into Jessica Hernandez too with connection to the bombing, but he is clueless as to who sanctioned the explosions. He's working with a few of our agents, but I want the credit. This is my case."

\*\*\*

Kid was sitting in the window when two unmarked federal vehicles pulled up in front of his home. This was it. They finally had enough to arrest him. He was glad that Eshon was out shopping and hoped that she wasn't on their radar. He assumed that they had already picked up Devon and Papa John. For a split second he wanted to call them and warn them but knew that his phone would be confiscated and didn't want to lead them to his friends. Thinking quickly, he took out the phone's SIM card and flushed it.

The hard knock on the door was reminiscent of better days when Kip was alive. Kid wheeled himself to the door to see Jackie with her identifiable law enforcement gear and two male coworkers. Kid opened the door and wheeled himself backwards.

He looked bewildered. "Jackie? What's going on?"

"Kid, my name is Agent Moore and these are my colleagues, Agent Lanier and Special Agent Hanks. You know me as Jackie, the eighteen year old ingénue." She looked down at her gear. "Obviously that was my cover. You have information we need to put a very dangerous person behind bars for the rest of his life. A man who murdered your brother. His real name is Akar Mudada, but you know him as Maserati Meek. Would you feel comfortable testifying against him? We could also offer you Wit-Sec."

Kid continued to feign shock at this revelation. Jackie was cold and standoffish as she detailed how their investigation had grown and how he connected the dots for them. He repeatedly said he was terrified of the warlord, and the feds insisted that he would be safe. That soon enough Akar would be off the streets.

"When is he being arrested?" Kid wanted to know. "Are you picking him up today?"

"Not that soon, but it's under control. Don't worry. We have men doing surveillance if that's what you're afraid of."

Finally Kid complied. "Whatever I can do to help put my brother's murderer away, then I will."

Before she left, Agent Moore lingered behind. When Lanier and Hanks were out of eyesight she smiled at Kid and whispered, "Keep that window unlocked."

\*\*\*

Maserati Meek had been anticipating word from Ghost. When he got the video, a small wave of relief washed over him, but it wasn't over yet.

The call came early that evening. Meek had the money, three million dollars—1.5 million in each of the two duffel bags as he was instructed. But he wasn't ready to give it up without a fight. Ghost and his cronies had to meet him face-to-face—he assumed, and when they did, Meek would be ready to go ham on them. However, he needed the safe return of his parents first.

In six black Tahoes, Meek and his men drove to the location in the Bronx. They arrived at an abandoned baseball field not too far from City Island. The area was somewhat secluded, and a few trees covered the vicinity. A few yards away was an open field adjacent to a bay.

The doors to the Tahoes opened, and several armed men removed themselves from the vehicles. There was no one there except for them—a mass of killers ready to react when told. Meek looked around. He was certain it was the location that he was told.

"Are we in the right place?" Amir asked him.

"Yes. Baseball field, it's correct."

"So where are they?"

Maserati Meek didn't want to be bothered with questions. His main concern was getting his parents back safely and destroying this character named Ghost. A few minutes went by and still nothing. It was at a standstill in both directions of the road.

Then the burner phone sounded and Meek quickly answered it. "I'm here, waiting as instructed," he growled at the caller.

"I see you brought some company with you. You were supposed to come alone."

"Wherever I go, they go with me. No exception, eh."

The caller Ghost chuckled. "I can respect that."

"What do you want us to do now? I have the money."

"Just wait. You'll see soon."

The call ended, leaving Meek baffled.

Five minutes later, something caught Meek and his men's attention. It was coming from the bay, something hovering; it was approaching them at a moderate speed. Each man looked up and was transfixed. Unbelievable. There were two huge phantom drones, their propellers buzzing noisily and fast like wings on a bee. The drones were specially equipped with a carrying mechanism—four iron claws underneath each of them. They landed in the field. Meek was in awe. He watched these machines, and the machines watched him with their cameras.

The phone rang, and Meek answered. "Attach the bags to the drones, and I'll do the rest. You do anything stupid, and your parents are dead."

The realization of how clever this heist was didn't go over Meek's head. He did what he was told. His men attached the duffel bags to the iron claws, and their grip around the bags tightened. He couldn't believe what he was witnessing. There would be no face-to-face with the man named Ghost. He seemed to have thought of everything.

Once the bags were secured, the drones started to lift from the field, hovering with 1.5 million dollars under each of them. The weight of the bags was tested earlier, and the creator of the specially made drones assured Kid that it would work. The drones hesitated to lift higher for a split moment, due to the weight of the cash—but in due time, they elevated into the air and headed toward the bay—headed toward the direction they'd come from.

For a moment, Meek and his men stood around watching, still in awe. The drones were flying over the water and fading from their sights. Then suddenly, Meek yelled out, "Follow them!"

The men hurried into the trucks and tried to give chase, but the spot Ghost had chosen was for a purpose. A body of water and marshlands surrounded the area, and to attempt to follow the machines would be futile. No matter how hard they drove, the drones were quickly lost.

Maserati Meek cursed, banged his fists against the dashboard, and shattered the window with the butt of his pistol. Somehow a stranger had outsmarted him, and the fate of his parents was unknown.

*** 

The door to the dark and moldy basement opened, and The Kid, Papa John, and Devon descended the wood stairs and entered into the concrete room where Shahib Abu and Asma Mudada were barely alive. The couple lay in waste and blood, their movement sluggish.

The men were extremely happy. They were rich men. The heist had been implemented without any problems. It was all thanks to a man named Spirit—whom The Kid used to chat with and had befriended while gaming online. Spirit was also a mechanical engineer, and they were able to obtain the money without incident or exposure because of his hi-tech creation. Who would have thought—drones? Not in a million years.

The Kid looked down at the Mudadas. He had no more use for them. They were dead weight now—despicable to themselves and mankind. The Kid had never intended to set them free. He wanted them to die—to suffer first, and then die. He removed a .45 from his waistband and stepped to Asma first. He pointed the barrel of the gun at her face and fired—Boom! Her brains decorated the concrete floor. He stepped to the husband next and aimed his gun at his head, and did the same—Boom! The bullet tore through his forehead and sprayed his blood everywhere.

Papa John and Devon simply watched the execution in silence. It was still a shock to see Kid kill. He was more heartless and colder than Kip.

"Bury these muthafuckas somewhere. Meek will never see them alive again, nor will he see them dead."

"What about Meek?" Devon asked.

"What about him?" The Kid replied.

"He's still breathing."

"And?"

"I thought we wanted him dead too."

"I wanted him to feel the pain I felt when he took my brother from me, and now he's gonna feel it. We took three million dollars from him, kidnapped and killed his parents—and he'll be left in the dark wondering who it was. I think that's pain enough," The Kid proclaimed wisely.

But Devon was still longing to kill Maserati Meek.

"Trust me. Meek will pay for his crimes. Listen, we're about to retire from this shit and live a good life someplace far from here. Let's get the girls and go," The Kid said.

Shahib Abu Mudada and Asma's bodies were left buried in a deep grave in upstate New York. It brought pleasure to The Kid knowing that Maserati Meek would never know where his parents were and that he would never be able to give them a proper burial.

***

There was still no word from Ghost, or any clue what had happened to his parents. Maserati Meek had waited impatiently for a call that never came. He knew that he would never see his parents alive ever again. The rage and fury that bubbled inside of him nearly turned his blood into melting lava. With Panamanian Pete dead, Kip and his little brother and crew dead, he had no idea who had taken his three million dollars and most likely killed his parents. The individual who named himself Ghost had done just that—he became a ghost.

Meek vowed to find this person and skin him alive—and make him pay drastically for all he'd taken from him. It wasn't over. He was willing to spend his last dollar on finding this Ghost and implementing his revenge.

# 36

The Kid had help with getting his wheelchair out the yellow cab, and he had help into the cemetery where his brother was buried.

"I got it from here," he told the driver. "Give me ten minutes."

The driver nodded and walked back to his cab parked on 155th Street. It was dawn, with the sun bright in the sky and the temperature soon to reach ninety degrees. It felt like the perfect time for a visit.

Clutching some flowers, Kid wheeled himself toward his brother's grave. He hadn't been to it since the funeral, and he felt self-centered for taking this long to visit Kip. He reached the grave and placed the flowers against the stone. He released a deep sigh and stared at the writing on the granite. He managed to smile, and then he frowned.

"I know I haven't been around to visit you lately, but I felt that I couldn't come around until I corrected things—until I avenged your death, Kip. I miss you so much."

He sat silent for a moment, overwhelmed with grief and nostalgia. Being there was taking a lot out of him, but Kid felt he needed to be strong. He had come a long way. He looked around the area, making sure that he was completely alone. He was. So he slowly removed himself from the wheelchair and stood over his brother's gave. He lowered himself down on his knees and dropped his head as if he was about to pray.

He released a heavy sigh. "I destroyed that muthafucka for you, Kip. I got him good. I made him pay for what he did to you. He took you from me, so I took his parents from him, and I took his money. I outmaneuvered Maserati Meek, Kip. You should have seen me. I know you would have been proud of me."

Kid's knees pressed into the grass. He placed his hands against the tombstone and traced his brother's name carved into the granite with his fingertips. He was silent for a moment.

"I have a confession, Kip. I've been able to walk for more than five years. I know you wanted to see me walk when you were alive and I kept that from you. I don't know why, but it tears me up to know that you died thinking I was still a cripple when you tried your best to get me the best physical therapy money could buy. And me being foolish, I kept it a secret from you to keep you close to me. It haunts me that I did that to you. I'm sorry about that, Kip. I truly am. And I'm going to have to live with it for the rest of my life."

Kid released a few tears and let them trickle down his face.

"I just came by to say goodbye, big bro. I'm leaving the city. I don't know for how long, but I know it's time to go. But no matter where I'm at, I'm gonna always keep you close and you will never be forgotten. Oh, and I met someone too. You should see her, Kip. She's beautiful and smart. And guess what? She beat me at chess, Kip. Can you believe that? I actually lost, and I lost to a girl. But you know what? She was definitely worth losing to."

The Kid kissed his brother's grave and stood back up. He planted his butt back into the wheelchair, took one memorable look at the site, exhaled, and started to leave. He had a plane to catch soon and a new life to live, away from Harlem and New York.

✳✳✳

Officer Spielberg sat at the uptown bar and downed a shot of vodka. It frustrated him that the two bombings were still unsolved and they had no one in custody yet. He had worked tirelessly with the FBI, but still nothing. With Jessica dead, her being their only lead, and Eshon lost in the wind, he was greatly frustrated. But he wasn't about to give up. He was determined to investigate this case night and day. The feds were relentless too. These certain terrorists seemed to be tricky, but Spielberg and his colleagues had the law and the manpower on their side to keep hunting. He just needed to take a step back from it all and get a closer look at things.

One good thing about the case was that he had been promoted to Detective Third Class. He was climbing the ranks in the NYPD, and from detective, he was determined to make sergeant.

He finished off his drinks and left the bar. Outside, he took in a breath of fresh air and studied his surroundings. The case never left his mind. He knew they were missing something, and he felt it was right in front of their faces. But what was it?

Meanwhile, Agent Daphne Moore and her team were moving in Maserati Meek's operation.

# EPILOGUE

St. Thomas was a paradise that stretched for miles and miles. With its ideal eighty-degree weather, the birds flying above in uncorrupted skies, the sun shining bright and friendly, and the rich blue ocean water so inviting and virtuous, the place was heaven. It was the perfect retreat for Kid, Eshon, Brandy, Devon, and Papa John and all seven of his kids and baby mommas, including Dina. Most surprisingly, Jackie, also known as Agent Daphne Moore, was there as well.

Jackie had called him and told him that they had arrested Meek and had enough evidence that the charges were going to stick. She didn't need him to testify after all. Kid invited her on the vacation and was delighted when she said yes. She had arrived late last night.

They'd done it. They'd escaped the city with their lives and an abundance of cash that The Kid laundered into their Caribbean accounts. In total, they each received six hundred thousand dollars. They'd traveled a long road, and there was suffering and pain, but at the end, it was all worth it. The beachside resort was flawless. They were seated in the white sand, relaxing with their tropical drinks, enjoying the tropical music and the approaching sunset.

Kid sat coolly and watched the kids splash and play in the ocean with huge smiles on their faces. He was extra happy.

All afternoon Kid and Jackie were openly showing each other affection. One of Papa John's daughters interrupted them by running over to play with him. She threw sand on Kid's lap and he laughed. He picked the young girl up into his arms and hugged her warmly. He gave her a few little tickles to her belly, and she laughed and laughed.

Papa John had his entire family with him. It was insane at first to think of him bringing all of his baby mamas and his children with him to the Caribbean, but everything seemed to work itself out. Back in New York, he had a court date next fall to answer for his father's shooting. Originally he thought he would run forever, but he thought about his children. He would be a man and face whatever punishment a jury of his peers deemed appropriate, but for now it was all about family.

Jackie stood up and stretched in her skimpy bikini. She looked around at the vast ocean and blue skies and drank in the tropical breeze. She turned around only to see Kid looking at her with a smile.

"What?"

"You're beautiful."

"And you're a tease."

He smirked. "Me? How?"

"You never left that window unlocked."

"Tonight, how about I leave my door unlocked so you can come and go like a lady? I want you to keep your virtue, Jackie. Or is it Daphne?"

"It's Agent Moore to you."

"Yes, ma'am."

"Ma'am?"

"That's how I address my elders," he joked because she was several years his senior.

"You want to take that trash talk to the chess board?"

"What are we playing for?"

"Your virginity."

Kid grinned. She had no idea what he was working with. "You gonna find out the hard way that I ain't no virgin, Mrs. Kane."

"Mrs. Kane? I might just let you make that come true."

"Might, huh?"

"No offense, but I have to test drive the package first."

"Then hop on!"

Jackie hopped on Kid's lap and he wheeled them off into paradise.